dare me
again

dare me *again*

An Angel Fire Falls Novel

SHELLY ALEXANDER

Montlake
Romance

Text copyright © 2019 by Shelly Alexander
All rights reserved.

Published by Montlake Romance, Seattle

www.apub.com

Amazon, the Amazon logo, and Montlake Romance are trademarks of Amazon.com, Inc., or its affiliates.

ISBN-13: 9781503905207
ISBN-10: 1503905209

Cover design by Erin Dameron-Hill

Cover photography by Sara Eirew

Printed in the United States of America

For my husband, because he gets me. And because he has spent twenty-six years letting me spoil our dogs.

For all the selfless people who dedicate their time helping our veterans when they come home. The Paws and Stripes organization in Albuquerque, New Mexico, is one such organization. Thank you for allowing me to go behind the scenes to see what you do for our community. The fact that you're willing to dedicate your lives to training and pairing rescue dogs with our nation's veterans is awe-inspiring.

For my middle son for letting me use his name (unbeknownst to him) and his personality for the hero in this book. I'm so proud of you, son.

And for the real Bogart (Bogey, as we so endearingly call him). You are a survivor, little buddy. Having only three legs has never slowed you down . . . much. ☺

Chapter One

#ThreeCupKindOfDay

"Now that's a set of balls," Elliott Remington said to his brother while staring down the barrel of his pool stick. The white cue ball cracked against the neat triangle of billiard balls at the far end of the pool table, sending a rainbow of colors whizzing in every direction. Two stripes disappeared into the corner pockets, and he stepped over to the window to peek through the shades of the state-of-the-art game room of the Remington Resort.

He looked one way, then the other, and saw no one. *Excellent.* Lily, the Remington's hospitality manager—who was hunting him like she was on safari—hadn't discovered his hiding place. Yet.

"Hey, butthead." Spence, younger by just sixteen months, perched on a new lime-green barstool and twirled his stick. "The game's over here, and how would you know anything about balls, since you don't have any?"

"You're in that much of a hurry to lose?" Elliott looked out over the expansive front lawn and the stillness of the resort where he and his two brothers had grown up. The resort they now owned. The usual Sunday morning rush was over, but it never failed to get him out from behind his desk for a few hours to help the guests with their luggage and see them off. Gave him a break from managing the staff, doing payroll, yelling at vendors.

Scratch that. Negotiating with vendors.

Yeah, he liked that term better. Sounded more professional. Less assholeish.

"The scenery outside hasn't changed since you looked two minutes ago," Spence said. Because they were both more than six feet with the same light-brown hair and green eyes, people often mistook them for twins. "It's only a matter of time before Lily finds you. You might as well enjoy the downtime before the next set of vacationers starts checking in."

Unwinding over a game of pool was a Remington brothers' tradition. A nice change from the hustle and bustle Elliott had grown addicted to while living in San Francisco.

Scratch that too. Grown attached to. Because the lightning-fast pace of the City by the Bay, where he'd spent the better part of a decade setting the financial district on fire, was a thrill. An adrenaline rush.

A distraction from painful memories.

So here he was, on the little vacation island of Angel Fire Falls, unwinding. Ish.

He finally let the blinds snap shut and circled the table, looking for a clean shot. "There's very little I wouldn't do to help the resort." Hell, he was still here, wasn't he? He'd come home for a long-overdue vacation several months back, only to stay indefinitely because of how much his family needed his help if the resort was going to survive. "But I can't take charge of the service dog camp Lily scheduled." He bent to line up a shot. "I don't know anything about dogs. I don't have time to *learn* anything about dogs." The camp had been scheduled at the last minute due to the original trainer and venue suddenly pulling out. "And even if I had more than a few days to brush up on my . . . dog skills"—he couldn't hide the eye roll in his voice—"dogs usually hate me because I'm—"

"An ass?" Spence said with a straight face.

Good to know sibling rivalry was alive and well, even in their late twenties. It was one of the things Elliott could count on. That and numbers. Numbers were safe. Secure. Steady. And never failed him, unlike the women in his life.

He took aim and sank the next shot. "I was going to say intense." Man's best friend didn't take to his Mach-5-with-his-hair-on-fire personality.

The feeling was mutual. Pets could run away, and he'd already experienced more than once the pain and disappointment of someone important disappearing from his life.

"Seeing as how you're still living with me instead of moving into your own place, I get to pick the words that best describe you." Spence scratched his scruffy jaw. "I say you're an *intense ass*, which is why I'm planning to pack up your crap and move you out myself."

Elliott moving into one of the cottages on the resort grounds like the rest of the family was out of the question, even if his family didn't understand why. Having a place of his own was too permanent, and he'd already stayed far longer than he should've. "Someone has to keep your sorry butt out of trouble. I guess that's my job." *For now.*

Elliott pretended to aim at another stripe, then straightened and circled the table slowly. Taking too long was the easiest way to annoy Spence and ensure victory.

Spence gave him a stony stare.

Criticizing Spence's work as a master builder usually shook his concentration too. The remodel was perfect, but pool wouldn't be as much fun if Elliott couldn't give his little brother hell. "Did you forget your level the day you installed those?" Elliott hitched his chin toward the shelves hanging over the new gaming stations that ran the length of one wall and were stacked with the latest video games. "Or were you in a hurry to get home and watch *Dr. Phil* with a box of tissues?"

Spence's jaw ticked.

3

Score. Elliott dropped another shot.

Spence leaned back on the barstool. "You're the one who secretly DVRs *Say Yes to the Dress.*"

Elliott flinched. Some of the brides were hot. Some of the dresses made the brides look hotter.

He scratched an imaginary speck from his cheek with his middle finger, the Remington brothers' code for *Up yours.* No one else was around, but it never hurt to be discreet, which was the reason they'd created the secret communication system when they were kids. Then he bent to line up a shot that would send another stripe flying across the new purple felt.

The door swung open, and Trace, the oldest Remington brother, walked in. He whistled a snappy tune with his son's pet duck tucked under one arm. "Thing One and Thing Two," he greeted them with the usual nicknames, then started whistling again.

Several months ago, Trace had walked around like he was shouldering the weight of the entire universe. The goofy smile on his face and the constant whistling were new since he'd fallen head over heels for Lily.

Chalk two up for Elliott.

He'd been the one to plant the seed of hiring a hospitality manager in his dad's head. Not only had Lily proven to be a prodigy in hotel hospitality management and was turning the resort around faster than any of them expected, but she'd managed to bring some well-deserved happiness to Trace.

Maybe the debt Elliott owed his family was a little smaller now.

"Waddles kept squawking, and Ben needed some quiet to finish his homework." Trace set the duck on the floor and pulled out his phone. "Lily's been looking for you, Thing One. I'll let her know you're here."

Elliott's stick scuffed the side of the white ball, and it rolled in the wrong direction. "Do you have a death wish?" He straightened. "'Cause I'm going to kill you in your sleep if you send that text."

Trace's face blanked. "What do you have against my fiancée?"

4

Waddles ruffled his malformed wing and wandered around the room. The limp from his bum leg caused him to rock like a boat in choppy water.

"Nothing." Elliott claimed the same barstool Spence had just vacated. "That's the problem. Landing the contract for a service dog camp—"

"Boot camp," Trace corrected.

Elliott tried not to roll his eyes. "Whatever. Landing a contract for an event that benefits veterans was brilliant, especially this time of year with summer winding down." Since he handled all things financial for the resort, he fully understood that the deposit alone, which the sponsor had paid to reserve the grounds and the rooms, was more than the Remington typically earned during the entire off-season. "I mean, who doesn't like either dogs or veterans? It's a win-win." As long as it was run by the right person. "Which is why it's going to be difficult to say no to Lily."

That and the fact she was like a lipstick-wearing pit bull when she was hell-bent on an idea to improve the resort or bring in new business.

"*Bullshit.*" Spence fake-coughed behind his hand. "He's *afraid* to say no to Lily." He banked a shot left to knock a solid into the side pocket.

Spence and Elliott might look alike, but their personalities couldn't be more different. Spence usually won the brothers' contest for biggest smart-ass—although Elliott had to admit it was a close call. But hands down, Elliott took home the award for the brother most likely to fail the family.

Being at the business end of a snarling dog wouldn't help make the event a success. An unsuccessful event would hurt the Remington, which would defeat the whole purpose of spending precious time trying to solidify the resort's financial future while his real job was on hold in San Francisco.

He didn't plan on dealing another blow to his family or the resort. The last blow had been bad enough to last a lifetime.

Guilt scratched at his stomach, and he tamped down the nausea that bubbled up every time he thought of his mother's accident.

"My fiancée barely reaches your elbows, but you're smart to be afraid." Trace grinned, dragging a barstool over to sit next to Elliott.

"Down Home Dog Food is a big corporate sponsor." Elliott scrubbed a hand across his five-o'clock shadow. "They can afford to hire an event coordinator with experience, and it's in their best interest to do so."

Trace shrugged. "They might be a big company, but their brand is more . . . well, down home. Lily landed the deal by pitching us as a wholesome family-owned business, so they want a Remington to take the lead and work with the trainer."

"I'm the least suitable person for this event." Elliott prided himself on knowing his weaknesses as well as his strengths. It saved him from making mistakes. Or at least from making the same mistakes twice. "Someone else in the family needs to step up."

"I'm busy with my new cargo delivery business, Lily's helping Howard's Hardware organize a community improvement month . . ." Trace nodded to Spence. "Thing Two has a list of remodeling projects that will keep him busy until the end of time, so you're the only one left."

"Not happening." Elliott rubbed the back of his neck. "Can you tell Lily? She'll accept my answer if it comes from you, since you're marrying her."

"*Aaaaand* we're back to you having no balls." Spence let his stick fly.

Trace's brow arched. "You obviously don't know women as well as you claim, Thing One."

"I dare you to take charge of the service dog camp," said Spence.

Trace rubbed his hands together. "Now we're getting somewhere."

The hair on the back of Elliott's neck prickled. Dares were another institution among the Remington siblings. Probably a sign they should

6

rethink some of their childhood shenanigans that had survived into adulthood.

"Lily really liked the dog whisperer she hired to replace the original trainer." An evil grin spread across Trace's face. "They conducted the interview through a video call, and Lily said she's an attractive redhead. You like redheads, right?"

Elliott's jaw tightened. A long time ago, he'd liked *one* redhead. Until he'd come home from his first semester at Wharton to find out she'd ditched him. Vanished without a forwarding address and no explanation except a kiss-off note she'd entrusted to Old Lady McGill at the ferry crossing. Not sure what that said about him, but it was enough to get redheads out of his system for good.

Spence missed, and Elliott got up, put the pool stick behind his back for show, and sank the next stripe. "Nice try, but I'm not stupid."

Spence scoffed. "Since when?"

"Then do it for the resort," Trace argued. "If we impress the sponsor, they might host an event here every year."

Hard to say no to that one.

Now that the Remington was coming off its first successful summer season in years, Elliott wanted to make sure they kept financial momentum going so the resort had a steady flow of income year-round. Then he could get the hell off the island and away from the haunting memories.

As soon as he figured out how to break it to his family that he wasn't home for good. Probably something he should've already mentioned before his dad signed over ownership to his brothers and him. Definitely the reason he was still sleeping in Spence's extra bedroom instead of claiming one of the vacant cottages in the remote part of the resort where the rest of his family lived.

He missed his next shot.

Yeah, no balls. Spence was right.

"We still have the little problem of animals not liking me." Elliott walked over to Waddles and knelt with his hand out.

Waddles squawked, shuffled away, and settled at Trace's feet, making a noise that was somewhere between a cluck and a cackle.

Elliott gave Trace a look that said *told you so*. "If I can't win over a duck, then I won't stand a chance with a bunch of dogs that have sharp teeth."

"Look, the trainer will be working with the dogs, not you. Down Home Dog Food has been promoting it as a community outreach program, and interview requests are already hitting their inboxes. All you have to do is be the face of the resort." Trace chuckled. "You know, stand to the side and look pretty."

Spence laughed, then sank the eight ball to win the game. "Mr. Congeniality here will be representing us in the news? We might as well board up the windows."

"Fine." Elliott hitched his chin at Spence. "But I'm only doing it to prove that asshat wrong." Never hurt to show up his brothers and let them know he was still a force to be reckoned with, no matter how old they got. "You two are going to owe me big for accepting this dare."

"Good." Trace stood as Spence racked and stacked the balls into a perfect triangle. "You can pick up the dog whisperer at the ferry terminal first thing in the morning. She's coming in ahead of the dogs and veterans to set up."

Elliott returned his stick to the wall rack. "I'm going to my office." He headed to the door. "I've got toilet paper to order, and we're getting low on the miniature shampoo and conditioner bottles we put in each room." His life was so damn exciting. If his buddies in the world of high finance could see him now.

Trace scooped up Waddles and handed him to Elliott. "Take him with you. He needs water."

Elliott gave his older brother a *not on your life* look.

"It's a duck, not a wolverine." Trace pressed the duck against Elliott's chest, and his arms closed around it instinctively. "There's a water bowl for him in Lily's office. Consider it practice for the canine boot camp."

Waddles squawked in disapproval and pecked Elliott's arm. *"Ouch."* He glared at the bird. "Do that again and duck stew will be our next meal."

Waddles settled into Elliott's chest but kept cackling his unhappiness.

Elliott pulled the game room door open to go knock out some of the tedious work he'd been putting off. If there were no shower caps and pillow mints in the rooms, this week's guests might riot. But if he could get ahead on his regular workload tonight, then give the trainer one thousand percent of his attention when she arrived tomorrow . . .

Scratch that. Two thousand percent. Because his driven personality required nothing less.

And if the service dog camp was a success, it might bring him that much closer to going back to San Francisco where he belonged.

Dog training and drinking strong coffee were Rebel Tate's superpowers, and today was a three-cup kind of day.

A buzz of anticipation raced through her as she leaned against the railing of the small ferry. It cut through the sapphire-blue water of the narrow channel separating Cape Celeste from the small vacation island. Showing up in Angel Fire Falls a day before she was due would give her extra time to set up before the dog matching boot camp started in a week.

And might help her get over the earthquake of nerves that was shaking her concentration over seeing *him* again before the campers arrived.

Time. Time—and a lot of it—had passed since she'd crossed the channel for what she'd thought would be the last time. Since she'd lost her mother and set out on her own as a homeless eighteen-year-old. Since she'd decided to end it with the love of her life because she knew he never would.

Yet it seemed like yesterday.

The furry shoulder of her retriever pressed into her thigh.

She stroked the young dog's head and adjusted his service vest. "I'll be fine, Rem." Besides the nest of angry hornets stinging her insides, she was as golden as the dog's shiny coat. After ten years, she was returning to Angel Fire Falls a different person than when she'd left.

Mostly.

No more ratty clothes that had drawn snickers from the high school mean-girls clique. No more taking care of her mother, who was either strung out or passed out every day when Rebel had gotten home from school. No more living in her car or sleeping on park benches once she'd moved to Portland when her mother was hospitalized for a failing liver.

The only things about Rebel that hadn't changed were her flaming red hair and love of animals. Okay, she still loved mocha java chip ice cream like a girl gone mad. Coffee, ice cream, and dogs weren't bad vices to have, considering her upbringing.

Rem leaned heavier against her side.

She gave his head a pat. "It's okay, buddy. I'm not that nervous."

His whine told her he wasn't any more convinced than she was. Obviously, his BS radar was just as sharp as his ability to detect rising cortisol levels.

She chuckled and scratched behind his ear, thankful for the comfort he provided. "It's just a town." A small town where her mother's humiliating lifestyle had overshadowed Rebel's entire youth. "I doubt anyone will remember me." She'd lived life on the fringe, never accepted by the cool kids. Except for one. Elliott Remington had taken an interest in her during a calculus class. They'd both been smart, tough survivors.

No doubt he'd remember her.

No one forgot their first love. Especially when one of them walked away with no explanation, asking to be left alone. For good.

The ferry's deep horn echoed through the light fog rolling in off the ocean. The rocky cliffs of Angel Fire Falls rose out of the mist in the distance, and the late-afternoon tide beat against the white sandy beach as the ferry drew closer to the terminal.

She zipped her heavy windbreaker, pulled out her phone, and took a photo of Rem staring at the coast. Tapping on the screen, she uploaded the picture to her Instagram account, @WestCoastDogWhisperer. She stared up at the overcast sky before typing the caption *Homecomings can be stressful, but my service dog is on it!* Then she added the hashtag #ThreeCupKindOfDay and posted it.

Social media had been instrumental in building her clientele as a dog whisperer. But not nearly as instrumental as the service dog matching camp would be in securing a training facility of her own. The accelerated schedule was definitely going to be a challenge, but the small fortune Down Home Dog Food had offered for stepping in at the last minute would fund her business plan and provide the down payment for a building. The media coverage the sponsor had planned for the event might help her solicit donations once she opened a nonprofit facility.

The boot camp might've been last-minute, but the timing couldn't have been better. The abandoned shelter she had her eye on wouldn't stay on the market forever. Someone else would eventually realize what a hidden jewel it was and snatch it up.

Unless she made an offer on it first.

There was just one little catch that had Rebel's anxiety soaring as high as the rocky cliffs that were drawing closer. One tiny problem that could derail her focus on the camp and send the emotions she'd learned to keep in check spiraling.

The camp was hosted at the one place she'd never been able to forget because of the fond memories. Memories she'd held on to for years, locked away in her heart because they were the only good things she had from her life on the island. She'd worked at the resort to spend time with Elliott, and his family had become hers. The Remington had been her refuge.

And *he* was there. She'd perused the resort's website and social media pages, her breath catching on the pictures of Elliott.

She glanced down at Rem as the foghorn echoed through the mist.

He pressed into her like he was trained to do when she got upset. The tightness in her chest eased.

"How 'bout we call you Buddy while we're on the island?" Coming face-to-face with the guy she'd walked away from was going to be hard enough. If Elliott found out she'd named her service dog after his family's resort, that she'd named every service dog she'd owned after the Remington, he'd probably start asking questions. Questions she didn't want to answer because there was no sense dwelling on the past.

Rem lifted his head to pant into the breeze, allowing the cool air to blow back his ears.

The loudspeaker crackled to life. "We'll dock in five minutes," the ferry captain said, as though he couldn't have turned around and spoken to her, since she wasn't more than ten feet away and the only passenger on the two-car ferry.

Rebel drew in a deep breath, letting the fresh, salty air of the Pacific Northwest fill her lungs. The first signs of the shifting seasons added a crisp edge to the atmosphere, and she pulled the neck of her windbreaker over her chin.

As if to hide.

When she'd accepted the job, she knew returning to the island would be hard, but why did she feel like she was returning to the scene of a crime?

Anxiety bolted through her, and Rem looked up at her with a whimper.

Probably because she *was* returning to the scene of her mother's crime. Mom dying before she could fess up to what she'd done hadn't eased Rebel's conscience or brought justice to the other family who had been destroyed.

With Rem's leash in one hand and her suitcase in the other, she nodded to the captain and walked down the ramp. Her bag thumping behind her, she glanced at the sign at the entrance of the open-air terminal that said WELCOME TO ANGEL FIRE FALLS.

Her heart stuttered.

As she passed through the entrance, Ms. McGill's familiar profile and supersize backcombed hair greeted Rebel from behind the scratched acrylic ticket booth window. Half a dozen vacationers stood in line with their bags, obviously booking passage back to the mainland.

Rebel glanced at the shuttle schedule hanging on the wall next to the booth and stepped to the back of the line to pay for a ride. While she waited, she turned and took in the rocky shoreline to the left and the white sandy beach to the right. Her gaze landed on the small country road that led inland. Led to the Remington.

She swallowed hard.

Rem leaned harder and wedged the top of his head under her palm.

She moved up another space in line just as a scraggly mixed-breed dog that was missing a front leg hopped over to them. Rem growled playfully.

"Settle," Rebel said.

The three-legged dog seemed to like the attention and wanted to play. He sidled up to Rem, who proceeded to lick the dog's face.

"Rebel Tate? Is that you?"

Rebel jumped at Ms. McGill's scratchy voice and swung around. Rebel eased up to the window as the other passengers disappeared through the exit, ferry tickets in hand.

Mabel McGill hadn't changed one bit. Coral lipstick still bled into the deep lines around her mouth. Both bony hands lifted to her cheeks in surprise, and her sparkling blue eyes filled with warmth.

"Yes, ma'am." Rebel greeted her with a smile. "Good to see you, Ms. McGill."

"It's been an age. You're all grown up now, so you might as well call me Mabel. What brings you back to the island, hon?"

"I'm . . ." The reality that she was going to be living at the Remington for a little more than a month made her throat close. "I've been hired to work on an event at the Remington," she managed to choke out.

One of Mabel's penciled-on eyebrows lifted.

Rebel glanced away from that knowing look and eyed the cawing seagulls hovering for scraps of food. She chewed her lip before she said, "It's a service dog boot camp." She lifted Rem's leash. "I'm a professional trainer."

Mabel's eyes glittered. "That should be *interesting*." The way she stressed the last word said she wasn't just talking about Rebel's profession or the camp. No, she was talking about her long history with the middle Remington brother and the way Rebel had slipped away from the island right after Elliott went off to college.

The dog rolled onto his back in submission, and Rem nuzzled him. Rebel had enough experience to recognize the signs of a puppy, and she figured he was probably two years old or less.

Mabel leaned closer to the glass to look at the dogs. "He showed up on the island a few months ago, and no one has claimed him. I named him Bogart."

"He's not chipped?" Rebel asked.

Mabel shook her head, and not one backcombed strand of hair moved. "I took him to the only vet on the island, and Dr. Shaw couldn't find a chip. No tag either. So I feed him and let him stay in the booth at night for shelter." She paused. "Can't bring him home, though. My grandkids visit every weekend, and one has asthma."

Rebel had seen it a thousand times. Someone didn't have the compassion to bring him to a shelter, so they dumped him off and made him someone else's problem.

Rebel retrieved her wallet from the small fanny pack under her jacket. "I'm here a day ahead of schedule, so the Remingtons aren't picking me up. I need a lift to the resort."

Mabel punched a few buttons on her register and out popped a ticket. "Next shuttle should be here in a few minutes. It's running more often even now that tourist season is over on account of how busy we've been."

Rebel handed her a bill. "Thanks."

"We've also got bicycles and giant trikes if you want to take a ride around the island while you're here." Mabel slid the ticket across the counter. "Next summer we'll have scooters to rent out." Mabel shrugged. "Just FYI for next time you visit."

The chance of there being a next time was about as good as, say, Rebel living down her awful name. *Thank you, Mom.*

Mabel waggled her brows. "Business is good thanks to the Remington hiring that new hospitality manager. The whole island is flourishing again."

Rebel nodded. Lily was the one who'd contacted her about the job. She'd been persuasive and persistent, and Rebel couldn't have said no to her any more than she could've turned down Mother Teresa on a mission to save orphaned children. Even after she found out where Lily worked.

Rebel picked up the ticket. "Thanks. I'm afraid I couldn't bring Re—" She stumbled over the dog's name because one of Mabel's artistic eyebrows wouldn't just arch. They'd both disappear into the hairline of her large 'do. "My dog couldn't ride on a scooter." She let a playful smile settle on her lips. "Unless you'll be offering one with a sidecar."

Mabel picked up a deck of cards so worn the edges were frayed and started shuffling like it was her way of thinking. "Not a bad idea. I never thought my adult-size tricycles would be in high demand." She stopped shuffling long enough to wave a hand toward the beach.

Rebel turned to glance at the row of bikes and trikes chained to a bike rack, their blue-and-yellow flags swaying in the breeze. Half the slots were empty.

"I could hardly keep them in stock during the vacation season. Even now that summer's over, they're still popular." The zip of the cards made Rebel turn around again. "I bet scooters with sidecars would go over big."

"If the sidecar doesn't work out, I'll bring my own car over on the ferry when I—" Rebel hesitated. "If I visit again." She'd driven to the Cape but had left her car in long-term parking for fear the small ferry might capsize with an actual car on it.

"Good to see you again." Rebel grabbed the handle of her luggage and turned toward one of the wooden benches to wait for the next shuttle. She stopped and angled her body back toward the booth. "Um, Mabel . . ." She wasn't sure how to phrase the question she desperately wanted to ask.

Did you give Elliott the Dear John letter I was too chicken to deliver myself? How did he take it when he came home for the holidays and realized I'd abandoned him? Has he hated me all these years for dumping him even though it was for his own good? Or worse. Maybe he hadn't given her a second thought.

Her stomach did a flippity-flop.

How long had it taken him to realize she was an albatross who would've held him back from the bright future he'd had ahead of him? As smart as Elliott was, he'd likely figured it out before she had. His sense of duty, the way he'd looked out for her, was probably the reason he hadn't broken up with her first.

When Rebel couldn't speak, Mabel's expression softened. "I made sure he got your letter, hon, but I wasn't around when he opened it."

The buzz of an engine drew their attention, and a shuttle bus came over a rise in the road.

"That's your ride," Mabel said. "I hope your stay on the island is pleasant."

She wasn't the only one. Even if Rebel would be reporting to Lily, her path would cross with Elliott's. How could it not?

Rebel couldn't muster more than a half-hearted smile. "Thanks, Mabel. I owe you one."

She shrugged and shuffled. "I get that a lot. Don't mention it, hon. I'm here to help folks however they need."

The shuttle pulled to a stop in front of the terminal. Rebel lifted her chin and inhaled a cleansing breath, trying to relax. It might be the last time she could until she completed the camp and went on her way with the nice payday she needed to fulfill the dream that would finally give her the sense of purpose she'd been looking for her entire life.

Because she was not leaving this island a failure. Again.

Chapter Two

#EpicFail

Rebel peered through the shuttle window as it slowed along the circular drive and stopped under the covered portico of the Remington. Her former teenage sanctuary looked good. Fresh paint on the wood trim framed the stone facade, and double doors at the entrance shone with new varnish.

No one was waiting to greet her, just the way she'd intended. She'd wanted to arrive under the radar. Give herself a little time alone to adjust. Seeing the resort again was nostalgic. Sentimental.

Terrifying.

She drew in a breath and stood. As she led Rem down the aisle, she glanced out the front windshield. Two groundskeepers were busy manicuring a grouping of Oregon holly shrubs that were tinged with deep red. The island was technically part of Washington, but since it was right on the Oregon state line, Angel Fire Falls captured the charm of both.

She stepped off the shuttle with Rem at her side while the driver fumbled to unload her luggage. The way the nautical uniform swallowed his youthful frame said he was barely old enough to qualify for a commercial driver's license. The way he struggled with her suitcase said he was as inexperienced as he looked.

He gave her a nervous glance through the open door of the shuttle.

"Push the button on top of the handle." She smiled, hoping to reassure him.

Rem strained toward the kid, his keen ability to detect stress kicking in. Unfortunately, a service dog was supposed to respond only to its companion, not to everyone experiencing anxiety. Which was why he'd been rejected from a previous matching program and abandoned.

"Settle," Rebel said to him in a calm, low voice.

Rem plopped onto his haunches.

The driver knocked the bag over, and it tumbled down the steps of the bus, lodging in the open door.

"Need help?" she asked. The kid's driving had been stellar. Everything that had happened after the bus was in park was another story.

"No, ma'am," he insisted.

Ma'am? She looked old enough to be a ma'am? *Fanfreakingtastic.* No one wanted to reunite with old friends and acquaintances—and ex-boyfriends—looking like a *ma'am.* She stopped herself from frowning. Didn't frowns cause more wrinkles than smiles?

Rem got up and pulled toward the side of the bus, whining.

Rebel didn't move, waiting for the tension in his leash to relax. Rem was still young and a little jumpy, but she wasn't giving up on him like his previous trainer had. Giving up on a dog usually meant their time would be short. Without a supportive trainer, it was hard to find them a home.

That's what made her future facility so unique. She didn't plan to use pedigreed dogs specifically bred for service programs. She also didn't plan to use training handlers who spent two years with a dog before pairing them with a companion in need of a service dog. She planned to use rescues and match them right away with victims of traumatic brain injuries and anxiety disorders similar to the veterans who'd be attending this camp. She'd train the human, and the human could train the dog. Suffering people shouldn't have to wait years for a match, and the traditional training process excluded a lot of homeless dogs just because they were born into unfortunate circumstances. Both the rescue dogs and their recipients needed someone in their corner rooting for them, believing in them, willing to take a chance on them.

Rebel knew the feeling.

Finally, Rem eased up and waited for Rebel's cue instead of pulling ahead of her.

"Good boy."

But then he pulled free and took off at a dead run, disappearing around the rear of the bus.

"Re—" She stopped herself. "Buddy!"

She turned to go after him just as her suitcase sprang free and the driver tumbled out onto the curb along with it.

"Are you okay?" She bent to help him up.

The receding sound of Rem's barking told Rebel he was putting distance between them.

"Yes, ma'am." The kid turned bright red. "Sorry. I'm new at this job."

She never would've guessed.

The bus blocked her view of Rem, but his frenzied barks told her he was on the lawn that led to the resort's game room. A place she'd spent a lot of time. With Elliott. Working, playing, falling in love.

In the distance, Rem squeaked and barked violently, like he'd treed a terrorist.

She stuffed a nice tip into the driver's shirt pocket. "I need to go after my dog."

She left her suitcase on the curb and hurried around the bus.

Rebel's breath seized.

Across the lawn, a man dove for a flailing duck. The duck squawked and escaped as the man fell to the ground, empty-handed.

Rem pounced on the duck, pinning it with his front paws.

Oh. No. No, no, no.

The duck pecked Rem's nose, which sent him reeling backward with a whine and more barking. Having escaped, the duck went airborne for several feet, then lost altitude, and Rem pounced again.

She took off running. "Buddy, stop!"

Rem ignored her. The three-ring-circus act among the man, the duck, and the dog started all over again. The man dove, the duck escaped, Rem pounced, the duck pecked.

"Buddy!" She kept running.

Good Lord. She hoped no one was recording this, because #EpicFail wouldn't be the best advertising if the video showed up on Instagram.

She increased her speed. Only to stop cold when the man started to pull himself to his feet. Didn't matter that his back was to her or that he wasn't a teen anymore. No, this guy was all man now, and she'd know him anywhere. Inch by alpha-testosterone-inch, he rose until his T-shaped frame reached more than six feet tall. A gray thermal shirt molded across broad shoulders and a muscled back, tapering down to a slender waist. Nicely broken-in Levi's cupped a firm ass and molded to long, powerful legs. Wavy light-brown hair brushed the nape of his neck, just long enough to give him a bad-boy look.

He stopped, his body rippling with tension, and angled his head to one side. Not fully looking over his shoulder but listening, processing. Like he sensed an unwelcome presence.

He started to turn, the world around her slowing.

Rebel took a step back.

Her heart thumped and bumped against her rib cage, and she fought the urge to turn and leave. Retreating—running away, to be perfectly honest—wasn't an option this time. She wasn't a desperate eighteen-year-old girl anymore, and it was time to stand her ground. Face him head-on, even if he didn't need to know the truth behind her sudden departure.

They'd been kids ten years ago. Now they were adults with jobs to do. The past didn't matter.

Except that it so obviously still did if the shift in his sea-green eyes was any indication. They locked onto her, clouding over like one of the storms so common in the Pacific Northwest.

She forgot to breathe.

Time stopped as recognition registered in his gaze and a rainbow of emotions morphed from one to the other, finally settling on the most disturbing.

Cold indifference.

What bothered her the most was that she deserved it.

"Elliott," she said.

"What are you doing here?" His tone flatlined.

Rem's agitated bark provided a welcome interruption. He was still chasing the poor duck.

Luckily, the duck held his own with effective one-two pecks from his lethal beak. So Rem had resorted to barks and lunges without actually touching the bird, which had mastered Self-Defense 101.

"Heel, Buddy."

Rem whined but stilled.

"Sit." She walked to the dog with a steady gait so she wouldn't spook him.

He sat, keeping a bead on the duck.

She picked up his leash. "Settle."

The dog visibly relaxed and finally refocused on her instead of the bird.

"Good boy." She patted his head and forced herself to look at Elliott.

Like he wasn't going to budge until she answered his question, he crossed his arms. Nice strong arms, with muscles that rippled and rolled under his thermal.

Ladyland purred.

She forced her attention back to his dark stare and scrunched her brows. He'd asked what she was doing there.

Wait. Oh . . .

Elliott didn't know she'd been hired as the new dog trainer.

"What do you want?" he asked.

Right. This wasn't going to be awkward. Not in the least. "I'm here for the boot camp." Rebel chose her words carefully, the heat of his stare licking over her like fire.

Rem pulled on the leash, and she released enough slack for him to sit flush against Elliott, who immediately stepped away. Rem followed. Instead of taking another step back, Elliott focused on the dog, like he was really seeing the service vest for the first time.

His eyes widened.

"You're staying *here*? To train your dog?" His head snapped up, his voice a mixture of shock and disbelief.

"No," Rebel responded. "Well, yes. I'm the new tr—"

A horn beeped and a white Jeep appeared, coming from the lane she knew led to the residential cottages where members of the family lived. The Jeep pulled around the drive and parked.

A young boy jumped out of the passenger seat and lumbered toward the duck. "Waddles!"

It didn't seem to startle the duck at all. In fact, the duck waddled in the boy's direction as fast and furious as his legs would carry him. The boy scooped him up into a hug, and the duck settled against the kid's chest like they were long-lost pals.

Rebel had never seen anything like it, except with therapy dogs. But a therapy duck?

It was incredible. And totally awesome.

"Hi, Uncle Elliott," the boy half yelled. Then he skipped all the way into the game room.

So one of the Remington brothers had a kid.

A pretty woman with light-brown hair, about Rebel's age, climbed out of the driver's seat and hurried over with an iPad in her hand. When she got close enough, Rebel recognized her from their video calls. "Rebel Tate?" Lily offered a friendly wave as she approached.

"Yes." Rebel glanced at Elliott.

His hard body grew even more stiff, tension rolling off him. Rem whined and pressed into Elliott, who seemed to grow confused at the dog's attention.

Rebel tightened her grip on the leash to prevent a replay of the dog-and-hottie show she'd just witnessed.

"Ms. McGill just called me from the ferry terminal and said you were on your way." Lily stopped within arm's reach and held out her hand.

Rebel shook it. "I hope it's okay that I came early. I'm excited about the camp and wanted extra time to prepare." They didn't need to know the extra prep time was for her to get her bearings before the inevitable confrontation.

She glanced at Elliott's scowling face. Definitely an epic fail.

"It's perfectly fine. I see you two have met." Lily shifted her friendly expression to Elliott. "Rebel is the expert dog whisperer we've hired for the boot camp."

Elliott's scowl deepened like he was in physical pain.

Rebel stared down at a blade of grass like it was the most fascinating shade of green she'd ever seen. Besides Elliott's ridiculously beautiful eyes, of course.

Rem whined. Stepped toward Rebel, then back to Elliott like he couldn't decide who was the most stressed.

Lily's expression blanked, and she gave them both a confused look. "What's going on?"

When Elliott didn't offer a response, Rebel spoke up. "Elliott and I already know each other. I grew up on the island."

"Oh. Well, welcome back, then." Lily gave both of them an uncertain smile. "Small world, isn't it?"

Elliott shrugged. "Not really all that small. It's big enough for a person to run away and hide. For years."

That one stung.

"Look, I—" *Didn't want to let you go. Didn't want to drag you down.* She definitely didn't want to bring up their history right then and there. She lifted her chin. "I'm here to work, and I guarantee I'll do a great job with the camp."

"Great!" Lily obviously thought that settled it. "The sponsor put together profiles for each veteran." She tapped on the screen of her iPad. "I'm forwarding those to you as we speak. Why don't I show you to your room, then you can spend the rest of the day getting reacquainted with the Remington, since you weren't scheduled to start until tomorrow."

"Sounds good," Rebel said.

At the same time Elliott said, "Not happening."

That awkward pause was back, and Rebel cleared her throat. "I agreed to work with you, Lily. Whatever you want is fine with me."

"Actually." The nearly undetectable hesitation in Lily's voice made the hair on Rebel's arms prickle. "You'll be working with Elliott while you're here. He'll be in charge of the boot camp."

And the situation just skyrocketed from awkward to downright nightmarish.

Sibling rivalry was one thing, but Elliott didn't usually get seriously pissed at his brothers. Until today.

He stalked back to the game room to give Big Brother a chance to explain why he'd forgotten to mention who the new trainer for the dog camp would be. Before Elliott castrated him.

What were the odds?

As a college kid home from his first semester, there were limits to how far he could reach, how long he could search. Because hell yes, he'd looked for Rebel even though her note had clearly said not to.

The Rebel he'd known and been so close to wouldn't have walked away without telling him face-to-face. Or at least over the phone, since he'd been at school on the opposite coast. She would've broken up with him in person and given him a reason. Even if that reason was nothing more than "I don't love you anymore" or "We've grown apart" or "I've found someone else." It wasn't so much what her piss-off note had said. It was more what it hadn't said.

So he'd defied her wishes and looked for her anyway. To see if she was okay. To see if he could help.

To see if she still loved him.

He'd found nothing. Returned to school hoping she'd contact him eventually.

She never had.

Her showing up here, now, where they'd spent years planning their future, was . . . a shock. The old wound he thought had healed long ago started to throb with a soul-deep ache.

Especially since she still had a body that could stop traffic.

His strides lengthened.

When Elliott stepped onto the path that led to the game room, a small space between the slats of the shades snapped shut.

He threw open the door.

Cockroaches probably scurried less than Trace and Spence, who hurried away from the window and resumed their game of pool like nothing was wrong.

Elliott glanced at his nephew, Ben—who was playing a video game at one of the game stations, his pet duck sitting in the chair on the far side of him—and bit back a string of colorful language.

The duck cackled at Elliott like it had out on the lawn, right before it had tried to peck him to death. He glared at the bird. He could swear the damn duck glared back.

"Uncle Elliott!" Ben's volume was always dialed up ten notches above normal because of his Asperger's. "I'm joining the Frontier Scouts! When I earn my first badge, they'll have a pinning ceremony. Want to come?"

"Of course, little man." If he didn't go down for twenty-five to life for making Ben an orphan. "I never made it to Lily's office to get Waddles a bowl of water. Want to go take care of that?"

"Yep!" Ben scooped up the duck and thundered through the door.

Elliott moved to the side to let him through, then folded both arms over his chest, glaring at his older brother. "Care to explain why you tricked me into an event working with the one person on earth you knew I never wanted to see again?"

Trace straightened. "If the redhead outside is who I think she is, I didn't know." His sympathetic look said he was telling the truth. "I've never mentioned your history with Rebel to Lily, so this is purely a coincidence. A really bad one, but a coincidence nonetheless."

Elliott pinched the corners of his eyes with a thumb and forefinger. With a shove, he shut the door and slumped into the chair at the game station Ben had just left. "No way in hell is this happening." Just in case his brothers didn't get the message, he communicated the same thing in code by running the tip of his thumb all the way across his forehead.

"I'd trade places with you if I could, but you can't fly my planes." Trace tossed his pool stick onto the table and braced both palms against it.

"Same here," said Spence. "But you're not exactly a master when it comes to wielding a hammer."

True. Unless Elliott used it to bludgeon his oldest and most annoying brother for getting him into this mess. Then he'd rock at wielding a hammer.

"No one else in the family is available," said Trace.

"Bullshit." Elliott's heart pounded against his crossed arms. "Spence, your renovations can wait."

He shook his head. "I've got to pour the foundation for the new veranda and finish enlarging the parking lot before winter sets in." He hitched his chin up at Trace. "Asshat here has me renovating and expanding the boathouse into a warehouse for his cargo loads. It has to be you."

"No." Elliott's tone couldn't have gotten any flatter if a steamroller had hit him. His brothers needed to start learning to handle things without him because he wouldn't be around forever.

Tiny beads of sweat formed around his neck, and he pulled at the neckline of his shirt.

He hadn't meant to mislead his family about his plan to eventually go back to San Francisco. When he hadn't left the island right after the holidays, his dad had assumed he was staying. Dad had been so excited that, one by one, all his kids had come home. His dad had immediately handed off the resort's finances to Elliott, consulted with him on how to return the resort to its prime, and included him in the management decisions until Dad finally phased himself out completely.

After that, Elliott couldn't bring himself to let his dad down. Not again. Not since Elliott was responsible for making his dad a widower.

"You and Rebel were . . . uh, close once." Trace's tone wasn't even close to confident. "Maybe you'll get along fine."

"*Hell* no," Elliott fired back.

"We're talking about five short weeks. You've got a week before the campers start arriving and then a month for the vets to train with their new service dogs," Trace said.

"Those vets survived war," Spence said. "You can survive an old girlfriend for five weeks."

"That's low, even for you two idiots," Elliott huffed.

"It's your call." Trace slid a butt cheek onto the side of the pool table. "I'll cancel right now if that's what you want."

Elliott didn't know which would be worse—the loss of revenue, the loss of PR and press coverage the camp would bring in for the resort, or proceeding with the event with a dog trainer who couldn't control her own dog. Never mind that the trainer had made what had to be the quickest exit from his life in relationship history.

His background with said dog trainer and the fact that he knew as much about dogs as he did brain surgery made it an even bigger clusterfuck.

He wished like hell the Remington didn't need this event so much, but it did. Canceling because of an old flame would be a wuss move. Especially since they were grown adults now.

He could handle it for a little while. Didn't matter that she was still as gorgeous as he'd remembered. Didn't matter that he might need dentures by the time it was over because of the way he was grinding his teeth into dust.

"This is how it's gonna go down." He gave his brothers a pointed stare. "I'll take the lead for now, but I'm going to have Lily start looking for someone to take my place. She'll have to make the sponsor understand that putting a family member in charge of this event isn't an option right now."

It was the best he could do under the circumstances. If it didn't work out, he'd figure out another way to stabilize the resort's future and tell his family that he was leaving the island for the career he'd put on hold. For the partnership he'd earned. For the long work hours he'd used to keep his mind off the past.

His firm in San Francisco had been patient and understanding. Not common for a group of finance experts who thrived on risk and were constantly forging ahead to reach the next business goal. But they weren't going to wait for him forever, no matter how good he was at his job, how many lucrative clients he'd reeled in, or how much money he'd made them.

He might owe his family and the resort, but every man had his breaking point. Losing all the years of hard work he'd invested in that firm was his. So was working with the only girl who'd managed to rip his heart out of his chest while it was still beating.

Chapter Three

#$H!TGETSREAL

The next day, Rebel silently chanted the words *payday, payday, payday* over and over in her head as she started to set up for the boot camp. Elliott climbed into the last of the Remington's fleet of Jeeps and backed it out of the motor-pool garage, which was the designated space for the veterans and the service dogs.

Rebel tried to focus on the stacks of wire crates and boxed supplies that filled an entire garage bay. Down Home Dog Food hadn't skimped. For someone in her profession, opening that many boxes of canine goodies should've felt like Christmas. Instead, it felt like a bad dream thanks to the sour attitude of her helper.

She pushed a wire crate against the wall and went back for another.

She'd assumed her reception wouldn't be warm and fuzzy. Glacier cold would be a better description. How on earth was she going to make this work?

Better yet, what had she been *thinking*, coming back to Angel Fire Falls? Had she really been naive enough to think they could coexist on the same island? Had she really been stupid enough to think it wouldn't cut her to the bone to see him again, the kindness and love that used to be in his eyes when he looked at her turned to chips of ice?

Maybe she should give him an opportunity to vent. Tell him it was okay to get things out once and for all. Because she'd been back only one day, and she was already tiptoeing so much she might as well invest in a pair of ballerina slippers.

Elliott walked in and stood in one of the empty bays. "You're putting the dogs in cages?"

The sound of his voice slid through her like hot coffee on a cold afternoon. Not smooth, but bold and exhilarating in an edgy way that got her juices flowing.

Payday, payday, payday.

That commercial property was as good as hers. She'd finally have a bigger purpose in life. All she had to do was keep it together and not get too personal with the glowering hottie who was going to be her coworker for the next few weeks.

"They're crates, not cages." She kept her tone impersonal. Braced both hands against the crate and pushed it toward the wall, spacing it several feet from the other.

Rem matched her steps.

"Isn't that cruel and inhumane?" Elliott asked.

"Not unless the animals are neglected. Crate training solves half a dog's behavior issues and housebreaking problems." There. Keeping it impersonal could work.

The bottom of the crate caught on a lump in the concrete floor, and she stumbled. *"Ooomph."*

Elliott was at her side with near supernatural speed. One strong arm circled her waist, his other hand circled her arm, and he caught her before she tumbled face-first over the crate.

When she regained her footing, she looked up at him.

For a second, she couldn't breathe.

Those soulful green eyes stared down at her, filled with concern like they had been years ago when she'd spent an hour crying in the girls' bathroom at school because of her mom. Or when he'd shown up at her house the night before a big calculus test to make sure she studied. Or when he'd broken the news to her that he was going away to college, knowing she wouldn't have the same opportunity.

"You okay?" The cold edge in his voice was softer. Kinder. Less guarded.

She nodded, letting a sharp breath whisper through her lips as she forced air into her aching lungs. "Thank you."

He let go, his warmth draining away. "Be careful. The event can't afford to lose another trainer." The flatness of his tone was back. "I'll do the heavy lifting." He turned his back to her and picked up the crate, carrying it to the wall. "Where do you want it?"

Dangerous question with his perfectly worn jeans cupping and hugging in all the right places.

Her mouth turned to cotton. "Line them up around the perimeter." The scratch in her voice wasn't obvious. Not in the least.

He placed the crate against the wall and picked up another.

She followed him with a stack of waterproof foam pads, placing one in the bottom of each crate.

They worked fast and efficiently, the strained silence speaking louder than if they were communicating with a bullhorn.

When they were done, there was nothing left to *not* talk about.

He shoved both hands into his pockets. "What next?" Rem settled against Elliott. When he took a step to one side, Rem followed. Elliott's wrinkled forehead said he didn't know what to make of it.

"Come here, Buddy." She gave the dog a signal meant to draw him to her side.

Rem's tongue lolled out one side of his mouth, and he leaned harder into Elliott's leg.

Rebel studied them. This could be a problem. Rem's behavior was already regressing since she'd arrived at the resort. What kind of impression would that make on the veterans? She needed them to trust her instructions if they were going to make quick progress once they were matched with a service dog.

She drew in a long, slow breath and pointed to a large wooden pallet that had gigantic bags of Down Home Dog Food shrink-wrapped to it. "Put a bag at each station. We'll feed the dogs inside their crates to eliminate aggressive or territorial behavior at mealtimes."

He looked surprised. "I wouldn't have thought of that, but it makes sense," he grumbled as though it pained him to pay her a quasi-compliment. He retrieved a box cutter from a tool chest in the corner, went to the pallet of dog food, and started slicing through the plastic wrap.

"Most dog training is common sense. Patience is the key." Rebel rearranged several boxes that were sitting next to the stacks of dog food. Each box was marked with the company name and slogan: DOWN HOME DOG FOOD—THEY'RE NOT JUST PETS. THEY'RE FAMILY. "I'll unpack the boxes and see what we have to work with. I have no idea what supplies the previous trainer requested, but if we can set up each station so the vets have everything at their fingertips, it'll reduce their stress levels."

She tried to rip open a box, but she was no match for the amount of packing tape used to secure each one. "Wow." She straightened, a hand on her hip. "That could hold the Golden Gate Bridge together."

With the same scowl he'd been sporting since they first saw each other on the front lawn, he waved the cutting tool at the boxes to shoo her away without a word.

She stepped to the side. As he bent over a box and ran the sharp edge of the tool along a strip of tape, Rem bumped Elliott's leg. The box cutter slipped and nicked the tip of his thumb.

"*Damn it.*" He dropped the tool and stared at the red stream oozing down his hand.

"I'm so sorry!" She took the handle on Rem's vest and led him back a few steps. "He's still in training." And probably would be forever.

When she reached for Elliott's hand, his scowl deepened, and he recoiled.

She hissed in a breath and stepped back too, his reaction like a slap in the face.

Pay. Day.

She let her eyes slide shut for the briefest of moments to block out Elliott's magnificently square jaw. His ridiculously handsome face. His look of disgust because she'd tried to take his hand.

Big payday. Huge, even.

"You need to put pressure on it." She pointed to the area above the knuckle of his bleeding thumb. "Squeeze there to slow the blood flow."

It was hard to unlock her gaze from the light stubble across his strong jaw that was just enough to look ruggedly sexy. Slowly, he put pressure on his thumb right where she'd instructed.

"Where's the first aid kit?" Her gaze swept the room. "I know there's one here. Your dad always made safety a priority."

The air grew thick at her mention of the past.

Rem whined, looking from her to Elliott.

He notched his chin toward the tool chest. "Bottom drawer."

She found the kit and waved him onto a stack of dog food. "Sit."

"I'm not a dog." He reached for the white box with the red cross on top. "I can take care of it myself."

She moved it out of reach. "I know you can." She'd had to take care of herself since she was old enough to remember. Elliott had possessed the same independence and maturity that only came from having to grow up way too young. "That's one of the things I always admired about you."

They both froze.

The dog whined, straining toward Rebel, then Elliott, then back to her.

"Um." She grasped for a way to end the uneasiness. "It'll go quicker if I do it." Unable to hold his gaze, she opened the kit and rifled through it. "Sit down. Please."

He slid onto the stacked dog food. "Fine." He held out his hand, a drop of blood splattering the cement floor. "Then we can get back to work. We've got a lot to do before the campers arrive, and I've got a ton of work waiting on my desk."

Right! Work. This was about work.

His hand was rough against hers as she disinfected the cut. The heat of his skin sent a tingle skating up her arm. A tingle she remembered well. A tingle only Elliott had ever been able to create.

She dabbed the cut once more to distract her wandering thoughts. When she leaned in to apply a bandage, his warm breath coasted over her cheek, her neck . . .

She swallowed and grabbed a tube of ointment from the kit. With the tip of one finger, she gently smoothed the salve over his thumb.

She could swear his breathing grew heavier.

Her gaze snapped to his, and he ground his teeth so loud she was surprised he didn't break a tooth.

Rem whimpered, put his front paws on the stack of dog food, and nudged his head under Elliott's free arm.

Rebel let out a heavy sigh and straightened. She'd wondered how long it would take for shit to get real. Maybe there was a hashtag for that she could use. "Go ahead. Just say it."

He gave her a look that said he had no idea what she was talking about. "Say what?"

She crossed her arms. "Whatever's on your mind. Whatever makes you feel better, because there isn't just an elephant in the room. There's an entire herd of elephants, and judging from the sound of your grinding teeth, they're about to stampede." She cocked a hip and waited. Waited for the very thing she'd tried to avoid years ago. His disapproval. His disappointment.

35

Regret washed through her. Breaking up with him through a note had been cruel. But at the time, it was her only option. If she'd told him the truth about her circumstances, if she'd told him about the horrible secret she was keeping for her dying mother, she was pretty sure he would've given up his scholarship and come home to go to community college on the mainland just to be her support system.

That would've been the only thing worse than him hating her for leaving him without an explanation.

So it was time to face what she'd done, even if it meant hearing harsh words from the only man she'd ever loved.

Instead, he stewed in silence. She wasn't sure which was more awful.

His jaw hardened, and his eyes turned icy.

Yeah, the silence was much more awful.

"Go on." She couldn't stop her foot from tapping nervously against the cement. "I'm a big girl. I can take it. I've been through much worse than a few scathing words from an ex-boyfriend."

Rem moved to her side.

Elliott studied her, finally drawing in a deep breath. "It's ancient history. Forget about it. I know I have."

Oh.

Her foot tapping stopped.

"Let's focus on the camp," he said. "That's all I care about. Then you and I can go back to our lives."

She swallowed down the sting in her throat.

She thought he'd ask why, want answers, or just plain tell her off.

She'd been terribly wrong.

More than answers, more than having his say, what he obviously needed was for them to go their separate ways. Again.

Something sharp pricked at her heart. Breaking up had been the last thing she'd wanted, but what would a homeless teenager with no prospects have to offer a Wharton grad who was going to have a world of opportunities at his feet? Especially if the truth about what her mother had done ever came to light. So she'd broken up with him and told him to move on without her.

She just hadn't realized how much it would hurt if she got what she'd asked for, even after all these years.

◆ ◆ ◆

Since Elliott hadn't been able to get Lily alone long enough to tell her to find a replacement, he'd sent her a text first thing that morning. Her immediate response was, We'll talk later.

Damn straight they would.

He ignored his throbbing thumb as he opened the boxes so Rebel could examine the arsenal of supplies. After slicing through tape on box number two thousand and one, he straightened. "How much stuff does a dog need?" It was the first time either had spoken a word since he'd brushed off her offer to vent.

What could he have said that wouldn't have sounded like a sulking adolescent still holding a grudge over a wounded ego? Worse, he might've sounded like a grown man still smarting over a broken heart.

After she reminded him she'd been through far worse than getting an earful from an ex-boyfriend, no way was he going to vent. The things she'd endured while living on the island had been worse than him getting dumped by a high-school sweetheart. He'd suck it up and stay quiet until he handed the event off to someone else.

Trusting her was another matter entirely, though. She hadn't shown any remorse for kicking his family to the curb, even though they'd treated her like one of their own. That was something he couldn't ignore.

Rebel kept working, organizing the supplies at each station. "A lot of this is specific for service dogs." She held up a blue vest that had IN TRAINING stitched on the side. Then she pulled a tennis ball from another box. "The dogs will have been with training handlers for as long as two years. They'll already know the basic obedience commands, but we'll use some of the toys when testing the dogs for their matches." She tossed that back in the box and retrieved a fuzzy toy squirrel with an elongated body. "Some we'll use to teach skills specific to their companion's needs." She let the squirrel drop into a box and fanned a hand across the array of different boxes. "When it comes to household pets that aren't used for service, supplies are still big business. Have you ever walked into a pet store? They're more like department stores, especially the big chains."

"But they're *dogs*." He stooped over another box and sliced through the tape.

She shrugged and kept working. "They're family." She stopped, stared down at the bags of treats in her hands, and chewed the corner of her mouth. "Especially to someone who's alone." Her voice was low and wistful like she had firsthand experience.

He wouldn't ask. He wouldn't. She'd made her choice a long time ago, and that choice hadn't included him.

Anger flashed through him.

If she wanted him to know the details of her life after leaving the island . . . after leaving him, she'd have to spill them on her own.

He folded both sides of the box top back, and an assortment of colorful toys greeted him. He pulled a small chimpanzee out that had CHUNKY MONKEY embroidered across its chest and a pink flamingo whose wings crinkled. He squeezed the monkey, and it let out a squeak that sounded like it had just broken wind.

"Holy shit." Elliott's head snapped back. Then he took in the ocean of boxes. "I didn't have this many toys as a kid."

"Neither did I." She dug more supplies out of a box and stopped at the first station. "Mom got most of my toys from Goodwill and the Salvation Army." A sad smile turned up the corners of her mouth. "Or from dumpster diving."

Her mom. It was the first time Rebel had mentioned her troubled mother, and Elliott had been too caught up in feeling sorry for himself to ask.

"How *is* your mom?"

She didn't answer for a second, moving to each station without looking up. Finally, she said, "She passed a long time ago."

Well, didn't he feel like an ass. "I'm sorry."

"It's fine." Her tone went cold, and she focused on her work, making it clear the subject was closed.

They worked for several hours until half the supplies were unpacked. Elliott started breaking down the empty boxes while Rebel sorted the contents.

Finally, she put both hands on her lower back and stretched. "I drove in from Portland yesterday, and we've been bending and lifting all day. How about we call it a night and start early in the morning?"

"Portland." He tossed an empty box onto the pile. "Is that where you live?"

So his plan not to ask her about her life was shot to hell.

She fingered the zipper of her jacket. "Yes." Her voice dropped to just above a whisper.

"How'd you end up there?" He folded another box into a small square and broke down the next.

She turned a foot on its side and stared at her hiking boot. "My mom's doctors were there. So tomorrow morning, then?" She headed to the open garage door but stopped as soon as she reached it.

He took a few steps over to see what had caught her attention. The sun had slipped behind the mountainous landscape of the western side of the island, turning the sky bold shades of pink and orange.

Rebel's dog stood close at her side like he often did. "It's still as beautiful as I remember."

Yes, she was.

His lungs locked.

Wait. No. *It* was still beautiful, as in the sunsets that drew tourists to the island. Not *she*. Okay, she was still beautiful too, but . . . *Fuck.*

The cardboard box he was folding closed on his thumb. He let out a string of cuss words under his breath.

Rebel's dog trotted over and stood flush against Elliott's side, and she followed.

"How's the thumb?" She reached for his hand.

He pulled away, cradling it in his other hand.

She looked him in the eye, but her chin trembled so slightly that he would've missed it if he hadn't been looking. Taking in every detail of her pretty face, from the light dusting of freckles that sprinkled her nose to the small dimple in the middle of her chin that had always quivered when she was nervous. Or upset.

"It's good." Her closeness unsettled him, so he blurted the first thing that came to mind. "I forgot how nice the sunsets were until I moved back home recently."

A crease formed between her eyes. "You didn't come home for visits?"

He shook his head. "Not that often. A firm in San Francisco recruited me right out of college, and I worked most of the time. My brothers had all moved away, and Dad came to see us as much as he could." Elliott hadn't wanted to come back. When he was on the island, he couldn't think of anything else except his mother's accident and Rebel's abandonment. At least in San Francisco, work kept his mind from going there, even if his job was so demanding he'd never had time for anything else. "There wasn't much of a reason for me to come back."

That miniscule quiver was back, but this time her gaze darted away. Then she nibbled her bottom lip.

Which caused the dull throb in his thumb to spread to other parts of his anatomy.

"And now you're back on the island." Her voice was distant, like she was talking to herself more than to him. "And living in one of the family cottages. I loved those cottages."

So did he.

Elliott and his brothers had grown up in the largest of the cottages, located far enough from the main lodge to give the family members privacy. Now Spence lived in one of the smaller cottages, Trace and his son occupied one two doors down, and Lily lived in another up the road.

"They were so quaint and warm and said 'family,'" she said wistfully.

Her home had been a pigsty, her mother letting her latest boyfriend and crazy friends mess it up every time Rebel had cleaned it. Eventually, she'd started spending most of her time at the Remington. If she wasn't working, she was goofing around with the family.

Or escaping into a remote spot on the grounds or vacant cottages for alone time with him.

He gave a half nod, half shrug. "I'm staying with Spence." *Because I never planned to be on the island long enough to move in to one of the vacant cottages and make it my own.* His mind raced to find a change of topic. "What's with your dog?" He stared down at the furry guy. "He likes me."

She chuckled. "You find that surprising?"

He raised both brows and tilted his head in agreement. "I do, actually. He's the first dog I've ever met that isn't either scared of me or growling at me."

She studied both Elliott and the dog. "He's trained to identify anxiety. That's why he leans."

Elliott gave the dog an approving nod. "That's pretty damn smart."

"It is. Unfortunately, he responds to whoever is most stressed in the room, instead of only to his companion. Because of it, he was released from a previous service dog program and dumped in a shelter. I found him right before his time was up. He may never be a great service dog. So I'll keep him instead of pairing him with someone else."

Elliott couldn't help but frown. "It's strange he didn't respond to my nephew out on the lawn earlier today. Ben has functioning autism, and his anxiety usually runs high."

"Ah, that explains the therapy duck." A glimmer of approval lit her stunning hazel eyes.

Dammit. The churning sound in his ears must be his man card circling the bowl because guys did not use words like *stunning*. Especially when describing the eyes of a woman they had zero interest in beyond a working relationship. And he was trying like hell to get out of the *working* part.

"The source of the anxiety doesn't matter to the dog, whether it comes from autism or PTSD or any other cause. They can start to identify triggers for their companions, but it's the anxiety itself the dog focuses on and how to help their companion get past each episode."

Elliott stopped to listen. Amazing how the confidence in her voice skyrocketed when she talked about dog training. He had to respect someone so obviously dedicated to her profession. He also had to wonder why she'd decided on a career as a dog whisperer.

"Could be Re—" She shoved both hands in her pockets. "Maybe Ben's anxiety level wasn't as high as yours, so the dog stayed at your side." Her expression softened. "Or maybe he's finally found his match."

"No. Way." Pets didn't fit into his lifestyle in San Francisco. From day one, he'd set the pace at his firm for logging more work hours than anyone else. Hell, his laser-sharp focus caused him to crunch numbers and make trades in his dreams most nights. When he finally did finish his leave of absence and return to his old job, he'd have a lot of caching up to do to prove he was still their champion racehorse. "I don't have time to take care of a dog." Elliott went back to breaking down boxes.

"It's more about the service dog taking care of their companion, not the other way around," Rebel said.

He gathered up the rest of the trash and tossed it onto the pile. "My lifestyle doesn't lend itself to pets."

Scratch that. Neither his eighteen-hour workdays nor his penthouse apartment in Pacific Heights, which he was subletting until he moved back to San Francisco, lent itself to pets. He'd spared no expense furnishing his place, which had a view of the bay. It was what his firm had expected from their movers and shakers.

Seemed like a waste, since he'd spent most of his time at the office, chasing after the next brilliant business opportunity for the firm's clients.

He loved the thrill of it all. And his job left no time for dwelling on regrets from the past.

He retrieved a gigantic square trash bin with wheels from the corner and started filling it with trash. "Dinner's still being served in the main lodge, if you're hungry." They were swerving too far into the personal realm with talk of her mother, his lack of visits to the island, and the possibility of him owning a dog, so he changed the subject.

"I'm starving." Rebel scooped up an armful of trash and dumped it into the bin. "Haven't eaten all day."

"Charley runs the restaurant with a friend of hers," Elliott said as they tossed in the last of the trash.

"Really? Charley left Seattle and moved here permanently?"

"Yep. She and her daughter, Sophie. The food's excellent." He pushed the wheeled bin toward the door. "Get the lights, and I'll roll this over to the dumpster."

Rebel grabbed two bowls and a small sack of dog food from the arsenal of supplies, flipped off the lights, and followed him outside.

He stepped over to the control panel attached to the metal garage and punched in the code. "You can get in and out of the garage this way." As the door slid shut, he said, "The code is zero, four, one, six, enter." As soon as the words left his mouth, he wanted to snatch them back. Why in the hell hadn't he thought to change the code? The sixteenth day of the fourth month was Rebel's birthday.

When a sharp intake of breath whistled through her lips, he refused to look at her. If he did, he'd be so busted.

"My dad sets the code," he blurted. *Liar, liar.* If the uncomfortable heat welling in his center was any indication, his boxer briefs were probably on fire, because *he'd* reset the code right after moving back to the island. "Dad resets them every few months for safety reasons."

His eye twitched.

He hadn't consciously realized he'd used her birthday as the code until now.

Coincidence. Nothing more.

They stood there, silent.

"Well." She picked at a cuticle. She finally lifted her gaze to his, and her chin trembled. "I guess I'll see you tomorrow. I need to go unpack."

"You didn't unpack last night after you got here?" he blurted.

She looked away, the quiver in her chin turning to a quake. "I wasn't sure if I should stay. It didn't seem fair to you once I realized you hadn't been informed that I was the trainer."

Ah. She'd considered pulling another disappearing act. His gut twisted.

"Well, my suitcase isn't going to unpack itself." She turned to go.

His eyes stayed anchored to her back as she headed toward the main lodge with her dog at her side. Long locks of silky red hair swayed with each step.

Right. Unpack. He'd been back on the island for several months and still had a suitcase full of suits sitting in the spare bedroom of Spence's cottage he'd never bothered to unpack.

The last several months, he'd used his business sense to help guide the resort into a much better position, but he'd been on sabbatical long enough. It was time to confront Lily and demand she find a stand-in. If the sponsor wasn't on board without a Remington taking the lead, that was okay.

Hell, who was he kidding? It was anything but okay. But just in case, he'd double his efforts to come up with a brilliant idea that would keep the resort coffers full every season of the year. Then he could get back in the game of high finance. There was a corner office down the coast with his name on it, and he wasn't about to give up everything he'd worked for.

Now more than ever, there was no reason for him to unpack that bag. No reason at all. And he'd make sure to keep it that way.

Chapter Four

#Hangry

Juggling a bag of Down Home dog food and two bowls, Rebel hurried over to the main lodge to unpack and feed Rem. She ignored her rumbling tummy and bypassed the delicious aroma coming from the dining room. She and Rem took the stairs to the second floor two at a time.

I'm such a chicken.

After spending a year homeless, she'd never been able to get past the sheepish feeling that came over her when she had to eat in front of people. She preferred to eat alone, for fear of making an uncouth fool of herself.

If that didn't cause her enough social anxiety, she still hadn't met up with the rest of the Remington clan. Truth was, facing Elliott for the first time was only half her worries. As uncomfortable as it had been all day while setting up in the garage, at least the initial shock of seeing him again was over. She wasn't looking forward to facing his family. They'd treated her like family when she was a teen, and she'd repaid them by disappearing without so much as a thank-you.

And everyone on the island knew the Remingtons stuck together. They were good people, but if you crossed one, you crossed them all.

When she reached the landing, she turned right and headed down the long corridor. A middle-aged couple came out of a room on the left and smiled at Rem. Rebel nodded and hurried to the end of the hall. She tucked the bowls and dog food under one arm, swiped the card key across the panel, and let herself into the room. As soon as the door clicked shut, she leaned back against it and closed her eyes.

Her rush to get to her room might've been to avoid seeing the rest of the Remingtons, but her racing pulse was because of the garage door code.

Elliott had brushed it off like it was nothing. No show of emotion. No sign that it had been anything more than pure coincidence.

Still, when he'd spoken the numbers out loud, it'd hit her square in the chest and knocked the wind from her lungs.

Rem's round, furry head came up under her free hand, and she molded her palm to it.

"Thanks, boy." She'd never really needed a service dog of her own, but she had to admit they were a big comfort when her stress level spiked. Ever since the first stray dog found her sleeping on a park bench in Portland right after her mom died in the hospital, she'd had a dog at her side. Eventually, the comfort and companionship that dog provided had evolved into a career.

Thankful didn't begin to describe how Rebel felt for her life turning out the way it had despite where she'd started. All because a lonely, abandoned stray had taken a chance and approached her with its tail between its legs.

She didn't deserve that kind of unconditional love from either a human or an animal after covering up her mother's atrocity, but that dog's trust had saved her and given her something to hold on to.

She crouched and gave Rem a tight hug. "Ready to eat?"

He barked.

"I hear ya." She rubbed her growling tummy as she filled the two bowls with water and food, then set them on the balcony.

Rem watched patiently until she gave him the signal that it was okay to eat. He dug in, devouring the chicken-and-rice-flavored food.

While he ate, Rebel took in the view. The full moon had risen high enough to outline the silhouette of the rocky tips of the mountains that bordered the island to the west.

The night chill bit at her cheeks, and she wandered inside, leaving the sliding glass door cracked for Rem.

She took in the room as she opened her suitcase and pulled out comfortable clothes. She had to hand it to the Remington. The inside of the resort was just as nice as the outside. The place was in great shape and seemed to be thriving.

She took a quick shower, arranged a stack of sweaters in a drawer, then started on the rest of her clothes.

Her stomach growled.

Last night she'd eaten the only protein bar in her purse and had nothing left but a few sticks of gum. Maybe the resort had installed vending machines on each floor like regular hotels, because now she wasn't just hungry. She'd crossed that threshold and had breached the *hangry* zone.

Not a pretty sight.

Her mood could scare off a pack of rabid dogs when she went too long without eating.

She dug a few bills from her wallet, grabbed her room key, and went in search of sustenance. When she didn't find a vending area on her wing, she passed the landing to search the other wing.

Nothing.

She wandered back to the landing and stared down the stairs where they bent and descended in the other direction. If she ventured downstairs, the likelihood of running into at least one Remington was better than good. She wasn't ready for that after spending her first day on the job working with Elliott.

She crossed her arms and tapped a foot.

Her kingdom for a Twinkie. Or any other food that spit out of a machine with just the input of a little money and a punch of a few buttons. Soon she'd be desperate enough to eat the packaging too.

Oh, for God's sake. She was being stupid.

She went to the top step and grabbed hold of the thick, old-fashioned banister. The overhead chandeliers glinted off the glossy finish of the dark wood.

Rebel prided herself on being tough. She'd survived a childhood with an addict for a mother and no father. She'd survived as a homeless teen with no one to turn to.

So why was she scared to face the Remington family? They'd probably forgotten her long ago.

She squared her shoulders and forced herself to take the first step. Then another.

See? Piece of cake.

Her confidence increased with each step until she'd almost reached the switchback in the staircase.

"Find someone to replace me." Elliott's voice filtered up from the lower level. "As soon as possible."

Rebel stopped, her fingers tightening around the banister.

"I'm sorry," Lily said. "Trace said you had some history with Ms. Tate, but no one else in the family will do it. It has to be you."

So the entire Remington family did hate Rebel.

How nice.

Wasn't their little reunion going to be cozy?

"This isn't a request." Elliott's tone was stony. "I'm not working with her."

"You agreed." Lily's voice was calm and encouraging. "I've already told the sponsor we'll be ready. The service dogs arrive at the end of the week, and the veterans will be here a few days after that. They're coming from all over Oregon and Washington."

"Lily, I know you're thinking of the resort, but this crosses a line. Whether you know it or not, finding a replacement for me is the least of your worries. I hope your trainer actually sticks around and doesn't disappear *after* the campers are here."

Rebel tried to steady her heavy breaths.

"She had a good résumé and even better references," Lily argued. "I don't know exactly what happened between you two, but it was a long time ago. She doesn't seem like the type to just disappear without a good reason."

Every ounce of air in the building vanished, and scalding heat crept up Rebel's neck.

A pang of guilt clawed at her insides.

"If you're concerned about her reliability, then it's best if you stay on as the point man for this event," Lily argued. "You could keep an eye on things."

"Find a replacement and make the sponsor understand it's for the best." Elliott's voice was controlled but hardened. "Or cancel."

No. Rebel's hand went to her mouth. This camp was her chance to earn the money she needed to make an offer on the abandoned shelter before someone else discovered its potential.

"Elliott, the sponsor wants a family member." Lily's tone turned desperate. "I don't have to explain to you what a setback it will be if the resort loses this event."

It wouldn't just be a setback for the Remington. It would likely be the death blow to Rebel's dream. The commercial property she had her eye on would eventually sell, and she'd never have the money to build one from scratch. Offers like the one she'd gotten from Down Home Dog Food didn't come along every day. They'd been desperate after the previous trainer pulled out so close to the start of the camp and had offered Rebel the moon. She needed the camp to work.

"We'll find another event to bring in revenue during the off-season." Elliott stayed firm. "This is something I can't . . ." He stopped. "Scratch that . . . this is something I won't do—"

Rebel shifted her weight, and a board in the step creaked.

Elliott and Lily went quiet.

Dammit.

Rebel didn't think. Didn't wait for them to walk up a few steps and find her eavesdropping. Instead, she turned and bolted up the stairs.

If Elliott found working with her distasteful enough to cancel such a lucrative event, then his hard feelings went far deeper than she'd imagined.

Her appetite gone, she ran to her room and slammed the door. Rem bounded in from the balcony and immediately pressed into her. She turned and locked the door for the night, shutting out Elliott's harsh words. Shutting out the Remingtons' low opinion of her.

Because it hurt. Hurt just as much as it would've ten years ago if she'd told them the truth, which was why she'd quietly snuck away. And why she'd leave again as soon as her job was done.

Rebel had paid her dues in life. Paid enough dues for the entire population of North America. She couldn't deal with the hurt anymore. No matter how deserving it might be.

Hell. Elliott and Lily stood at the bottom of the staircase looking up.

Her eyes grew round. "Was that . . . ?" She pointed up the stairs.

Without a word, he nodded. Let his head fall forward in defeat as the sound of Rebel's retreating footsteps faded.

"Well, now I need to do even more damage control than usual." Lily excelled at putting out fires and defusing difficult situations. Everyone walked away happy when Lily was on duty.

He scrubbed a hand down his face. "I'll put out this fire. I'm the one who started this conversation right here in the open instead of insisting we go to my office." He would not send Lily to do his dirty work.

"Maybe it wasn't Rebel." Lily's tone turned hopeful. "Maybe it was a guest."

"It was her." He'd only been able to see the shoes, but there was no question it was Rebel. Because try as he might to pretend she had no effect on him, he remembered every detail of her hair and the way her wispy red locks caressed her cheeks. Remembered every detail of the way her practical clothes showed off her exquisite body, all the way down to her all-weather boots.

How could he not remember every detail?

She was a knockout. The kind of woman who made a guy take notice. Made a guy look twice. Made a guy afraid to stand up in a crowded room until he thought of something really disgusting like the saggy old men who wore Speedos at the beach during the summer.

Elliott shivered in disgust as his pants grew looser around the middle again.

Whew.

Worked every time.

"We can't afford to lose Ms. Tate," Lily said.

"Which is why I'm stepping aside." Mostly. No one needed to know how the old feelings already churning in his stomach scared the living shit out of him. "If I stay involved in the camp, there's a good chance something will go wrong. We're better off trying to get the sponsor to see why this is the best way, and I'll focus on coming up with a backup plan in case we lose the event."

"I'll go talk to her." Lily tried to sidestep him to reach the stairs.

Elliott held up his hand. "Just try to find someone to replace me right away. In the meantime, I'll make things right with Rebel." He wasn't sure how, but he could start with bringing her a peace offering.

One of Charley's gourmet doughnuts or pastries could go a long way toward pacifying just about anyone.

He left Lily, passed the hostess working at the entrance of the dining room, and walked toward the kitchen. The dinner hour was winding down, and only two tables were still occupied, with one server waiting on both sets of guests.

Elliott pushed through the double doors and let them swing shut in his wake. "Hey." Charley and her business partner, Briley, were putting away the extra food.

Briley waved and disappeared into the pantry.

A kid who looked barely old enough to have a job washed dishes in the industrial sinks on the opposite side of the large kitchen. The island's sudden resurgence of tourism had created more jobs than the local population could fill, but the kids who lived on the island year-round loved the selection of new employment opportunities because they no longer had to take the ferry to the Cape every day for an after-school or summer job.

Elliott shoved his hands in the front pockets of his jeans and rocked back on his heels.

Charley stopped and stared him down like she figured he wanted something.

His cousin knew him so well.

"I screwed up with the dog whisperer who's here for the camp." He cut right to the chase.

"Of course you did." Charley went back to sealing a large pan of lasagna with plastic wrap. "And you want me to help you fix it."

Okay, she knew him better than he knew himself sometimes.

"You could turn loose of one of your precious doughnuts and a cup of coffee," Elliott said. "I'll deliver it to her room when I apologize for being a jerk."

Charley came from a coffee magnate family in Seattle, so her coffee was almost as legendary as her pastries, and she was pretty stingy with her baked goods. Probably because the Remington brothers would eat all her profits and bankrupt her if she let them. Whoever said the way to a man's heart was through his stomach was pretty damn clever.

"Wouldn't you rather bring her a hot meal?" Charley got a plate from the cupboard, peeled back the plastic wrap, and dished up a nice serving of lasagna. "Rebel hasn't made it to the dining room for dinner since she's been here, so unless she's got a stash of food in her room, she probably hasn't eaten."

Huh. She'd said she was starving.

"So you already know who the dog whisperer is." Elliott sank onto a barstool at the counter across from Charley's work space.

She nodded. "Spence stopped in earlier." She added a breadstick to the plate. "So how uncomfortable is it seeing Rebel again?"

"On a scale of one to ten?" He braced both elbows against the stainless-steel counter. "At least a twenty-five, and that's probably a conservative estimate."

Charley added a helping of salad and poured Italian dressing over it. "Are you sure you *want* to fix things with her?" When they were growing up, Charley was the only person with a mean enough punch to send the Remington brothers running for cover, but she was fiercely protective of them too. She covered it with a metal lid, put it on the tray, and prepared a glass of ice water with a lemon wedge.

He shrugged. "The camp is worth saving, so yeah, I need to try to smooth things over." If that was possible. Not trusting Rebel was one thing. Being an asshole about it was another. Yet, continuing to work with her seemed like a train wreck waiting to happen. *Dammit.* Now that he thought about it, he was screwed either way. "Come on." Elliott tried to sound desperate. "Throw in a doughnut just in case she's *really* pissed."

Charley gave him an exaggerated eye roll, but then she plated a doughnut. She pushed the tray across the counter. "Don't eat it before you get to her room." She wiped her hands on a towel and went back to storing the leftover food. "The rest is up to your charming disposition."

"Thanks, Cuz." Elliott picked up the tray and headed for the door.

"You owe me," Charley called after him. "I'm keeping track too."

Elliott made his way up the stairs, rehearsing what he was going to say to Rebel. How he was going to explain that he wasn't cut out for the camp, how she'd be better off working with someone else.

How it'd been torture working with her for one day. No way could he keep himself in check for an entire month.

He reached the landing at the top of the stairs.

Nah. He'd leave the last part out. And the part about having to constantly think of old, wrinkly, half-naked guys to get her out of his head.

When he got to her door, he stood there staring at the number, trying to get up the nerve to knock.

A whine came from the other side.

Rebel's muffled voice gave the dog a command, and then she must've looked through the peephole because a few seconds later, the deadbolt turned and the door swung open.

Their gazes locked, and Elliott could swear time stopped. She'd changed into black spandex leggings and a microfiber tank top that showed every dip and curve of her incredible body. Her hair was clipped up into a messy pile with wavy tendrils framing her face and brushing the creamy skin of her neck.

"Uh . . ." His voice turned to gravel.

Nice.

There went that charm he was so famous for.

The dog trotted into the hall and leaned into Elliott.

The dishes on the tray rattled as the weight against his leg jostled his balance. *Jesus.* He widened his stance to keep his peace offering from clattering to the floor.

Rebel didn't try to help. Instead, she crossed her arms and leaned a shoulder against the doorframe.

"What can I do to get your dog to like me a little less?" Not words he ever thought he'd hear himself say.

She ignored the remark. "Is that food?"

Oh. Right. "Charley hasn't seen you in the restaurant, so I brought dinner to you."

Rebel studied him through narrowed eyes. Finally, she pushed off the doorframe and reached for the tray.

He moved it out of reach. "It's heavy. I'll get it." He wasn't giving her the chance to shut the door in his face before they talked. He wasn't sure yet what to say to make things better, but if the food and doughnut didn't work, he wasn't above groveling.

How was it that *he* was the one willing to grovel when she'd been the one to skip out on their relationship? Seemed ass-backward to him, but the camp was already at risk with him stepping aside. Losing Rebel would seal its fate, so he'd take one for the Remington team and just deal.

"Some of the animals I work with are eighty pounds or more. I can handle a tray of food." She didn't budge.

He tilted his head. "I can take this back to the kitchen if you don't want it." He wasn't above bribery either.

Her eyes darted between him and the tray, then back again.

When Buddy returned to her side, Elliott knew he'd won the throw down.

She turned to the side and held the door open with her back to it.

He angled his body to ease into the room, his backside brushing against her front.

Old wrinkly guys, old wrinkly guys . . .

He hurried to the table in front of the sliding glass doors and bent to set down the tray. The door shut behind him, and he turned to find Rebel standing at the end of the bed. Staring at his crotch. Which meant she'd been checking out his ass.

He couldn't stop a smile. Not that he cared what she thought of him personally, physically, or any other way. But shaking her resolve might help him with damage control.

When she lifted her gaze to his, he let his smile widen.

Her face went up in flames, matching the color of her silky hair.

"You were starving in the garage, so here you go."

"I had an extra tube of toothpaste." She shifted from one bare foot to the other. "It was cinnamon flavored and filled me up in a pinch."

He blinked.

"I'm joking."

Humor. Right. His mind wasn't firing on all cylinders. It wasn't because of the way her hair was just messy enough to look like she'd been in bed. It wasn't because her bare feet revealed a toe ring and purple-painted toenails. It wasn't. He was just tired because he'd been working multiple jobs around the resort, taking up the slack everywhere he could because the rest of the family seemed to have a real purpose. A real direction. Everyone besides him, which was why he needed to salvage the camp and come up with fallback ideas to give the resort a cushion of income, so he could return to his firm in the city where he belonged.

"Thanks." She leaned a thigh against the end of the bed. "I *am* hungry, but after I unpacked, I needed to feed . . ." She chewed the corner of her mouth. "I needed to feed Buddy. Then I went in search of a vending machine, since it was almost closing time at the restaurant, but . . ."

Her plump bottom lip disappeared between her pearly whites, and it took every ounce of self-control Elliott could muster not to lick his lips.

"But you overheard me being a dick," he deadpanned.

She didn't miss a beat. "You said it, not me." She went to the tray, occupied one of the two chairs around the small table, and removed the lid. Leaning over the plate, she inhaled. "This smells incredible." She inhaled again. Her eyes slid shut, and she moaned.

Old wrinkly guys in Speedos!

Elliott quickly claimed the other chair, sitting with his arms over his lap so he could salvage some dignity. "Listen, about me being a dick . . ."

With the lid in her hand, she waited for him to finish.

"The camp is better off without me." He bounced a leg.

Slowly, she replaced the lid.

"Aren't you going to eat?" he asked.

She didn't answer. "After you explain why the camp is better off without you."

"I don't have the disposition for it. I'm not exactly a nurturing person."

"That's not true. You can be very nurturing when you want to be." Her big hazel eyes coasted over his face. "You were very"—she glanced away—"devoted and protective once."

And you still dumped me.

"Has that changed?"

Hell yes. His leg bounced faster, so he crossed them at the ankles. "Ten years is a long time. A lot has changed."

Rebel's dog sat equidistant between them, but he moved to Elliott's side.

"Well, if that's your final decision . . ." She let her disapproval hang in the air.

"It is." He nodded.

She folded her hands in her lap. "Then I guess we're done here."

He decided to mimic her blasé attitude and didn't respond.

She lifted a brow. "Aren't you going to leave?" She mimicked him right back.

Guess she could still give as good as she got.

So could he. "After you explain why you're not eating when you're so hungry."

She stared at him.

He didn't budge.

With measured, mechanical movements, she removed the lid and forked up a tiny piece of lasagna. Her hand trembled ever so slightly, bumping the side of her lush mouth and leaving a dot of sauce there. Then the fork found her mouth.

Holy shit, that mouth. It cast a spell over him as he watched it close around the fork. When she pursed her lips and chewed, he wanted to groan.

She swallowed and slowly wiped her mouth with the cloth napkin, missing a tiny speck of sauce at the corner.

He ran his hands down his thighs, letting the coarse denim fabric dry his damp palms. "I'm out as soon as Lily finds someone to take my place."

"But their last name won't be Remington, which might be a problem for the sponsor." She twisted the napkin.

"True, but Lily has a way of fixing things. The sponsor won't stand a chance." He smiled.

Rebel didn't.

Slowly, she set the spiraled napkin on the tray. "I came a long way for this boot camp, and I did so in good faith."

"Except for the part where you didn't unpack last night because you were considering skipping out?" he smarted off.

Her lips thinned. "If you want to risk blowing this opportunity for both of us, I can't stop you." She pushed out of her chair.

Elliott followed. "It's not personal."

Her eyes flashed, and that fiery personality he knew and loved showed in the way she lifted her chin to stare up at him. "I may not have the college education you have, but I'm smart enough to know that it's very personal. I'm perfectly capable of managing the camp on my own. A replacement isn't necessary, and the sponsor won't know the difference. If I need anything, I'll ask one of your employees, so you won't have to be around me." She held up both hands. "See? Simple solution. You're off the hook because I don't need your help."

His chest tightened. Why did it feel like she was digging out his heart with a spoon all over again?

He wasn't sure why he did it, but he stepped around the dog and closed the distance between him and Rebel. She tried to take a step back but came up against the chair. Her eyes widened when he dipped his head so that his face was a fraction from hers.

Her rapid-fire breaths washed over his jaw.

"I'm well aware that you don't need me. You made that painfully clear a long time ago." With the pad of his thumb, he touched the corner of her lush mouth.

When her lips parted, it was nearly his undoing.

Her long, glossy eyelashes fluttered down in a slow blink to brush the velvety skin under her eyes. When she opened them again, a storm raged there, and she leaned toward him just enough for him to know she expected him to kiss her.

At that moment, he didn't want to only meet her expectations. He wanted to surpass them, but he'd have to be out of his mind.

He gathered every bit of willpower he possessed and then some and swiped at the corner of her mouth like a parent would a child. "You had sauce . . ." He held up his thumb. Resisted the urge to put it in his mouth.

Or even better, her mouth.

Dammit. Not better. Much, much worse.

Without breaking eye contact, she tugged the napkin from the tray and held it up between two fingers. "That's what napkins are for." She wiped her mouth with controlled movements to make her point. But the way the soft skin just above her V-neck tank rose and fell in rapid-fire succession told him she wasn't as composed on the inside as she wanted him to believe.

"I'll see you tomorrow." He stepped away.

With a hand on the edge of the table, she steadied herself like his sudden movement set her off-balance.

"Lily *will* find a replacement because we're not keeping the truth from the sponsor while I disappear into the shadows. That might be how you roll, but I don't work that way." He didn't wait for her to respond. Instead, he strode to the door and got the hell out of there before he did something he'd regret.

Something that would open him up to another *decade* of regret.

Chapter Five

#ItsAThang

As soon as the first blush of dawn cascaded through the crack in Rebel's curtains, she was up and at 'em. She pulled on athletic clothes.

After two more days of working nonstop, she and Elliott had everything ready for the dogs, who were arriving the next day. The sponsor was smart to deliver them and their handlers a few days before the veterans so the dogs could get acclimated to their new surroundings. The garage was ready with stations for each dog and their companions, and an obstacle course was arranged in the center of the garage. Each guest room reserved for the camp was equipped with supplies so the dogs could stay with their handlers and then their companions once they were matched.

She sat on the end of the bed to put on running shoes.

She was exhausted from the long hours, and it was just day four. She wasn't sure how she'd make it through the next month with little sleep because of the tension between her and Elliott. He so obviously didn't want to be around her. So much so that he still had Lily out looking for a replacement at the risk of ticking off the sponsor. Putting distance between him and her for the remainder of the camp was probably a good thing. She might get more rest.

When he'd come to her room with a food offering and claimed not to be nurturing enough for a dog camp, she'd wanted to remind him that he was the only person who'd ever loved her unconditionally. Which was why she'd found working with dogs much more rewarding than working with people.

She got out her smartphone and earbuds.

For now, most of the prep was done, so she might as well get in a morning run before starting to work.

It wasn't just Elliott's thumb brushing across her mouth that had kept her awake every night since. It wasn't just the way his breath had washed over her, making every nerve ending in her body roar to life with a needy ache.

There was a bit of personal housekeeping Rebel needed to get out of the way or she might not sleep at all during her stay on the island. That dark secret she'd kept hidden away for ten long years had been niggling at the back of her mind, pecking at her conscience since the moment she stepped onto the ferry bound for Angel Fire Falls.

She tucked a few things into a fanny pack and slung it around her waist. Before dealing with Elliott handing off the event to someone else, Rebel wanted . . . no, she *needed* to see the damage her mother had caused with her own eyes.

She wasn't sure if seeing her mother's handiwork firsthand would help or make her stay on the island unbearable. Either way, it was something she had to do.

She hustled down the stairs and out the front entrance so Rem could get in his morning walk. He seemed to be more focused if they started the day with both physical and mental exercise, and it had become their daily routine.

The cold morning air raced through her, and she zipped her jacket. She looked up and took in the overcast sky as Rem tortured every shrub on the front lawn. A fine sheen of cool mist settled over her skin. A few pillowy clouds were darker than the rest, but that wasn't unusual for the area. She should be able to spend a few hours outdoors without an umbrella.

"Come on, boy." She put her earbuds in, turned on the music, and set out jogging at a steady pace. The town was just a few miles away, so she reached the outskirts within thirty minutes.

She slowed to a walk on the main drag so she and Rem could catch their breaths. Since it was still early, not many people were out and about except a few shop owners who were getting their stores ready to open along Marina Boulevard. An old pink-and-white VW van that had been cleverly converted into a food truck was parked a little farther down the street. The steam swirling from the top and the delectable scent coming from the open window told Rebel there was coffee to be had. She stuffed her earbuds into her pocket and headed in that direction.

Briley's Burgers & Brews was painted on the side of the van, and Rebel stepped up to the window.

"Coffee, please," she said to the twentyish young woman working the window.

"Coming right up." The server moved to one side of the small space inside the van to make the coffee.

The only other person who could fit inside turned around and froze when she saw Rebel. She was a pretty blonde who seemed vaguely familiar. She wiped her hands on a towel and stuck her head through the window. "Rebel?"

"Um . . ." She hadn't thought anyone would remember her. Now that someone had, she wasn't sure if it was a good thing or not. "Yes, I'm Rebel." She still couldn't place the familiar face that stared back at her.

"I wondered when I'd see you." Her voice wasn't quite friendly but hovered somewhere over the neutral zone. "Welcome home."

Home. That word knocked the air from Rebel's lungs. She hadn't thought of her return to the island quite like that.

"I . . . I don't mean to be rude, b-but . . ." Rebel stammered.

"But you don't recognize me." The blonde slid cream and sugar packets through the window. "It's okay. I only spent summers here when we were growing up. You haven't been to the dining room at the Remington since you arrived, so I haven't had a chance to reintroduce myself."

Rebel pulled her brows together. "Charley?"

"The one and only." She took a piping-hot cup from the server and handed it to Rebel.

The transformation was remarkable. Charley was no longer the plump teenager who used to torment her three cousins with a mean left hook.

"I, um, I've been ordering room service because we've been working so late." Really, she still hadn't been ready to face Elliott's family. "I'm sorry. You looked familiar, but I couldn't place you. I guess it's been too long." Rebel retrieved money from her fanny pack and exchanged the bills for the cup of liquid gold.

Charley gave her a thin smile. "No worries. I finally lost my baby fat. Took me a couple of decades longer than most kids, but better late than never, right?" She tapped fingers against the counter like she was sizing up Rebel.

Rebel shifted from one running shoe to the other as she fixed her coffee. "Elliott said you took over the restaurant at the Remington." She'd thought changing the subject would dial down the discomfort level, but the mention of her cousin's name only made Charley's bland look turn more suspicious. "Um, is this yours too?" Rebel scanned the length of the van.

Charley leaned through the window and pointed to the sign painted on the side. "Briley's my business partner. We're keeping the food truck open for sentimental reasons, since it was her first establishment. Plus, it's really popular with the tourists. We couldn't just close up shop and disappear when a better offer came along." She folded her arms. "It would've been like breaking a promise to the people in this town who count on us being here."

Rebel had to stop her head from jerking to the side, the words like a smack across her face. There was the proof of those strong Remington family ties she'd once loved.

Rem leaned heavier against her side.

She tossed the stir stick in the small tabletop trash bin and schooled her expression. "It's incredibly clever." She lifted her cup. "Thanks. This is exactly what I needed before walking back to the resort."

Charley's brow knitted. "You walked into town?"

"Ran." Rebel lifted Rem's leash. "It's our morning *thang.*" She smiled.

Charley didn't.

"Um, well, good to see you." *Sort of.* "See you around the resort." Unless Rebel's plan to steer clear of as many Remingtons as possible was a success.

"Need a lift back?" Charley didn't look at all certain that she should offer. "I'm just dropping off pastries and coffee beans. I'll be heading back to the resort in a few minutes to help Briley with breakfast."

Rebel shook her head. "I . . ." She glanced up the street toward her final destination—Morgan's Market & Produce. "Thanks, but no. I'll get reacquainted with the town before heading back. I enjoy the time outdoors." She gave Charley one last uncertain smile and headed up the street.

The tightness in Rebel's chest that she hadn't realized was there released.

One more Remington down.

She ticked another name off her mental list. Three more to go.

Just like that, the tightness was back.

She meandered up the street, taking in the familiar setting. A few new businesses had replaced the ones that had closed since she left the island. She walked past the Fallen Angel, a place that had been off-limits when she lived in Angel Fire Falls because of her age. And because her mother had practically lived in the old honky-tonk. It looked fresher than it had back then, obviously trying to attract a different breed of clientele than it had in her mother's day.

Rebel settled on a bench across the street from the market to enjoy her coffee, and Rem laid his head on her knee to comfort her. Another ten cups or so and she might get up enough nerve to go inside.

Childish, since no one knew her mother had been driving the car that had changed the course of the Morgans' lives. But *she'd* known. Her mother had told her so, and she felt partially responsible because she'd kept the secret so well. Rebel sipped her coffee and stared at the storefront. Her mother couldn't have gotten a liver transplant if she'd been sent to prison for a hit-and-run.

And she couldn't have confided in Elliott because he wouldn't have stopped trying to help. Wouldn't have stopped trying to fix it for her. And it would've tainted the course of his life just as it had Rebel's.

When the cops didn't show up on their doorstep, Rebel had packed up what they could fit in her mom's old car, handed off Elliott's letter to Mabel McGill when they boarded the ferry, and left the island bound for the hospital so her mom could wait for a transplant.

Rebel let another sip of bold brew coast over her taste buds.

The front door of the market opened, and a young man with brown hair stepped out and started cleaning the front windows.

A chill slithered through her.

He walked with an unusual gait. Despite the slight contortion of his facial features, he seemed happy and innocent, his brain too stunted from the accident to be anything else.

She watched him until he finished the task, the window so sparkling clean the glass was invisible except for the store name that was stenciled on with gold-and-black lettering. He went into the store and started on the inside of the window, even though it seemed spotless from where she sat.

She barely noticed the crack of thunder. She didn't run for cover when the misty air turned to a light drizzle. She just kept staring at the raindrops sluicing down the squeaky-clean window, even after little Danny Morgan—who wasn't so little anymore—moved away, undoubtedly to do some other menial task for his parents' store.

The dull ache of sorrow made her want to run straight for the ferry crossing and disappear like she had years before.

Elliott upended his double-walled coffee tumbler as he sat behind his desk in the resort's administrative offices and sent the week's payroll checks to the printer. He'd placed the weekly supply orders, paid the resort's taxes, ran profit projection reports based on their upcoming bookings for the month, and sent off all the bills that were due.

He glanced at the clock on his computer. All before eight thirty in the morning so he could work with Rebel as soon as she came downstairs.

He leaned back in his chair and rubbed his eyes with one hand, dog-tired from working at an even faster pace than usual.

Scratch that. Tired from not sleeping because of working with the only person he'd ever allowed to cut out his heart with a rusty knife. Tired from the excitement that rushed through him, making all his limbs prickle when he thought of spending more time with her.

Dammit.

Lily needed to find that substitute sooner rather than later.

He snatched up his phone and sent her a text.

Any ideas on where to find a replacement?

She texted right back.

Working on it as we speak.

He'd expected nothing less from his future sister-in-law. Her efficiency to solve any problem should have set him at ease. She'd find someone more suitable to work with Rebel, and he'd be off the hook. Except instead of setting him at ease, it only kicked up an ugly case of heartburn.

Dammit to hell.

What had Elliott done to make the universe hate him so much?

Guilt tickled his stomach like a feather.

He and he alone knew what he'd done. He'd spent the years since his mother's death trying to make up for it.

He let his head fall back against the chair, and he stared at the blank white ceiling.

He needed to go back to San Francisco. Back to the partnership he was neglecting. Back to the adrenaline rush the world of high finance offered and the fast-paced life that kept his mind off the past.

The printer spit out the last of the payroll checks, then went silent.

Hell, who was he kidding? It wasn't just that his pulse still kicked when Rebel looked at him. Or that his mouth still watered when she got too close.

His protective instincts still reared up when he thought of the hardships she'd endured because of her mom. He wasn't sure what she'd been through after her mom passed or how Rebel had survived, but he hoped it had been an improvement over her rocky childhood.

He grabbed the paychecks off the printer, signed the top one, and shuffled it to the bottom of the stack to sign the next.

When he got to his own check, he stared at the modest amount on the right.

Just a few months ago, he'd been making exponentially more zeroes.

He picked up his phone and dialed the senior partner's office number, certain most of the partners had already been at work for several hours. That was how they got to be partners.

Mick picked up on the first ring. "McPhearson."

"Answering your own phone?" Elliott kept his tone upbeat, not wanting his dark mood to trigger an alert with the man who'd recruited him right out of college, then spent years as his mentor.

"My assistant quit," Mick grumbled.

Elliott snorted. "How many assistants have you burned through this year?"

"You'd know if you'd actually been here," Mick shot back. "Please tell me you're calling because you're coming back to work soon."

Finally, Elliott could deliver good news. "As a matter of fact, I am. I need another month, then I'll be occupying that corner office." One month, some solid ideas to generate more revenue during the off-season, and a successful service dog event with lots of press and a satisfied sponsor would put the Remington right where Elliott needed it to be. Hopefully.

Silence hung in the air.

A desolate feeling gnawed at his gut. The same feeling he got when a particular stock was about to plummet. It was a sixth sense, a natural gift, and it had saved his clients from substantial losses. Now that sixth sense told him his value to the firm was about to free-fall.

"Listen, about that." Mick's typically solid voice came out just above a whisper. "I had to give it to Lucas Foster. He's a partner now."

Elliott bolted out of his chair. It rolled backward and bumped against the oak credenza behind his desk. "What the hell?" He ran a set of fingers through his hair to calm his temper. Foster was a clown who had latched on to Elliott's talent and ridden his coattails by mimicking all his trades. The fact that one of the senior partners was Foster's uncle hadn't hurt his climb up the company ladder. "I've run circles around that joker for years."

"I had no choice. We've landed some big new clients, and we need all the help we can get. Lucas is actually here. Working." At least Mick had the decency to sound sympathetic.

"I've given two thousand percent to the firm since the day you hired me." Elliott paced the length of his office. "And now because I needed a personal leave of absence to help save my family's business, you're giving away my office?" He paced back toward his desk. "An office I paid dearly for, I might add." When the firm required a buy-in from new partners, Elliott hadn't hesitated to write the check. Unlike most of the others, who spent everything they made living the life and keeping up the image, Elliott paid cash. Everyone else had to have the firm loan them the money.

"What do you expect, Elliott? You've been gone for months." Mick sighed into the phone. "Look, you know I have your back, but I've only got one vote. The other partners are getting antsy, and if they decide to vote you out, there's nothing I can do about it."

Elliott let his head fall forward. "When's the next vote?"

"Don't know," Mick said. "Nothing's on the calendar yet. Mainly because I don't have an assistant to keep my calendar organized."

"Then do me a favor." Elliott pushed his chair under the desk and headed to the door. "Hold off the other partners for one more month. That's all I need, then you have my word I'll be back." He stopped in the doorway. "And I'll be ready to work twenty-four-seven to make it up to the firm."

The sound of crickets was deafening.

Finally, Mick said, "One month. Then your ass better be back here, even if your office is the copy room. Got it?"

The hard edge to Mick's tone was oddly comforting. The challenge in his voice and the way it never failed to get Elliott's hackles up was exhilarating and motivating.

A certain redhead who'd just shown up again out of nowhere was having the same effect on him.

Which was unacceptable.

"Got it." He flipped off the light switch and headed toward the main lodge's front door. Now all he had to do was tell Lily to forget about a replacement, take charge of a dog event he knew absolutely nothing about, work with a woman who already had his pulse racing through his veins even though he knew he couldn't let history repeat itself, and break the news to his family that he wasn't staying in Angel Fire Falls. All in a month's time. He pulled up a mental calendar in his head to tick off the days until the camp would be over.

No worries.

What could go wrong with such a perfect plan?

"And, Elliott?"

"Yeah?" Elliott pushed through the front door and stepped into the chilly morning air.

"Don't let me down," Mick said.

Well, hell. Letting people down was what he did best. But not this time. He was determined to break the curse. "I don't plan to." Elliott reached his Jeep and opened the door.

"If you do . . ." Mick hesitated.

Which had Elliott stopping cold. He turned around and leaned back against his Jeep to wait for Mick's other four-hundred-dollar Italian shoe to drop.

"There's a clause in your contract that stipulates the firm doesn't have to pay back your buy-in if there's evidence of negligence."

Elliott nearly choked. The buy-in the firm required for new partners had drained his life savings.

"Taking an indefinite leave of absence could definitely qualify as negligence. I don't want to see that happen to the best protégé who's ever crossed the threshold of this firm. So get your ass back here in a month. No later." The line went dead.

Elliott stared at the phone.

When he finally climbed into his Jeep and fired it up, the phone rang again. Excellent. Probably Mick calling back to tell him it had been a cruel joke. He answered it without looking at the number. *"Yeeel-low."*

Charley let out an exaggerated sigh. "I was making the morning deliveries to the food truck in town, and your girlfriend showed up."

"If you didn't make such killer pastries and coffee, I'd hang up on you." He backed up the Jeep.

"I *am* the best pastry chef in the world, aren't I?" She didn't wait for him to respond. "I'm on my way back to the resort, and it's starting to rain."

He threw the gearshift into drive and headed toward the garage. "So?"

"*So*, Ms. Tate wouldn't ride back with me. She jogged into town with her dog and was still sitting on a bench across from the market when I left. Just thought you should know, in case you want to pick her up."

Underneath Charley's *I protect my family at all costs* attitude, she was a soft marshmallow with a big heart.

"She's a grown-ass woman who doesn't want my help." She'd told him so. Several times. "I'm sure she'll be fine."

"If the weather kicks up into a full-blown storm, they'll shut down the shuttle until it blows over, and she'll have to walk back in the wind and rain. I wouldn't want your dog trainer to come down with pneumonia before the event even starts," Charley said like a mother hen.

"I'll take care of her." His eyes slid shut. "I'll take care of giving her a ride," he corrected.

"Mmmm-hmmmm." The sarcasm in Charley's voice practically dripped through the phone.

"Whatever." He ended the call. Instead of taking the road that led to the garage, he veered left and headed to the resort exit.

At least he'd already discovered that losing his partnership along with his life savings was the one thing that could go wrong with his not-so-perfect plan.

Scratch that.

He thought of Rebel sitting on a bench in the rain, flowing red locks of hair sticking to her neck, long eyelashes starred with wetness.

He'd discovered *two* things that could go wrong and screw up his life for good.

He set his jaw with determination.

His brothers could suck it, because their childish dare for him to take charge of the camp was back on. He'd keep his contact with Rebel all about work and do a kick-ass job with the event, set the resort's off-season income up nicely by landing Down Home Dog Food as a repeat sponsor, and show his brothers who was really boss, all at once.

Not a bad day at the office, all things considered.

He could leave the island feeling good about his contribution to the resort. Nothing he could do would fully repay the debt he owed his family. Not even close. But since he couldn't bring back his mother, maybe it would help assuage some of his shame over causing her death.

Because twenty years was a long time to carry around guilt.

Chapter Six

#MeantToBe

With three cups of coffee down, Rebel had only seven more to go. Even with the weather getting worse, it was going to take a lot of caffeine for her to muster enough nerve to get off the bench across from Morgan's Market & Produce, cross the street, and step inside the store.

She gave Rem the signal to lie down under the bench so he'd be sheltered from the thundershowers.

Coming face-to-face with the family her mother had devastated would be hard enough. Keeping the secret as a scared teenage girl because her mother begged her to, because her mother stood a better chance of survival if she wasn't in prison, was something Rebel couldn't run from anymore. She had to face them. See if there was a way to help, even if telling them everything wasn't an option.

Maybe coming back to the island was providence. Karma. Payback. Or all of the above.

She sipped her fourth cup of fresh coffee and crossed her legs. Every now and again, Danny Morgan got close enough to the store window for her to glimpse his unnatural gait and his twisted facial features brought on by a traumatic brain injury. She kicked her foot back and forth at a rapid clip. Consuming so much coffee probably wasn't the best idea without a public restroom nearby and a two-mile hike back to the resort ahead of her.

Another crack of thunder made her jump, and the drizzle that already had her soaking wet and shivering turned to pouring rain. Still, she didn't move off the bench. Instead, she pulled her hood farther over her forehead and kept staring at the market.

"Rebel?" a familiar brusque voice said from the sidewalk behind her.

She clamped her eyes shut. Elliott was the last person she wanted to see her sitting in the rain, staring at the market like a lunatic stalker.

"Rebel, is everything okay?" His tone grew gentle, telling her she hadn't misread the impression she was making. When his footsteps shuffled around to the front of the bench, Rem whined and shot out from under his makeshift shelter.

She forced her eyes open to find Rem brushing against Elliott's side. The hood of the dark-green rain slicker framed his handsome face and turned the color of his eyes to emeralds.

"I'm fine. Why?" She tried to sound business-as-usual, but her stare trekked back to the store window. It was almost magnetic, snagging her attention and not letting go.

His wrinkled brow and worried look said he wasn't buying it. "Well, you're sitting in the rain without an umbrella or rain slicker." He scanned the empty coffee cups scattered next to her on the bench. "Apparently, with enough caffeine running through your system to power the entire island."

When his gaze followed hers to the front of the market and his worried expression grew even more troubled, she knew she'd made a serious mistake. "I just wanted to get reacquainted with the island." She stood and gathered up her trash.

"What's up with the market?" His gaze shifted from her to the store and back again.

"Nothing!" she blurted far too quickly and dropped the trash, scattering it across the sidewalk.

Rem was back at her side in a flash.

"Okaaaay." Elliott bent to help her pick up the mess.

She snatched up a cup and two lids, only to drop them again.

His strong, warm hand closed around her wrist as she reached for the trash again. "Sit."

The fact that he'd snapped at her for giving him the exact same command when he'd nicked his finger wasn't lost on her. As a reminder, she gave him an exaggerated glare.

"Please sit." His fingers didn't loosen against her wrist, and he guided her to the bench. Then he picked up the trash, walked to a nearby garbage can, and tossed it in.

She let the cup hover at her lips as she took small sips. "Sorry I'm late for work. Buddy needed exercise, and I took a run. I didn't plan to be gone so long, but I saw Charley, and her coffee is delicious, so I guess I got carried away and kept ordering more from that cute little food truck of hers, and . . ." Rebel couldn't stop gushing because Elliott's expression told her he was suspicious. "I decided to wait out the storm here."

"By sitting outside instead of ducking into one of the stores?"

He had her there. *Sip, sip, sip.*

He sat down next to her on the bench and braced both elbows on his knees. "How long have you been here?"

She had no idea. Time had slipped away from her once she'd seen Danny Morgan. "Not long." That sounded stupid even to her. Anyone could look at her and tell she'd been outside much longer than she should've. She took another long sip to keep from spewing more nonsense.

He took off his weatherproof jacket and draped it around her shoulders. "Want to tell me what's going on?"

"Thank you." She snuggled into the jacket. "What makes you think something's going on? I lost track of time, that's all."

He laced his fingers and didn't seem to mind that he was getting drenched. "You only ramble when you're upset."

"*Pfft,*" she huffed with the wave of a hand. "I ramble sometimes. I can be a rambler."

Good God. Lightning should go ahead and strike her down just to put her out of her misery.

He leaned back on the bench and studied her. His hair and clothes were already soaked. It was so unfair that it only made him look sexier, while she probably looked like a drowned rat.

She chewed the corner of her mouth.

Finally, he shook his head. "You're too smart to be a rambler unless something's wrong. So what is it? Maybe I can help."

At that moment, she'd like nothing more than to unburden herself. Tell him everything. But she couldn't. If it got out that she hadn't come forward with information about a crime, her professional reputation would be ruined. How could she repay her mother's debt to society if no one trusted her or wanted her help?

How unfair would it be to place that burden on his shoulders too? No, she'd left him once in order to protect him. Telling him now would be selfish.

A movement from the market window caught her attention. Danny stood inside attaching sale flyers to the glass that could be read from the street. He dropped the sheets of paper, and they fluttered to the ground. He got down on his hands and knees to pick them up. When he pulled himself to a stand, he glanced through the window and waved to Elliott.

Elliott returned the greeting, and Danny's wave sped like an excited child. Then he disappeared. The door opened and out he stepped, pulling on a raincoat with a compact umbrella in his hand. He looked both ways, then loped across the street.

"Hi, Elliott!" Danny said, his speech slower than the average person's. He threw his arms around Elliott.

"Hey, Dan." Elliott hugged him back.

"I, I br . . . brought you an uuuumbrella." Danny held it out but dropped it because of the tremor in his hand. "Preeeetty dog. Can I peeeet him?"

Rebel nodded. Technically, it was poor protocol to allow someone to pet a service dog while they were working, but how could she say no when someone wanted to show her dog affection? Especially *this* someone.

He bent down and gave Rem a scratch.

"Thanks, man." Elliott opened the umbrella and handed it to Rebel. "I'll get it back to you soon."

When she didn't take it, he stared at her.

She couldn't peel her eyes from Danny. "Um." She chewed her lip harder. "Hello, Danny."

"It's Dan," he said sternly. "I'm noooot a liiiiittle boy." Rem moved to his side and leaned, which prompted *Dan* to pet him more.

"Dan, she didn't mean anything." Elliott stepped closer to hold the umbrella over her, and she realized she still hadn't taken it from him.

She put a hand over his and lifted it higher so he was protected from the rain too. "I'm sorry, Dan." For so many things. "I haven't seen you since you were a kid, and everyone used to call you Danny back then."

"I'm noooot a kid."

Rem moved in closer to Dan.

"She knows that, Dan. She's been gone from the island for a long time, that's all. Do you remember Rebel Tate?" Elliott shifted under the umbrella, closing the small space between her and him. Their shoulders brushed, and his warmth wrapped around her.

Suddenly, she wanted to throw herself into his arms and get lost. But if she hadn't been convinced of her unworthiness before, looking at Dan Morgan's distorted face and awkward stance persuaded her otherwise.

Dan shook his head adamantly.

"That's okay," she said. "I didn't expect many folks around here to remember me."

"I liiiiike dogs." He ran both hands over Rem's ears and scratched his neck. "I dooooon't have one."

"His name is . . ." She resisted the urge to bite her nails. "Buddy. His name is Buddy. I'll bring him back to visit you sometime." Rebel couldn't change the past, but she might be able to make a difference in Dan's future. "Would you like a dog of your own?"

"Suuure!" Dan said.

"How about talking to your parents about it first? If they say yes, I might already have a good match for you." She turned to Elliott. "Can we go? There's something I need to do."

They said their goodbyes and walked to Elliott's Jeep, which was parked along the curb past the food truck. When they were inside, he turned up the heat and made a U-turn on Marina Boulevard.

"Take me to the ferry terminal."

He stomped on the brake. "Why?"

If she hadn't had on a seat belt, she'd have flown into the dash. She grabbed the bar above her door. "Good Lord, do you really think I'd bolt so quickly?"

Apparently he did, if his raised brows were any indication.

Rem stuck his head through the front seats and nudged her shoulder, then Elliott's.

"Fine." She settled back against the seat. "I suppose I deserve that. There's something at the terminal I need to pick up." With any luck, it would have a positive impact on Dan Morgan's life.

Elliott punched the gas, and they headed out of town. With a hand slung over the steering wheel, he said, "Why wouldn't you expect people to remember you? You grew up here."

"There's not much to remember. I spent most of my life trying not to bring attention to myself. If people noticed me and associated me with my mom, they usually whispered something hateful behind their hands." She wrapped both arms around herself and tried to rub out the cold. "I guess I liked staying in the background, so why *would* anyone remember me?"

"Because you're quite unforgettable." His voice was almost a whisper.

Her breath caught in her throat, and she pressed a hand to her chest. She wanted to reach out and brush the wet waves of hair off his forehead. Tell him he was the unforgettable one because of how much kindness and compassion he'd just shown Dan. Just shown her. Elliott had looked out for her the same way in high school. That tenderhearted boy who often stayed hidden inside a determined and strong-willed shell was still there. He'd grown into a man who shouldn't have given her a second thought.

He propped an elbow against his door and rubbed his temple like he'd said too much.

The squeak of windshield wipers and the splash of water as they rumbled through mud puddles were the only sounds that cut the uncomfortable silence. Even without saying a word, his presence was so larger-than-life that it filled the cab and pressed her against the door.

Ten minutes later, the rain had slowed to a sprinkle as they pulled to a stop in front of the open-air terminal.

"I'll be right back," Rebel said.

Elliott threw the gearshift into park and killed the engine. "Not a chance. I'm coming with." He got out and jogged around to Rebel's side. He opened her door. "Until this camp is over, I can't risk you disappearing again with Old Lady McGill's help."

Ouch.

When he put it like that, the truth hurt worse than usual.

Rebel tilted her head. "You're the one who's bailing this time."

"Change of plans. I'm sticking with the event." He swiped his arm in a downward arc to usher her out of the car.

"Why? You were so adamant about handing it off."

"I have an investment to protect here at the resort," he said.

"Your investment is the same today as it was yesterday," she countered.

A muscle in his jaw tensed. Finally, he said, "Yesterday you seemed to be concerned about the consequences of me *not* being involved in the camp."

Touché. He was still evading her question, though.

She should know. She was the queen of evading sensitive questions.

Could it be that a seed of forgiveness might be starting to sprout in his heart? His big heart that was encased in a hard, muscled, droolworthy chest.

"My brothers dared me to take the lead on this event. You know I could never resist an opportunity to show them I'm superior in every way."

Oh. Right. She remembered the tight-knit Remington brothers and all their sibling rivalries. She climbed out of the Jeep, called for Rem to follow, and headed straight for the ticket booth.

Bogart darted out from behind the booth and hopped over to Rem. They greeted each other like pals.

Rebel knelt and gave the handicapped dog a thorough scratch around his neck.

A wrinkle appeared between Elliott's eyes. "He's missing a leg."

"Really?" Rebel smarted off. Paybacks were hell, after all. "I hadn't noticed. Good catch."

Elliott gave her a stony stare.

Which she ignored.

She waved to Mabel, who put down her deck of cards and opened the window. "Need ferry tickets?" Her eyes twinkled with mischief.

"I'm here about Bogart." Rebel led Rem to the booth and leaned an elbow against the ticket counter. Bogart followed. "Any chance you'll let me take him and train him as a service dog? I know someone who might be a good match for him."

"I thought you'd never ask, hon. When you arrived and said you were a professional dog trainer, I knew it was meant to be. Knew you'd come back for him because you need each other." Mabel's glittering eyes trekked to Elliott. "The best ones are usually wounded, either on the inside or the outside, and they're always worth the effort."

Rebel couldn't stop her eyes from flying wide. Then she cut them at Elliott.

His Adam's apple bobbed, and the ropy muscles in his neck flexed as he swallowed. His granite stance said he hadn't missed Mabel's insinuation. And didn't like it. Not a bit.

Rebel's grip tightened around the leash until her nails dug into her palm. The ride back to the resort was going to be eternal.

Elliott had done Rebel a solid by driving her to the ferry terminal in the middle of a thunderstorm. As a reward, Mabel McGill had compared him to the three-legged dog that was now riding in his back seat next to Buddy.

Elliott steered the Jeep around a deep puddle as they made their way back to the resort. He leaned in to the door to escape the slimy tongue that kept licking his ear.

He'd much rather the beautiful redhead who was riding shotgun do the licking, but he shouldn't let his mind go there.

Scratch that. He *couldn't* let his mind go there.

Even though he knew better than to get too personal with his ex, he still wanted to know what had her upset enough to sit in the cold and stare at the Morgans' store in the pouring rain, wearing flimsy spandex running gear and a thin jacket that wasn't even waterproof. The sixth sense that guided him through turbulent stock market trends told him her odd behavior had something to do with the Morgans. He just wasn't sure why.

When Bogart wouldn't stop getting way too intimate with Elliott's ear, he shooed him away with the flick of a wrist.

Rebel put a hand over her mouth to cover a grin. "He likes you." She grabbed the *Oh shit* bar above her door as the Jeep bounced through a pothole. "Both Bogart and"—she hesitated, her tone shifting—"and Buddy like you."

That was a record. Two dogs and neither was growling at him. He supposed the dog licking his ear was better than it biting his ankle. Or humping his leg.

Bogart moved to the other side of the back seat, stuck his head through, and gave Elliott's left ear a bath.

"His name should be Willie because he keeps sticking his tongue in my ear," Elliott complained, scrunching his shoulder up to block the next onslaught of licks.

Rebel's deep, hearty laughter filled the cab and took him by surprise. He'd forgotten how much he'd loved her laugh. Her home life had been so difficult when they were teenagers, so he'd tried to make her laugh as much as possible. Something shifted in his chest at the memory of Rebel showing up at school with dark circles under her eyes and no homework to turn in because of her mother's latest drinking binge.

He leaned forward and draped both forearms over the steering wheel to escape the dog's tongue. "Seems to me Bogart needs a service dog of his own."

Rebel giggled again, and his heart thrummed.

"He'll never be a dog for someone with a severe physical handicap, but he'll be fine with a companion who needs comfort more than anything else." Her voice turned small. Almost frail. "He won't be able to go on long walks, but he might be able to pick up lightweight things that his eventual companion drops, like sunglasses, car keys . . . compact umbrellas."

"Ah, Dan Morgan," Elliott said. He had a brain injury from when he was a kid. If memory served, it had happened right after Elliott left for college. Maybe seeing Dan in the window of the store was the reason for her strange behavior. Rebel had always had a big heart.

She nodded. "Bogart's handicap might be advantageous. He'll be able to keep pace with Danny . . . um, D-Dan," she stammered. "Dan moves slowly, so a dog with too much energy would be overwhelming." She turned away to stare out the passenger window, the reflection off the glass showing a sadness that ran deep. "I accepted Lily's offer to take over the boot camp because training and finding matches for PTSD and traumatic brain injury is my specialty. Those injuries are more prevalent among veterans, but I'll work with anyone who's suffering."

"How did that become your specialty?" Elliott guided the Jeep along the meandering road that edged a pond on the right, the water jumping from the drizzling rain.

"Um . . ." She nibbled at the corner of her mouth in that sexy way that mesmerized him. Every damn time. Her chin trembled, and her dog stuck his head through the front seats to prop his chin on her shoulder. She gave his head a pat. "There are different types of handicaps and different types of service dogs for each. I've trained them all. Now that I've built a solid reputation, I'd rather help people with specific problems."

That didn't exactly answer his question, but she was finally talking. Opening up. Try as he might to stay detached from Rebel and her past, his curiosity was getting the better of him. So he let her keep talking.

"In my experience, people who suffer internally tend to be overlooked because their injuries aren't visible or obvious."

As irritating as it had been to be compared to a maimed dog, hadn't Mabel McGill just said as much?

He turned in to the resort, passing between the stone columns on each side of the entrance with a wrought iron arch stretching overhead that fashioned the words THE REMINGTON in rugged lettering.

"So you don't help wealthy families figure out why their pampered dogs keep tearing up four-million-dollar leather sofas like they're giant rawhides?"

She tugged at an earlobe with a *guilty as charged* expression. "To be honest, I've done exactly that. Many times. Helping a family bond with their pet is never a bad thing, even if it's more of a first-world problem. It's usually the human's fault, not the dog's."

"So dogs hating me, present company excluded"—he glanced into the rearview mirror at the two lolling pink tongues—"it's my fault?"

She gave him an unapologetic shrug. "They can sense when a person doesn't like them."

"How?" This he had to hear, because he wasn't so sure he bought into it.

She turned to study him. "Well, the first clue is the human's body language. Say, someone leaning forward to keep a dog from touching them, their shoulders bunched up around their ears." She folded both lips between her teeth to hide a grin and wasn't quite successful.

That grin made his heart sing. Made his pulse rev. Made heat creep up his skin until he wanted to pull at the neckline of his shirt.

He flipped the knob on the dash twice, turning down the heater.

"Very funny." He'd give her that one just because it'd made her smile. "So were you lurking outside the market this morning to see if Dan might need a service dog? Or was there another reason?"

Her smile faded. Her body stiffened from the top of her wet red hair to the tips of her soaked, squishing running shoes.

Another question she wasn't willing to answer, and this one had her clamming up completely.

He passed the main lodge and followed the road around to the motor-pool garage, flicking off the wipers, since the rain had stopped.

Well, he could find Lily and tell her he'd changed his mind. Tell her he was prepared to see the boot camp through. Tell her to kick his ass if he let himself get too close to a woman he shouldn't trust.

When he pulled to a stop alongside the other Jeeps, one of the garage bays was already open.

"Thanks for the ride." Rebel had one leg out the door before he even cut the engine.

"Hold on a sec." He reached for her arm to keep her from bolting from the Jeep. "What's going on with you this morning?"

She sighed, pulled her leg back inside the Jeep, and let the door ease shut. "Really, it's nothing."

"Right. I call bullshit," he deadpanned.

She let her head rest against the seat. Long lashes fluttered down as she closed her eyes on a slow blink. "It's nothing you need to worry about."

Elliott wanted to reach out and cup her cheek in his palm. Taste that lip that she kept worrying between her teeth.

Fuck. He was losing his shit. Maybe telling Lily he wanted to stick with the camp wasn't such a great idea after all.

Then again, it might be his only chance to get the answers he'd been after for ten long years. And God help him, he did want answers, even though he shouldn't.

A rap on the window had him jumping like a wussy kid at a horror flick.

Elliott's head snapped around to find Lily standing at his window, her usual bright, hospitable smile in place.

He turned off the engine and got out, shutting the door before his new furry friend jumped out after him and really did start humping his leg.

"Hey!" Lily bubbled with excitement. "Guess what?" She didn't wait for him to respond. "I found a replacement!"

"Oh, uh," was all Elliott could think to say. Yeah, that Ivy League degree was coming in handy.

Rebel got out with the dogs and brought them around to join the conversation.

"Isn't that great?" Lily was so wired over her accomplishment, she didn't even notice Bogart or his missing leg. "It helps to have a fiancé who's also a pilot. He flew me to the Cape, and I popped in to the local shelter, wielding my powers of persuasion."

Of course she did. Lily didn't fail at anything. Damn her.

A guy Elliott didn't recognize walked out of the open garage door. He was big, built, and what Elliott guessed most women would consider good-looking. The guy's gaze locked onto Rebel, and one corner of his mouth cocked up in an *I like what I see* kind of way.

Elliott disliked the asshat already.

"This is Jax," Lily almost shouted with enthusiasm. "He's getting familiar with your setup."

Jax? Nobody was really named Jax. Had to be fake. Probably a name he invented while moonlighting as a male stripper.

"Hiya." Jax stared at Rebel with a goofy smile that said he probably wasn't very bright. "I stalked your Instagram account on the way here. Gnarly work you do. WestCoastDogWhisperer is a bitchin' handle." He gave both dogs a playful scratch, and they wagged their tails, their full attention firmly on him.

Elliott found it oddly irritating that the dogs liked *Jax.* He found it even more annoying that Jax had found Rebel on Instagram. Elliott rarely bothered with social media, a habit he'd have to change. He actually had to download Instagram first, though, because he'd never had time for social media because of his demanding hours at the firm.

"Um, hello," Rebel said.

"Cool place," Jax said. "It's my first time visiting the Rem."

Rebel's dog barked and spun in a circle at the mention of the resort, like Jax had issued some sort of command.

"*Shhh!*" she hissed, shushing Buddy with an impatience Elliott hadn't seen from her.

"Jax works at the shelter on the Cape," Lily explained.

"Oh." Rebel's one-word response had way too much approval in it. So did her full, honest smile. "That's fantastic."

No, it wasn't. It sucked, actually, because Elliott was going to have to explain to Lily why he'd changed his mind after she'd gone to the trouble of finding someone with more experience than himself.

"Welcome." Rebel grasped Jax's hand between both of hers and shook it. "This is an immersion program—"

Jax's brow scrunched like he didn't understand what that meant.

"It'll be very fast-paced so we can teach the matches as much as possible while they're here," Rebel kept explaining. "I'm going to need help once the campers arrive tomorrow."

Wait. What? She'd tried to convince Elliott since day one that she didn't need help. Or maybe it was that she didn't want *his* help.

He took a step back. "So, Lily. I've decided to stay involved with the camp."

"Oh. Well, great!" Lily beamed. "Keeping a Remington at the helm will make the sponsor happy." She said her goodbyes and hurried off to rule the world with her iPad in hand.

Elliott's jaw hardened, and his stare slid to Jax. "Thanks for coming all this way, but we won't be needing you after all. The resort is happy to compensate you for your trouble. Just leave us your mailing address, and I'll cut you a check." He glanced at his watch. "Next shuttle leaves in fifteen."

Jax looked confused. Not in an "I don't understand why I'm being let go" kind of way, but more like "I don't understand the word *compensate* because it's more than two syllables."

Rebel gave Elliott a patient smile. "Nonsense. We need all the help we can get, and having Jax here is a win-win." She turned to Jax. "I'll show you around."

"Aiya," he said.

Rebel started for the garage, then stopped. "Oh, here ya go." She swished her shoulders to shuck Elliott's jacket. "Thanks for letting me use it."

He held up a hand. "Keep it." Unable to stop himself, his gaze slid all the way to her running shoes. "It looks better on you."

She stilled, the tip of her pink tongue slipping through her lips to trace her mouth.

Hell. *Old wrinkly guys in Speedos.*

"Go on." He hitched his chin toward the garage. "I'll catch up in a sec."

Elliott stayed rooted in place, watching her disappear through the open bay with her new protégé in tow. Why was he pissed at Rebel for being so enthusiastic over having help from a fellow dog lover? Better yet, why was he pissed at Lily for having the audacity to do exactly what he'd asked of her?

It damn sure wasn't a win-win. He was supposed to be in charge of an event he had absolutely no idea how to handle, working with a woman he absolutely shouldn't trust beyond her knowledge of dogs. He was torn between wanting to ask questions about her past and being scared of the answers. And now he had to run interference for a guy who seemed to have half the IQ of Rebel's dog, if even that, but would probably be better than Elliott at the task ahead.

Chapter Seven

#TrainWreckInTheMaking

Rebel wasn't sure why Elliott had such a problem with their new assistant. The only thing she *was* sure about was that he definitely had one. He'd been quiet, distant, and brooding since Jax's arrival yesterday.

"Nice weather." Rebel made small talk as the three of them waited on the dock behind the resort for the service dogs to arrive on Trace's plane.

Rem leaned hard against her side.

Elliott stood farther down the dock, his eyes hidden behind a pair of Oakley sunglasses. He kept his attention on the inlet's glassy water.

Jax shifted his stance, and his arm brushed hers. And stayed there. "Aiya, good weather."

Elliott's exasperated sigh wafted on the breeze.

Okay, she could see how Jax might get a little annoying. He had a sweet smile that lit his eyes. Unfortunately, that light was on but no one was home. It wasn't his fault, though, and even if he didn't understand the boundaries of personal body space, he seemed harmless. He wasn't a trainer, but at least he had experience with animals, working around them every day.

She fiddled with the new leashes in her hand. "So, Jax, how did you come to work at a shelter?"

"I like dogs. They like me too."

Simple but honest.

"My boss lets me keep a set of weights at the shelter so I can work out on my breaks," Jax said randomly.

Her foot tapped against the wood planks. "Well, connecting with dogs is something we have in common." She pointed to his biceps. "And the weight lifting is certainly working."

Elliott's head swiveled in her direction.

Good Lord. She bit her tongue to keep from rambling more nonsense.

Elliott went back to brooding at the water. It was unnerving how well he pulled off that look. How was it possible to make a flannel shirt over a thermal, a faded pair of jeans, and all-weather boots look as classy as a tailored suit, just because he'd added sunglasses?

She clenched everything from the waist down.

Elliott possessing an unfair amount of swagger was another reason she needed to stay detached. Cool. Indifferent.

Or at least pretend to be all those things because her mind couldn't stop wondering *what if?* Her uterus—rebellious floozy that it was—couldn't stop turning flips like a high-school cheerleader either.

She'd come by her name honestly.

She clenched harder.

Rebel moved a step to her right and gave Rem the signal to come to her side. He eased in between her and Jax, and Bogart followed.

She glanced at Elliott.

His jaw relaxed, but he kept his distance.

She wouldn't let Elliott's dismissiveness bother her. Not a bit. The more distance they kept between them the next month, the better. He was already asking questions. If the older, more experienced Elliott was anything like the young, keen Elliott she'd known, his inquiring mind wouldn't stop until he'd pieced together the entire puzzle.

She couldn't let that happen. The shameful truth had been buried right along with her mother, and that's exactly where it could stay.

Tap, tap, tap, tap. Her foot clicked against the dock at machine-gun speed.

Jax shifted closer. "Too much caffeine this morning?"

Not nearly enough. She stepped in the opposite direction to put more space between them.

Rebel closed her eyes and tipped her head back so the sun could soak into her cheeks. So her mind could stop wandering. So her body could stop clenching.

A whirring noise sounded in the distance, and she opened her eyes to see a dot in the sky. It grew bigger, the sun glinting off the metal.

"'Bout time," Elliott grumbled.

When the floatplane touched down, slid across the mirrorlike inlet, and coasted to the dock, Elliott moored it with a thick nylon rope.

"Coooool," Jax said. "I couldn't see the plane land while I was riding in it yesterday."

Oh boy.

Elliott gave him a look that said *that's as moronic as it sounds.*

Jax closed in on her again, standing flush against her side.

Elliott stilled, staring at them.

Could he be . . . *jealous?*

Nah. He obviously didn't care enough about her to be jealous.

The engine shut off, and a chorus of barking filled the air.

Elliott stepped back like he'd been bitten.

Rem whined.

Bogart cocked his head to one side, and his ears pitched forward.

What on earth? If the dogs were all barking at once, the training handlers weren't doing their jobs.

She held her breath as Trace climbed out of the cockpit, ready for her first face-to-face with another Remington.

"Rebel." He gave her a single nod that wasn't accompanied by a smile.

"Hi, Trace," she said. "Thanks for picking up the dogs and their handlers."

His forehead wrinkled. "I don't know anything about handlers, but that was one noisy ride. Not to mention dangerous."

"The training handlers didn't introduce themselves?" she asked just as an earsplitting howl came from inside the plane. Several other dogs joined in.

Trace and Elliott hurried to the cargo door in the center of the plane, working as a team to open it.

"They've likely never ridden in a plane, so it upset them." Rebel stepped forward as Trace unlatched the door. "Once we get them out of their crates and walk them around, they'll settle."

"Yeah, about the crates. Whoever built them needs their asses kicked." Trace pulled open the door.

A dozen overly excited Labradors of varying colors dashed down the ramp.

Rebel's jaw dropped. "Are you kidding me?" They were allowed to run loose in the cargo hold?

"Whoaaaa," Jax said.

At the same time, Elliott said, "Holy shit."

Half the dogs galloped to the giant pampas grass that divided the dock from the resort grounds and proceeded to relieve themselves. The other half rushed Elliott, obviously sensing his tension. They surrounded him like a pack.

His eyes flew wide.

Rebel would've laughed if the situation wasn't already so far out of control. She stepped toward the plane, straining to see inside. "Where are the handlers?" And why did the handlers leave the dogs unrestrained and howling like a pack of wolves?

"I don't know what handlers are," Trace said.

"The dogs' *trainers*." She couldn't hide the desperation in her voice as she hurried up the ramp to look inside the plane. Besides the crates, the cargo hold was empty.

"I thought you were the trainer," Trace said.

"Call them off," Elliott said from the center of his furry horde. One stuck its nose in his crotch while the other goosed him from behind. He put a protective hand over each side of his privates. "I'm no longer feeling like this is a safe place."

Walking—no, stomping down the ramp, she ignored his plea for help until someone gave her answers. "I can't possibly handle this many dogs on my own. We need the handlers who've been training the dogs since they were puppies. *Where are they?*"

Rem came to stand firmly at her side, and Bogart followed.

"The manifest the sponsor sent Lily said to pick up twelve dogs," Trace said. "And that's what I did."

"Are the handlers coming on a different flight?" Surely he was going back to the Cape to pick them up.

He shook his head, disappearing inside the plane.

Rebel smoothed a palm across her forehead. Obviously, she'd been so dumbfounded by the amount of money Down Home Dog Food had offered that she hadn't asked enough questions before accepting the job.

Trace carried out a crate in each hand. They weren't made of wire like the nice crates the sponsor had delivered with the other supplies. They looked homemade from flimsy plywood, which was splintered and broken. "These are garbage. As soon as I took off, the dogs went apeshit. The cages literally collapsed. I was airborne and couldn't do anything but keep flying."

"Ahem." Elliott's voice couldn't have gotten more disgusted. "While you two are catching up, I'm being molested by a bunch of dogs."

She handed Jax half the leashes. "Can you manage that many?"

"Sure can." Jax had the dogs that were torturing the grass leashed in seconds.

Which seemed to irritate Elliott even more because he actually moved his hands away from his privates to cross an inflated chest.

"Take them to the garage and give them fresh water," she said to Jax.

He disappeared around the barrier of giant grass, heading up the path.

She pulled a training clicker from her pocket. Present or not, if the handlers knew their stuff, the dogs would respond to the noise. So far, her expectations weren't running high, though.

Here goes nothing.

She squeezed the clicker. The dogs stayed crowded around Elliott, but they settled and focused on her.

Thank God.

It was a small victory, but she'd take it. She leashed the dogs but didn't lead them away from Elliott. While she had his attention, she was going to make use of it by laying some ground rules. "*You're* representing the resort for this event, Elliott. You didn't know the handlers wouldn't be arriving with the dogs?"

"No, I didn't. I don't know anything about service dogs or camps or handlers, which is why I wanted to delegate my responsibilities to someone else. But there is no one else." He glowered in the direction Jax had just gone. "At least no one I trust."

Rebel dug deep for patience.

Trace stepped out of the plane with more crates and walked them to the dock.

When a particularly friendly black Lab jabbed his nose into Elliott's crotch again, he went back to guarding his privates.

Trace stopped next to his brother. "Maybe you should go take a shower."

Elliott moved the hand from his backside long enough to scratch his nose with a middle finger.

She waved both arms in the air. "I assumed the sponsor would send someone who knew what they were doing." Apparently, that was too much to ask. Down Home Dog Food didn't appear to know any more about running an efficient camp than the Remington Resort.

"We need better communication. If you're staying on as the resort's rep, then take the reins. You and I should speak with the sponsor—no one else."

"You're right." The tension in Elliott's voice escalated. "But give me a break here. It's taken me longer to wrap my head around this event because I'm not a dog person, and—"

The dogs crowded in on him again.

His arms flailed for balance.

She didn't try to hide a cocky *serves you right* smile as she let the dogs have their way with him.

His raised arms stilled against his privates again. "You're really going to let them rob me of my innocence?"

"You and I both know you're not at all innocent," she blurted before she could stop herself.

They both stilled. Both stayed quiet. Like they were both thinking of the not-so-innocent times they'd spent together so many years ago.

Involuntarily, the tip of her tongue darted out to trace her lips.

A muscle in Elliott's jaw tensed.

Which got the dogs excited all over again.

She pressed the clicker, and they focused on her. "They sense your uneasiness."

Trace emerged with more crates. "That's all of them. I'm heading back to the mainland to pick up a load of cargo." He tossed them onto the pile with the rest of the tattered crates and climbed into the cockpit.

"We need to move the dogs away from the plane, since the engine obviously upsets them." She handed Elliott a couple of leashes. "Can you walk two of them if I take the rest?"

"Of course." He grabbed the leashes, but his expression wasn't nearly as confident as his words.

She led her dogs up the path. When they got to the playground, she stopped for a brief training session. "Hold your hand palm down over their heads so they know you're the dominant figure."

Elliott's movement was far too fast, and a yellow female Lab squatted on his shoe to relieve herself.

Rebel clamped a hand over her mouth to cover a belly laugh. "I'm sorry." She chuckled against her cupped hand. "When a dog piddles, it's a sign of submission, which is a good thing in a service dog."

His scowl said he didn't believe a word of it. "Piddles?"

"Yes, piddles."

His scowl deepened.

"When they're scared or excited, they lose control of their bladder."

"I am not saying that word out loud," Elliott huffed. "Ever again."

She fought off another smile at the alpha hot guy with the high-dollar education who was so bothered over a simple word. "How about twizzles?"

"I quit," he deadpanned.

This time she tilted her head back and laughed.

Which seemed to lighten his mood and ease his scowl.

And for a second, everything else melted away, and it was just her and him. Staring deep into each other's eyes. Each other's souls.

The plane's engine whirred to life in the distance.

Elliott's lips parted like he was going to speak. Maybe say something sweet. Or something sensual. Like he used to.

Instead he said, "This is going to be a train wreck."

Her lungs deflated, her heartbeat a dull thud against her rib cage.

Train wreck? Probably. On so many levels.

Chapter Eight

#SnowballsChanceInHell

Rebel stood under a copse of red-and-orange-tinged trees by the garage and worked with one dog at a time, testing for personality traits, strengths, and weaknesses. Since she was the sole trainer, she'd been able to assess only half the dogs since they'd arrived the day before.

It would be an understatement to say her frustration level had run high when the handlers didn't arrive with the dogs. Rem and Bogart hadn't left her side since.

Rebel threw a ball to analyze the energy level of a chocolate Lab named Elsie. The dog took off after it.

What kind of company sponsored a boot camp and delivered the dogs unattended with one trainer to manage them all? The term *boot camp* made it obvious the event would be immersive, intensive, and condensed. Seemed common sense that those conditions would require the dogs to be accompanied by their handlers. At the very least, the sponsor should've hired more than just Rebel as a trainer.

Wrong. She shook her head and leashed the Lab as it dropped the ball at her feet.

At the very least, the sponsor could answer Elliott's calls, which Rebel had insisted he march to his office and make right after he'd admitted the camp was going to be a train wreck. He'd been trying to call the sponsor ever since.

She would not join in with his glass-half-empty attitude. She would not admit defeat so easily. Which meant she would *not* mention that she'd slept in the garage last night to calm the howling dogs.

He wouldn't understand that it had been the only way to keep them quiet after they'd been separated from their handlers, then gotten so worked up on the plane ride. He wouldn't understand that this was her job, and no way would she ask him or Jax to do anything she wasn't willing to do herself.

He wouldn't understand that sleeping in a garage was much better than some of the places she'd had to sleep right after she'd left the island.

She handed the leash to Jax. "Crate Elsie and bring out the next." Rebel rubbed the kink in her neck from sleeping on a makeshift bed in the garage. Then she picked up her pad and jotted down notes under Elsie's name.

"'Kay." Jax did exactly what Rebel asked. No hesitation. No questions.

No chemistry pulling her thoughts away from her task. Her goal. Her future.

"Still no luck getting the sponsor on the line." Elliott strolled up behind her.

Her skin prickled. *Dammit.* Less than a week back on the island and just the sound of his voice made her want to drop to the ground, roll onto her back, and ask him to pet her tummy. Among other things.

She pressed down so hard on her mechanical pencil that the lead snapped.

She didn't turn around to look at him. "Keep trying. We need to find out what happened to the handlers and see if Down Home Dog Food will fly them here to help." She clicked the top of the pencil and finished her notes on Elsie. "Amazing that a company would invest so much in an event, then drop the ball with communication. Not telling us the handlers weren't coming is kind of a big deal."

"I've left several messages, a few of which informed them to communicate with no one but me or you," he said. "Hopefully, nothing else will slip past us."

A wonderfully familiar aroma teased her senses. She spun around before she could stop herself. "Is that Charley's coffee?"

He boosted the drink carrier in his hand that held three piping-hot cups of coffee. "Doughnuts too. I figured we could use an afternoon snack." He walked over to a stump and set everything down.

Jax led a strapping yellow Lab out of the garage. He handed the leash to Rebel and bent to look at the tag dangling from the collar. "This one's Oscar. Yo, dude." Jax greeted Elliott like he should be catching a wave on the beaches of Malibu. "Thanks." He headed straight to the tree stump, didn't touch any of the cups in the carrier, and grabbed two of the three doughnuts instead. He took a big bite and nodded to Elliott.

Rem and Bogart trotted to Elliott and brushed against his leg.

"One of those was mine, but sure," he deadpanned. "Help yourself."

"Awesome." Jax took another gigantic bite.

Elliott responded with a *you've got to be kidding me* look.

Rebel tossed her notepad and pencil to the side, pulled the clicker from her pocket, and pressed it. It chirped, and his gaze snapped to hers.

She challenged him with a smarty-pants smile and nodded at the dog on the end of the leash. "Now that I've got your attention, can we focus on Oscar?"

"Very funny." Elliott stalked to the stump and pulled two cups from the tray. He brought one to Rebel.

"Thank you." She took a long drink, and then she lowered her voice so Jax couldn't overhear. "But a cup of coffee won't get you off the hook for wanting to start a pissing contest every time you're around him. We need his help." She cut her eyes at Jax, who was preoccupied with his doughnuts and a very large dragonfly that hovered a few feet away.

Oh boy.

Elliott leaned in. "I doubt we need to whisper." He lowered his voice to mimic her. "He won't know you're talking about him unless you call him by name."

"Now you're just being mean," she scolded. "He's good with the dogs, and we're shorthanded, in case you forgot."

"I never forget." He took a sip, staring at her over the rim of his cup. "Ever." His piercing gaze said he wasn't just talking about not having enough help with the camp. He shoved his free hand in his pocket and rocked back on his heels. "Work your magic, Dog Whisperer." He hitched his chin at Oscar.

"Uh-uh." She held out the leash. "You're going to work the magic."

His eyes flew wide. "I'll deal with the sponsor, but you've got to manage the dogs." Then he glanced at Jax. "Have him do it. Didn't you just say he's here to help?"

"Hey, Jax?" She didn't look away from Elliott. "Can you rotate the dogs out of their crates for fresh water and a bathroom break?"

"Gotcha." He stuffed the rest of the doughnuts into his mouth, brushed his hands off, and walked into the garage.

"He's busy." She tilted her head to one side and gave Elliott a challenging look. "I dare you to work with Oscar. You like dares, right?"

Without breaking eye contact, Elliott slowly took the leash from her fingers and replaced it with his cup of coffee so that both her hands were full. Still staring into her eyes, he stepped close, reached for her waist . . .

Her lips parted, and she let out a tiny gasp as his soapy scent mingled with the blessed coffee and made her light-headed.

"Challenge accepted." The zipper of her fanny pack whizzed as he opened it and plunged his hand inside. He leaned in, his mouth so close to hers she could almost taste him. "You don't mind me getting a treat, do you?" The fanny pack adjusted to the weight of his searching hand and slid low on her belly.

Ladyland didn't just purr. It roared to life like a mountain lion in heat. Desire scorched through Rebel's veins, setting her limbs on fire.

Her throat closed. "Not at all." Her voice turned to gravel, but she wouldn't give in to his taunt. He had no idea who he was dealing with. As a single young woman alone in the world, she'd fended off more than a few innuendoes. "I don't give my treats out to just anyone." To give him a little taste of his own medicinal smart-assery, she put her mouth at his ear and whispered, "But in your case . . ."

When she leaned back to look at him, his green eyes dilated like he was remembering, and his hand stilled inside the fanny pack. Stilled against her belly just above her thighs.

Breathe, breathe, BREATHE!

His fiery gaze raked her face, and he leaned in like he was going to devour her lips with his.

Rem whined, and he, Bogart, and Oscar crowded her and Elliott.

She tried to appear calm and confident. "I'll make an exception, since this might be the only way for you to get any." She paused for dramatic effect. "Any treats, that is."

He lowered his voice and said, "Great dog whisperer. Terrible liar." He dropped his voice a little more and glanced down at the notch where her neck met her shoulder. "That fearless expression you're wearing doesn't quite add up with the pulse that's pounding away at your neck."

Her lips parted to tell him he was full of it, but she couldn't form words as his tempting mouth hovered a breath from hers.

Abruptly, he stepped away.

Ladyland growled and clawed until Rebel had to tighten everything from the roots of her red hair to the tips of her curling toes. Swear to God, even her toenails clenched. Clenching was her only option because shouting "Down, girl!" at her crotch probably wouldn't build confidence in her abilities as a trainer.

He walked Oscar to the center of the grassy area. "So what do I do?"

Besides put his lips on hers, trail kisses along her neck, and use an assortment of body parts and appendages to give Ladyland the real treat she was craving?

Dammit. Rebel needed a mocha java chip fix, and fast. Because her favorite ice cream was the only kind of satisfaction she was going to allow herself while in Angel Fire Falls.

She marched over to the stump, exchanged Elliott's coffee for the only doughnut left, and took a huge bite. *"Mmmmm,"* she moaned out loud and let her eyes slide shut.

Only to open them and find him frozen in place again with a sultry look that said she'd struck a nerve. A nerve that was probably located somewhere a fanny pack would cover. Except he wasn't wearing one.

He shifted uncomfortably and glowered.

She smiled and washed down ten thousand calories or so with a drink of coffee. "Put your hand flat against his haunches and press down."

It took him a second to refocus on the dog. Finally, palm down, he smoothed a hand along Oscar's back. When Elliott got almost to the tail, he hesitated.

She discarded her food onto the stump and retrieved her notepad and pencil. "That's it. Now slowly apply pressure to see how much he can withstand."

"What's the purpose?" Elliott asked.

"Oscar's big and strong. He might be a good match for a veteran who has lost a limb or is disabled physically. We need to make sure Oscar can handle pressure from body weight." She twirled an index finger as if to say *proceed.*

"If you say so." Elliott pressed down on Oscar, and the dog didn't budge.

"Excellent!" She picked up two sticks, found a comfy spot under the trees, and sat cross-legged. Rem and Bogart flanked her. "Now, hold the treats in your fist, and keep your fist at your chest. Say 'look' and just stand still, looking straight at him until his attention is firmly on you and nothing else."

It took less than ten seconds for the dog to look up at Elliott and still like he was in the zone.

"Good," she said gently. "I'm going to beat these sticks together. Don't look at me, and don't move. Stay exactly like you are now." She pounded them together like drumsticks.

Neither the dog nor Elliott moved, and their attention didn't waver.

Rem, on the other hand, skittered away and hid behind the stump.

"Good. Oscar doesn't get distracted when he's working." She put the sticks down. "Now, tell him to sit with a firm tone—"

"Sit," Elliott growled before she could finish explaining the proper way to issue a command.

The dog's ears folded back like he'd been scolded.

Rebel slowly blinked. "I said be firm, not sound like Attila the Hun."

Elliott scrubbed his knuckles across his five-o'clock shadow, the stubble just visible enough to look sexy.

Meow.

"My tone is authoritative," he said.

"You just keep telling yourself that," she countered, forcing her thoughts back to the dog. "Try it again, and the second he obeys give him an enthusiastic *yes*, then hand him a treat."

Elliott blew out his cheeks like she'd asked him to disprove Einstein's theory of relativity. He was probably smart enough to do just that, which made it even more hilarious that a guy who had both brains and brawn couldn't manage a dog who was already trained with the basics.

She was about to give up on the training tutorial, but he issued the command. When Oscar plopped onto his haunches, Elliott looked stunned.

"*Yes,*" she mouthed.

"Yes," Elliott repeated, and gave Oscar a treat and a pat on the head. "That's amazing. I can't believe I'm training a dog."

"Actually, you're not." She stood with her pad and brushed the grass off her bottom. "His handler already trained him with the essentials." She gave Rem the command to follow her, and he finally eased out from behind the stump. "My job is mostly about training humans." She joined Elliott with Rem and Bogart at her side. "Once the human is trained, the dog follows suit."

"Huh." Elliott processed that. "If you were training me, where's *my* reward?"

"I thought you got plenty?" She moved on. "Let's try the touch command next. It can eventually transition into turning on light switches and such for a disabled companion."

"Really?" Elliott asked, all wide-eyed and wonder.

"Yes, really." She led him through the basic commands, making notes about Oscar.

When they were done, she said, "He's going to make a great service dog."

"Hiya." Jax sauntered out of the garage carrying a bundle.

She felt another eye roll coming on when Elliott stiffened.

"I found someone's pillow and blanket in the garage," Jax said. "Mind if I hang out on it later and read when the furry bros are eating in their crates?"

Oh God. She did not want Elliott to know about the damn pillow and blanket. She should've left them in her room and slept on the concrete floor with nothing but a big plush dog toy as a pillow. She'd certainly endured worse when she was a homeless teen.

"He can read?" Elliott whispered.

She glared at him. "Be nice."

"Jax, what are you reading?" Elliott asked.

"Graphic novels," Jax said.

Elliott lifted a brow.

At least the bedroll hadn't sparked any questions.

"Jax, can you take Oscar? And they need a potty break when they're done drinking. Elliott and I are going to try to reach the sponsor again."

Jax nodded and took Oscar away.

"He's very obedient," Elliott said with a cocky smile. "So is the dog."

"I'd hire Jax in an instant when I get my own facility." She clamped her mouth shut. The less Elliott knew about her life, the easier it would be to keep their time together about business.

A wrinkle appeared between his eyes. "You don't already have your own place?"

Dammit. "I work freelance." She didn't want to talk about her business plan. Not only could it give him more food for thought, but also because it still seemed too good to be true. It was like the abandoned property had been waiting just for her, a perfect ready-built solution offered at a bargain-basement price to finally make her dream come true.

A dream that would allow her to give back after all her mother had taken away.

The camp brought that impossible dream closer, but it wouldn't be a done deal until she could make an official offer.

"So." She changed the subject. "How about we call the sponsor again, then test the rest of the dogs. Maybe you can try out some of what you've learned on Bogart."

"You want me to train a dog who could qualify for a handicap sticker himself?" Elliott huffed.

"Don't flatter yourself," she shot back. "I'll be doing most of the training. It'll be more like practice for you."

Ten minutes later, they were sitting in Elliott's office. He'd claimed the chair behind his desk and dialed the phone, while she got comfortable in the armchair across from him. The call must've gone to voice mail again because Elliott all but growled. "Mr. Collins, this is Elliott

Remington *again*. I've called. I've left messages. And I've called more. It's time we conduct business like professionals, or we'll have a problem on our hands. Aren't there interviews lined up? Lots of eyes on this event in both the community and the press?"

He didn't use the same flowery tone Lily wielded like a weapon. Elliott's was different but just as convincing in an *I'm a formidable businessman who you don't want to mess with* kind of way. "Call me back by the end of the day." He hung up, leaving off an "or else" that was oh so apparent in his voice.

She blew out a breath. "Hopefully, they'll get back to us soon."

"If I have to go to their office and beat down the door, we'll speak to them." He leaned forward with his elbows propped on the desk. "I may not know anything about dogs, but I know plenty about business. You have my word, they *will* answer your questions."

Not only did she believe him, but his take-no-prisoners attitude made a tingle start way too far south of the border.

She crossed her legs and clenched again. Good Lord, she was going to have buns of steel by the time the camp was over. "Thank you." She examined a cuticle. "This evening, we can compare my notes with the veterans' profiles. Maybe pick three or four potential matches for each vet."

"Over dinner." He used the same self-confident, take-charge tone.

Her head popped up. Having dinner with him was not a good idea. Not at all. "I don't—"

"Hey there," a strong masculine voice said from the doorway behind her.

"Hi, Dad." Elliott's chair creaked as he leaned back.

She cringed. Drew in a deep breath and pushed out of her chair to face Elliott's father for the first time since she'd arrived. "Hello, Lawrence." Besides the white hair and a small spare tire around the middle, age hadn't changed him that much. "It's so good to see you." And it was. He'd been like the father she'd never known.

"I heard we had an expert dog trainer in the house who was an old friend." His voice was cautious, but his eyes sparkled with affection. "Why am I just now seeing you, Rebel?"

Because she'd been busy. Places to go. People *not* to see.

"I'm sorry." She had a hard time meeting his gaze. "Taking the job was so sudden, and I've been playing catch-up since I got here because I didn't have time to prepare ahead of time." Sounded legit. Even if it was a load of dog poo.

He took her in, his posture relaxing. "Time doesn't stop, does it? You're all grown up now, just like my boys. Right, son?"

Elliott didn't respond. Instead, his gaze coasted over her.

Her cheeks must've gone up in flames because the room suddenly grew so hot she wanted to fan herself.

"I always wanted a daughter just like you. Give me a hug." Lawrence held out his arms.

When she stepped into his fatherly embrace, her eyes grew wet.

"I heard the service dogs arrive," Lawrence said as he let her go.

Elliott's head bobbed. "Trace flew them in yesterday."

Lawrence cupped a hand around his ear. "I mean I actually heard them when I was in the main lodge last night. So did our guests."

"I checked on the dogs pretty late, and they were worked up," Rebel said. "Probably separation anxiety because they've been taken away from their training handlers."

"A dog spends two years with a trainer, and then it's taken away?" Lawrence asked. "That's cruel."

"It's definitely an emotional experience." Which was why she was going to do things differently when she opened her own facility. "The anxiety will get better once the dogs are matched. Once I got them calmed last night"—she picked at a nail—"I figured out a way for them to stay settled so they wouldn't keep everyone up all night."

Elliott frowned. "How?"

She would not let on that she'd spent the night in the garage. "Oh, you know." She flashed a brilliant smile at them both. "I worked my magic." She used Elliott's own words to deflect.

"I called your room to see if I could help you somehow with the noise," Lawrence said. "But there was no answer."

Well, poo.

Elliott folded his arms across his chest and pushed farther into the back of his chair.

"Would you like to see our setup in the garage?" She took a step toward the door. "I can show you right now."

"No." Elliott's tone had her stopping in her tracks. "We're waiting on a really important call from the sponsor. You can show Dad later."

"How's the camp coming along?" Lawrence asked.

She couldn't lie to him. "Well, it isn't—"

"It's great," Elliott said at the same time.

Okaaaay. Mr. Glass Half-Empty wasn't being honest with his father. But why would he lie?

"This is a really good thing you're doing for people who've served our country." Lawrence scratched his temple. "When I came home from 'Nam, there was no counseling or service dog programs. We had to deal as best we could on our own." He leaned against the doorframe. "Some adjusted to civilian life again. Some didn't."

She could relate. During the year she'd had nowhere to live, she'd visited her share of homeless shelters and soup kitchens. While they were a huge help, they didn't solve the bigger problem of getting lives back on track. She'd encountered a lot of different folks in those home-less hangouts, and many had been veterans. Some people found their way to a better life, like she had. Some were still holding signs on a street corner somewhere unknown.

Either way, the stigma of once being homeless clung to a person like a disease, and they were never able to completely shake it.

"Dad, can I catch up with you later? Rebel and I are swamped, and the veterans will be here tomorrow."

"Sure thing." He pushed off the doorframe. "Let me know if I can help."

As soon as Lawrence left, she tried to put on a bright face and said, "Ready to get back to work?"

"Shut the door." There went that authoritative voice again.

This time she didn't find it quite as admirable. Or sexy.

When she pushed the door shut, she turned and leaned against it.

He rested a hand against his jaw and tapped his forefinger on his temple.

Maybe his brilliant mind hadn't connected the dots between the pillow, the blanket, and her admission that she'd found a way to quiet the dogs all night long. Maybe his steel-trap memory had failed and he'd forgotten all about the pillow and blanket Jax found in the garage.

Maybe snowballs existed in hell.

"Want to explain why you slept in a cold garage last night with a bunch of dogs?" He pointed to the ceiling. "When you have a perfectly nice room inside."

Rebel sighed. It was going to be one hell of a month. "How I handle the dogs"—she put a hand on the doorknob and turned it—"is my decision. I'm the trainer. You just take care of the sponsor." She tugged the door open. "I'm going back to the garage to do what you hired me to do. Meet me there if you want. Or not." She stepped through the doorway. "It's your choice."

He opened his mouth to speak, but she closed the door in her wake and got the hell out of there.

Chapter Nine

#MannersMakeTheMan

After they finished testing the rest of the dogs, Elliott marched to the game room to blow off steam. *Steam* was putting it mildly. The sponsor still hadn't returned his calls; Rebel had been evasive about her questionable sleeping arrangements; she'd refused to discuss the potential matches over dinner, claiming she wasn't hungry; and he'd misled his dad about the event.

What good would it have done to alarm his father before Elliott had a chance to resolve the problems with Down Home Dog Food? If he could just get them on the phone, he'd straighten things out. Or die trying. Which he just might because his blood pressure had reached stroke level.

Once he'd discovered Rebel had slept in the garage with the dogs, he'd been simmering like a volcano ready to erupt.

Who did that? And why hadn't she asked for help? Better yet, why had she gotten so defensive when he'd questioned her about it?

When he reached the game room, he grabbed the doorknob but stopped. Turned to take in the colorful sunset.

Sunsets, playing pool with his brothers, seeing his dad, his nephew, and his cousin and her daughter had allowed contentment to bud in him for the first time since he went off to college. He was going to miss them when he left the island.

What he wouldn't miss were the constant reminders of his mother and his part in her absence. She was everywhere. He saw her in the paintings that hung in the family den, the way the kitchen was designed, and the shrubs she'd planted on the grounds when he was a kid.

Thank God he had a kick-ass job in Cali to go back to that kept his brain focused on the future instead of the past.

He threw open the door and stepped inside. "Whose ass am I kicking at pool today?"

With several balls left on the table, his brothers were obviously in the middle of a game.

Spence sank a shot. "In your dreams, asshat."

If his little brother only knew. Pool wasn't what Elliott had been dreaming about. Lately his dreams had been about flowing red hair across his pillow, plump lips, and moaning. Lots and lots of moaning.

Fuck.

"Thing One," Trace greeted him. "Where are your sidekicks? Lily mentioned something about a skittish Lab and a three-legged dog."

Huh. Elliott didn't think Lily had noticed Bogart's odd number of limbs. Then again, Lily didn't miss much, even if she didn't let on to it.

Elliott went to the dartboard and picked the darts from the cork. "They're with their master. She's taking a break in her room. We've been at it all day." Plus, she was probably exhausted from sleeping on the floor of the garage like a homeless person.

Something prickled down his spine, and he paused. He shook it off.

Pacing off roughly nine feet, he turned and hammered a dart dead-ass center. It hit the red circle with a *thud* that made the wall shudder and shake.

From the corner of his eye, he didn't miss the look his brothers exchanged. They came to his end of the room and slid onto the edge of the pool table to watch him chuck the next dart. Which he did with enough force that it could've landed on the mainland if the board hadn't been in the way. It stuck a pinprick away from the first dart.

"Soooo," Trace drawled. "I take it the camp isn't going well? Or are you in such a cheery mood because of having to work with your ex-girlfriend?"

"My mood is fine." Dart number three struck just outside the red center with a *thwack*. His overactive imagination was the problem. It kept forming images of velvety red hair against creamy naked skin that tickled his bare chest and his—

Not even the thought of old wrinkly guys in Speedos was working.

"Right." Spence wrapped both hands around his stick and leaned forward, bracing his weight against it. "Then why're you throwing so hard those darts could drill a hole through the wall?"

"I'm tired of these childish dares." Elliott stalked to the board to retrieve the darts.

"They're fun," Trace said. "That's how I found Lily."

"They're stupid." Elliott hoofed it back to the other side of the room. "And you'd have met her anyway." Another dart plunged into the cork just outside the red bull's-eye. "Since she works here and all."

"If you want to be the asshat who ends our brotherly tradition, then be that way." Spence blew out a breath. "You always were a killjoy."

"Oh no. You're not getting off that easy," Elliott said on a sarcastic laugh. "Trace and I have both been in the hot seat. The dare tradition won't be over until you've had your turn. And I'm going to make sure it's a whopper." He pounded the board with another dart. "I'll be in the front row watching the shit show like when we were in high school and dared you to play in a basketball game"—he lifted a brow—"unencumbered."

The color drained from Spence's face.

Trace threw his head back and bellowed with laughter. "I'll bring the popcorn and sodas."

Spence's lack of proper athletic underclothes had been quite a sight. Until the ref pulled him from the game because several mothers left with their hands over their children's eyes.

"I got suspended from school for a week, and Dad grounded me for even longer," Spence groused.

When Trace finally stopped laughing, he said, "Is the camp really that bad, Thing One?"

"No." Elliott's last dart smacked the red circle and stuck. "It's a million times worse than bad." Before he could launch into his bullet list of complaints, Ben burst through the door.

Meeting in the game room after school several times a week was another Remington brothers' tradition that had carried on between Trace and his son.

"Dad! Grandpa just picked me up from Frontier Scouts!" His little body hummed with excitement. "Guess what?" He didn't wait for his dad to respond. "I'm going to work on my community service badge."

"That's great, son." Trace ruffled his hair. "What can I do to help?"

"Can you help me think of ways to earn it?" Ben kicked the floor with a tennis shoe.

"Sure. Let's give it some thought tonight when we have dinner at Lily's," Trace said. "Among the three of us, I'm sure we can come up with an idea."

"The service dog camp is a community service event. He could take my place," Elliott joked. "He'd probably be more useful." He threw each dart in rapid succession, and they hit the board with a bruising *whomp*, *whomp*, *whomp*. "We don't have enough help, and the help we do have can't add two plus two with a calculator. Yet he's still more valuable than I am when it comes to this event."

"I don't suppose that's wounded your ego?" Trace asked.

Elliott glanced at his nephew, then responded with the code for *Kiss my ass*.

The truth hurt like a mother.

"A dozen vets are showing up tomorrow expecting us to have our shit together. Trust me when I say our shit is nowhere close to being together." He stomped to the board and pulled the darts free, thinking about Rebel sleeping on the cement floor instead of delegating to him or Jax. "And I'm not at all certain our dog whisperer was the right choice. I'm questioning her leadership skills."

Because her decision to spend the night in a fucking garage while he was tucked in a warm bed made him feel like shit.

"I guess she was a last resort, since Lily had to scramble to find a replacement at the last minute," Spence said.

Elliott turned to pace back to his throwing spot but stilled.

He hadn't heard the door open, but it was cracked about six inches. Rebel stood in the opening. Even from across the room, he could see her chin quivering.

Hell. He let his eyes slide shut.

With an index finger, she gave the door a nudge so it swung wider. Buddy and Bogart were at her side. "Hello, everyone."

Trace and Spence hopped off the edge of the table and spun around to face her. They were as speechless as Elliott.

"Hi." Ben rubbed his thighs with his hands. "I like your hair. It's a pretty red." He made a face. "Not like my teacher's hair last year. It was blue."

Elliott had to admit, at that moment his third-grade special-needs nephew had more sense than the three Remington brothers combined.

"Hi, Ben." Her thinned lips curved into a barely there smile. "How's your duck?"

"He's great!" Ben hollered in his usual volume. "Want to play with him sometime?"

"I'd love that," she said. "Want to pet Buddy and Bogart?"

"Yeah!" he cheered.

She gave Buddy the signal to go to Ben, and Bogart followed.

Rebel's eyes trekked back to Elliott and narrowed. "Our new camp assistant may not have great arithmetic skills, but he has kindness, compassion, and manners. Didn't Mrs. Ferguson used to say, 'Manners make the man'?"

She did. And if the woman who'd helped finish raising him and his brothers after their mother died had overheard the conversation, she'd be pulling them into the family den by the ear for a good scolding. Which made Elliott feel like one of the big brown piles the service dogs had been leaving on the grounds where Jax took them for potty breaks.

It killed him, but he had to be honest with himself. He was jealous of Jax. *Jax!* Jealous of the fact that Jax was more useful to Rebel than he was. Jealous of the fact that she seemed to enjoy the company of someone so simple over spending time with him.

Spence looked at Trace and pulled at his left earlobe, their code for *Let's get the hell out of here.*

"Ben," Trace said, finally unrooting himself. "Why don't we go over to the kitchen and see if we can bribe Charley out of a snack."

"I'll come with." Spence was first to the door. He paused in front of Rebel. "Good to see you again, Rebel."

"Really?" she asked matter-of-factly. "I would've never guessed."

At least Spence had the decency to look contrite as he nodded to her and left.

Trace started to lead Ben toward the door.

"I have an idea for Ben's Scout badge." Rebel gave Ben another warm smile. "If it's okay with your dad."

Trace stopped, closed his fist, and rubbed his knuckles along his cheek like he was scratching it. Seemed like an innocent gesture, but really it was code for *Can she be trusted?*

Elliott flicked the tip of his nose with a thumb. More code for *It's a go.* Which made his chest tighten. Because he was starting to trust Rebel, and he wasn't sure if that was wise or if it made him the stupidest smart guy on the island.

Rebel's chin quivered again, and the dogs crowded in on her. She'd known about their code years ago. She just couldn't decipher it because it'd been a secret kept between the brothers. But she was smart enough to know that she was probably the topic of their private conversation.

"We're all ears." Trace playfully tugged at the cusps of Ben's ears.

Ben giggled and swiped at his dad's hands.

"If Ben found a way to bond with a duck, then he can do the same with dogs." She stuffed both hands into her jacket pockets and walked to the pool table. "Elliott's right about *one* thing." The way she stressed the word hung in the air, making him feel even smaller. "We do need more help. Ben could help with feeding, walking, bathing." She ran a long, slender finger along the edge of the table. "I could show him how to teach Bogart basic commands that will transform him from a stray into an animal with a valuable purpose—"

"Hold up," Elliott interrupted. She'd earmarked Bogart for Dan Morgan. If Ben got attached, he'd be heartbroken when the dog went away.

Elliott's mouth turned to cotton.

Was he really thinking about the pain Ben might experience over losing something he'd grown to care for? Or was he thinking about his own pain over losing the girl he'd once loved?

He swallowed back the bitter memory. "I'm not sure this is a good idea." He looked from Trace to Ben. "He'd spend a lot of time with Bogart, then he'd have to give him away."

"That's where the community service part comes in." Rebel took a purple ball and rolled it across the table until it banked in front of Elliott. "He'd know going in that he was doing this as a service for someone who needs Bogart. I'm not saying it'll be easy, but letting go is a life lesson everyone has to learn." Sadness filled her eyes for a fleeting moment. "When it's for such a good cause like helping someone less fortunate, there's a lot of personal growth involved."

Trace rubbed the back of his neck. "Ben, do you understand you wouldn't be keeping Bogart?"

"I've got Waddles." Ben bounced on the balls of his feet. "Can I, Dad? *Please?*"

Rebel braced a hip against the table. A slender hip with just enough fullness to be perfect. Elliott didn't care much for a rail-thin woman. He liked at least a little curve and contour because it felt good under his palms as he explored every inch of her naked body—

Trace cleared his throat. "What do you say, Uncle Elliott?"

Somehow he managed to unhook his gaze from Rebel's lovely hip, which attached to nicely shaped legs that would wrap perfectly around his waist. *Jesus.* "Huh?" *Christ.* And he'd had the audacity to mock Jax's elementary vocabulary?

"Pay attention, Uncle Elliott." Ben's tone couldn't get more exasperated if he'd tried. Nothing like a kid with no filter to keep adults in line. "Can I help you train Bogart?"

Wait. What? "Help *me?*"

"Yes." Ben's head bobbed up and down.

"Rebel just said you were in charge of training Bogart," Trace said.

Elliott must've missed that while he was busy gawking at that perfectly formed hip attached to the perfectly formed legs. "I thought it would be more like practice for me, and you'd be doing the actual training?" he asked Rebel.

She nodded. "Yes. But practice means you actually have to be doing the work, so you and Ben can learn together."

Trace rubbed his son's shoulders. "Ben can help out after school and on weekends, so that means he'll be hanging out with you, Thing One."

Rebel's eyes glittered with laughter at the nickname.

"Anything for my nephew." Because Elliott had so much spare time on his hands lately. Still, he couldn't say no to the buzz of excitement that had Ben supercharged with joy. He wouldn't be seeing the little guy every day once he returned to San Francisco.

"When can we start?" Ben blurted.

After Elliott got the sponsor on the phone and demanded the handlers come to the island. "Soon."

At the same time, Rebel said, "Now."

Of course she'd want to get right to it. Because on top of Elliott being inadequate with the camp, he was also inattentive to his nephew's problems. Because instead of listening to Ben and helping him get started on his badge right away, Elliott had thought of his own problems and packed schedule.

Because Rebel was proving to be the same generous, kindhearted person he'd known her to be in high school.

Not at all the type of person who would walk out on the person who'd loved her, whom she'd loved back with that big, kind heart, not to be seen for ten long years. And not the type of person who wouldn't offer some sort of explanation.

That uneasy prickle slithered down his spine again.

He knew a thing or two about skipping out on the people he loved and who loved him. They didn't know it yet, but he was about to do it again. He had his reasons. Some professional. Some private and humiliating from his childhood.

The blood in his veins pumped hot as he turned a silent, contemplative stare on Rebel.

For the first time, he realized she might have her own dark, shameful secrets that she'd rather not share because of the pain.

Chapter Ten

#DogsBeforeDudes

"Run through each command a few more times, then we'll call it a night," Rebel said to Ben and Elliott. Darkness had settled over the island, and the landscape lighting had switched on, casting a glow over the lush lawn behind the resort. The gentle lapping of water against the dock carried on the gentle breeze.

After leaving the game room, she'd checked on Jax and the dogs. They were quiet as long as someone stayed with them. So she'd asked Jax to hang out there for most of the evening, then she'd take over once everyone had gone to sleep. And by *everyone* she'd meant Elliott, who seemed to have a problem with her sleeping in the garage.

She snuggled deeper into her down jacket as she sat at one of the picnic tables and watched Ben and Elliott work with Bogart. Rem lay on the cool grass at her feet.

"Go ahead." Elliott handed his treats to Ben and joined her at the table, sliding onto the bench at her side.

"Watch," Ben said to Bogart with his fist at his chest and a treat encased inside his closed hand.

Luckily, Bogart was smart, caught on quickly, and had the perfect disposition for training. It took a few seconds, but he stilled and focused on Ben.

"*Yes.*" Ben rushed to hand him the treat. Bogart's ears folded back, and he cowered.

"Slow movements," she reminded Ben. Rewarding the dog seemed to be Ben's favorite part, and he did it with an extreme amount of enthusiasm. "He was a stray, so it's possible he was abused. He might be skittish until he starts to trust us. Soft voices and slow movements are the best way to handle him."

Ben nodded and kept working with Bogart.

"I wonder how he lost his leg," Elliott said.

She let out a sigh. "Rescues have often been through more than most people can fathom." Except Rebel. She knew exactly what strays went through before finding their way into a shelter or a new home. "Their scars run deep, so it's probably a good thing they can't talk about it. It'd be too heartbreaking for most of us to hear."

Elliott angled his body toward her. "Doesn't sound all that different from people." He was close enough that his warm breaths whispered over her cheeks, swirling tendrils of mist across her skin. "Most of us have scars and painful experiences we'd rather not talk about."

She couldn't hold his intense, questioning gaze because that gaze seemed to be searching for answers.

With a thumbnail, she traced a notch in the picnic table.

Elliott angled more toward her. His muscular thigh pressed into hers.

A tingle shimmied up her leg to settle in places it shouldn't.

"I'm glad Mabel didn't turn Bogart over to a shelter. His chances of adoption are almost nil with one leg missing," Rebel said.

Elliott pulled on a jacket, shifting enough to close the small space between their arms. His powerful thigh and muscled arm massaged against hers.

Another shimmy and shake rocketed through her.

"How'd you learn so much about dogs?" His voice was soft. So soft that her heart expanded a little more with each word. "To my knowledge, you never had a dog when you lived on the island."

True. She'd been too busy taking care of her mother. No way could Rebel have taken care of a dog. Plus, the milk was usually sour for her own cereal—when they actually had milk and cereal in the house. How could she have fed a dog?

"I, u-um," she stammered. "Well . . ." She couldn't explain. Not really, because Elliott was too smart to leave it at *a stray dog found me not long after I left Angel Fire Falls. He saved me, gave me a new purpose. So now I return the favor.* No, Elliott would keep asking questions, keep digging until he got to the root of the matter.

"Career options are much more limited without a college education. I was given an opportunity to work with dogs." She scrunched her shoulders. "Turned out I was good with animals, so I rolled with it."

Ben let out a squeal of approval when Bogart obeyed the touch command, then quieted when Bogart cowered.

Elliott turned to watch his nephew, who was having a blast rewarding Bogart with far too many treats. "Thanks."

"For what?" She smiled as Ben dropped to his knees and threw both arms around Bogart's neck. "He's a great kid, and it looks like he's going to be a big help until we can get the handlers here." When Elliott's mesmerizing green eyes raked her face like he was memorizing every detail, she traced another notch in the table.

He blew out a gentle laugh. "Rebel Tate. The badass girl who raised herself is blushing."

"No, I'm not!" she argued way too fast. *Ack!* "It's just that you were looking at my freckles . . . and you know I've always been self-conscious of my freckles."

He reached up and smoothed a thumb across her cheek, then down her nose to tweak the tip. "Your freckles are . . ." He stopped.

Adorable? Sexy? What? WHAT?

A shiver raced over her.

Elliott's big, warm hand covered hers. She pulled in a breath and looked up into his ridiculously beautiful eyes.

"You're freezing." He took her hand between his and started to rub out the chill. "You didn't sign up to help my nephew earn a Scout badge. It means a lot to my family. Ben's mom doesn't come around much, and we're all so busy trying to get the resort back on a steady upward trajectory after years of decline that we have to work together so Ben and Charley's little girl aren't neglected. It takes all of us pitching in to look after them."

Try as she might to resist, Rebel fell a little in love with Elliott all over again. That family closeness, that family effort, that family willingness to look out for each other. She'd longed for it her entire life.

And had ruined her chance of ever attaining it after keeping her mother's secret. How could Rebel ask for that kind of loyalty when she hadn't given it in return?

Payday. Commercial property for sale in Portland. Payday. My one chance to open my own facility. Did I mention payday?

"We still have to go over the veterans' profiles, so we should wrap it up. Want to break the news to your nephew?" She pulled her hand free from Elliott's, immediately missing the warmth of his touch.

He hesitated. Studied her, then drew in a heavy breath. "Ben, it's getting late. Your dad's probably expecting you for dinner."

"Aww." Ben's bottom lip puckered. "I don't want to stop."

"It's rewarding when you see the dog learning, isn't it?" She'd never forget the first dog she'd trained. It had changed her life in so many ways. "But they get mentally exhausted when they're training. It takes a lot of brainpower for them to process what you're trying to teach them. They need a break as much as we do."

Elliott went to Ben and put a hand on his shoulder. "How about I take you home, little man?"

"Can Bogart and Buddy come see where I live?" Ben bounced on his toes.

Elliott shifted from one foot to the other. "I don't think—"

"Sure," Rebel said. Elliott had warmed up to the dogs quite a bit. The more comfortable he got with them before the vets arrived, the better. She leashed Rem and handed the second leash to Ben. "Ben, you walk Bogart, and your uncle can walk Re—" She bit down on her tongue so hard she could swear she tasted blood.

When she glanced at Elliott, her heart skipped a beat.

With narrowed eyes, he studied her with a curiosity intense enough to take down a big game cat in Africa.

"Elliott, you can walk Buddy." She stood. "I'll run up to my room and get the vet profiles and my notes on the service dogs. Meet me in your office in fifteen?"

She didn't wait for him to agree. Instead, she hurried away with his suspicious stare burning at her back, heating her more than her down jacket. But not nearly as much as his touch had.

She freshened up in her room, dug her iPad out of a drawer so she could access the vet profiles Lily had emailed, and grabbed her notepad. She all but skipped down the stairs with a bounce in her step.

The dreaded face-to-face meetings with each of the Remingtons were finally over. Each of them had shown distrust in some way, some more than others. But she hadn't received the frosty reception she'd expected.

She hit the switchback in the stairs, turned, and skipped the rest of the way down. And came to an abrupt halt.

Mrs. Ferguson, the woman who'd done most of the cooking at the resort back in the day and had kept motherly eagle eyes on the rambunctious Remington boys, stood at the bottom with a book held against her chest, the other hand resting on a very broad hip.

Where were sunglasses when Rebel needed them? The glare from Mrs. Ferguson's neon-pink spandex workout pants was blinding.

"Rebel Tate." Her voice was cooing and maternal, but it wasn't a greeting. An accusation would be a more accurate description. The woman always did run a tight ship. Somehow everyone knew not to mess with her, even with her Aunt-Bee-from-Mayberry vibe.

It was remarkable.

"Mrs. Ferguson," Rebel said. "I'm so glad to see you're still at the Remington."

"Thank you, dear. Lawrence told me you were in town. I hope you're enjoying your stay." She batted her eyelashes behind soda-bottle glasses. "I assume you won't be here long and probably won't return anytime soon. It's a wonderful place to visit, isn't it? But we can't stay on vacation forever, can we? Real life starts calling."

Good to know Mrs. Ferguson was just as savvy as she'd always been. Managing to invite Rebel to leave the island and not come back while sounding sympathetic was a true gift. She really was kind and sweet. Unless someone crossed one of her Remingtons. Then the woman put a bounty on their head.

Rebel had to respect that kind of loyalty. It would be interesting to know what price Mrs. Ferguson had put on Rebel's wanted poster after she'd disappeared from Elliott's life.

"Eventually, everyone who doesn't belong here has to go," Mrs. Ferguson cooed.

So Rebel's poster had probably said WANTED, DEAD OR ALIVE.

Mrs. Ferguson fanned herself with the book. "Sorry, dear. I'm having a hot flash."

There wasn't a bead of sweat visible.

Oh, she was good, all right.

But Rebel was better.

"I don't know how much Lawrence has told you." She let that sink in, because Mrs. Ferguson had always had a soft spot for Lawrence Remington.

Mrs. Ferguson's smile was replaced with uncertainty at the mention of Lawrence's name.

"The event is for war veterans." Rebel waved a hand around the resort's lobby. "Perfect place to host it, don't you think? Since *Lawrence* is a war veteran."

"You're so right, dear. Lawrence is like a son to me." Her free hand fluttered to her buxom chest. "I hope you do a good job for those young men and women."

Rebel nodded. "I'm going to do my very best. No matter how long it takes. No matter how long I have to stay here. Even if I have to ask the sponsor to extend the camp."

For a second, she forgot to breathe. She'd been on the island less than a week, and she'd already gotten comfortable. Comfortable enough to consider staying longer. Comfortable enough to wonder what life would be like if she stayed indefinitely. Which she couldn't. There was no training facility on the island waiting for her to occupy it. And even if there were, she couldn't live in a place where she'd bump into Dan Morgan on a regular basis. The guilt and shame would eat her from the inside out until there was nothing left of her to give back to the people she wanted to help.

"We're absolutely not asking the sponsor to extend the camp." Elliott's stony voice came from behind her.

She startled, her notes and iPad crashing to the floor. Thank goodness the iPad was in a protective cover.

Elliott helped her gather them up.

"Where's my dog and Bogart?" she asked as she scrambled for her notepad.

"I left them in the garage with Jax. I stopped in to check on things, and he said they needed to eat." He picked up her iPad and dusted it off.

Oh. She'd been so preoccupied she'd forgotten to feed the dogs.

Nice.

Hot ex-boyfriends did that to a girl. *Dogs before dudes* would make a great hashtag for female dog lovers.

Elliott handed her the notepad, and a muscle in his jaw tightened and released. "We're sticking to the original schedule."

Did he really loathe being around her that much? Because she'd thought he was softening toward her. To the point that she'd been wondering how to reinforce the invisible barrier he'd thrown up between them the day she'd arrived.

He turned to Mrs. Ferguson, took in her spandex attire, and backed up a step. His gaze flitted around, never dropping below her neck. "Hi, Mrs. F. What brings you here so late?"

She tapped the hard back of her book, which was still cradled at her chest. "My Fifty-Plus Book Club for ladies only met tonight." She smiled at Rebel. "I lead activities for our senior guests now that Charley has taken over the kitchen." She turned the book around to show them the cover and gave them a shy smile. A pair of legs in fishnet hose and orthopedic shoes was on the cover. It was titled *Ageless Erotica.*

"*Oh,*" Elliott wheezed out.

He could say that again, because Rebel had nothin'.

"I talked Lily into letting me discuss books with"—she batted her eyelashes several times—"mature content as long as the book club meets at night." She dropped her voice. "After the kids have gone to sleep."

Elliott grabbed the banister as if he needed it to hold himself upright. "I'll be in my office when you're ready, Rebel." Then the rat fink hurried away and left her alone to deal with Mrs. Ferguson's frightening choice of reading material.

"Well, I see you're still a firecracker, Mrs. Ferguson." Rebel winked. "I always admired that about you." She said her goodbyes and headed to Elliott's office. Too bad she didn't drink. She could use a shot of something, because fishnets and orthopedic shoes were likely going to give her nightmares tonight. And for many more nights to come.

She breezed into Elliott's office and then stopped cold. His desk was cleared of all work, replaced with two delicious-looking meals, two glasses of water, and two bottles of beer.

He was busy arranging the utensils and cloth napkins. "Hey." He glanced up. "Just in time. I had room service deliver dinner here. If I remember correctly, you like steak and lobster mac?"

She did. Very much. The incredible aroma had her tummy rumbling, but she'd planned to eat alone in her room. Having dinner with him was too much like a date. Not to mention, she wasn't keen on eating in front of others. "What's this?" She took a step back. "I told you earlier I wasn't hungry."

"That was hours ago, Rebel. *I'm* starving, and since we've still got work ahead of us, I wasn't going to eat in front of you." He nodded to the chair across from his desk. "Just have a taste." His voice turned smoky. "You might decide you like it and want more."

All the air disappeared from the room.

Finally he lowered his head and finished setting out the flatware.

She perched on the edge of the chair, her foot bouncing so fast it could've broken the sound barrier. "Still no word from the sponsor?"

He claimed the executive chair behind his desk and cut into his steak. "If he doesn't return my messages by tomorrow, I swear to God I'm going to have Trace fly me to their corporate headquarters." His fork hovered at his lips. Juicy and delicious looking.

The steak didn't look half-bad either.

"Ahem." He cleared his throat.

Her gaze flew to meet his, and the lazy smile that formed on his delectable mouth shone in his eyes.

He nodded to her notepad. "So how do we go about picking possible matches for the vets?" He popped a bite of steak into his mouth.

She couldn't help it. She just couldn't. She licked her lips.

Her fork clattered to her plate.

Lord.

"Well, um . . ." She shuffled through her notes. "First we need to review the veteran's profile, then pick out three or four dogs that might fit his or her specific needs."

Elliott put down his utensils, got up, and dragged his chair around to her side of the desk. Then he moved his food in front of him. He leaned closer to look at her notes, his scent, his body heat, his unfair amount of sex appeal triggering every pheromone in her body.

He twirled his fork in a circle. "You can show me while we eat."

She finally took a small bite of the lobster mac, and it melted on her tongue. She had to stop herself from moaning. While she savored the incredible bite of food, she pulled up the first vet profile on her iPad.

"This guy has an extreme case of PTSD. He needs a dog to take cues from his body language and identify his triggers." She thumbed through her handwritten notes on the dogs. After perusing the entire list, she pointed out three dogs. "I think we should start him with these three." She handed the notepad to Elliott. "Read my notes and see what you think."

While he examined her choices, she picked at her plate. If she really let herself enjoy the taste of food, it was like Homeless Hungry Rebel would take over and she wouldn't be able to stop shoveling it in. She supposed it was a form of PTSD from the trauma of being a homeless teen, which was why she was even more uncomfortable without Rem at her side. So she just moved the food around on the plate without taking another bite.

When she looked up, Elliott studied her with curiosity. His firm chest rose and fell with each heavy breath.

She shuffled more food around and even cut off a chunk of steak. "Briley and Charley are geniuses in the kitchen."

"Yes, they are." The roughness of his voice told her she hadn't misread the desire in his eyes. "Letting them take over the restaurant was one of the best things to happen at the resort, besides hiring Lily." He nodded and picked up one of the bottles of beer. "We're still building our team, fleshing out a long-term business strategy, but we're getting there. We just need a few solid events like this boot camp to keep signing up during our off-season, and we'll be good." He held up his bottle. "Here's to successful business plans."

She'd drink to that, just not with alcohol. She picked up one of the glasses of water. "I don't drink, but cheers all the same."

They both took long pulls.

"Did you swear off the stuff because of your mom?" He put down the pad and cut off a bite of steak.

"Yes. I was determined not to end up like her." Rebel concentrated on her food.

"You should be proud, then."

If that was a compliment, she'd take it. Her mother had been a good person once. But by the time Rebel was in middle school, the goodness had been drowned out by booze and poor choices.

"Alcoholism destroys more than just the person drinking themselves to death."

Was that her talking? Because her lips were moving, but she'd meant to keep her mouth shut so Elliott wouldn't keep asking questions.

"It destroys their family, their friends." She sighed inside. She'd kept quiet so long, kept everything bottled up inside, that it felt good to let out at least a little of the pain her mother had caused. Just a morsel couldn't hurt. It might even be cathartic. "It destroys innocent people who are unfortunate enough to be in the wrong place at the wrong time."

"Did that lead you to help veterans?" he asked, picking at his food.

She'd already swerved too far onto the information highway. "In a way." She forced a big smile and pushed her plate away. "Speaking of which, it's late. Let's get to work." She reached for her iPad and notepad, but his thick fingers circled her wrist.

A current of electricity shot through her. It was wonderfully exciting and terrifyingly dangerous at the same time.

"Come here," he whispered, his voice low and throaty and too damn sexy to resist.

Heat rushed from where his fingers circled her arm, up through her center, and turned her nipples to hard peaks. On her list of life mistakes, this had to be at the top. But she could no more stop her body from wanting him to kiss her than she could stop the sun from rising or setting.

"Elliott—"

He didn't let her finish. Instead, he crushed his lips to hers, devouring her mouth with a smoldering kiss. It wasn't gentle. It wasn't soft. It was desperate and urgent like they'd been deprived of each other for far too long.

Her heart punched against her chest, but she couldn't help herself. She opened for him, and his lovely tongue found hers. Desire crashed through her, sending shock waves of pleasure rolling through every nerve ending.

She moaned into his mouth, melting into him.

That urged him on, and he buried a set of fingers in her hair at the back of her head and tugged her chair flush against his with his other hand.

She molded a palm to his chest, sliding it up and then down again, and oh, he was just as firm as she'd imagined. Just as muscled as she'd remembered.

His lips moved to her ear, and he took her lobe between his teeth and nipped and tugged and sucked.

Lust rioted through her, and she lost all self-control. Good God, if he wanted to take her right there on the desk, she wouldn't be able to say no. His wonderful mouth feathered kisses down her neck that rocked her world, and she gasped for air.

His world must've been spinning off its axis too, because he let out a moan that was low and guttural and said he wanted her as much as she wanted him.

His phone dinged. He slowed the kiss, then went in for more, and she gave him what he wanted.

Another ding had him sighing against her mouth. He broke the kiss. He gently swiped his lips across hers one last time and then caressed his thumb along her jaw. "Hold on." He snatched his phone off the desk and thumbed the screen. "It's an email from Collins. He says he'll get with us tomorrow." He discarded the phone. Leaned over the arms of the chairs again and molded his fingers around the side of her neck, gently caressing her sensitive skin.

Her ovaries sighed as he leaned his forehead against hers.

"Why did you really become a dog whisperer?"

There it was. That inquisitive mind of his was shoveling away the BS from her past to get to the truth.

The sudden urge to blurt out the whole sordid mess welled up in her, threatening to spew.

To give back to innocent people who have been damaged for life. People who have served their country in the military. People who have been victims of the irresponsible behavior of others. Others like my mother.

"I . . . I told . . . told you." She stumbled over her words. "People's lives get destroyed. I like to help try to put them back together again."

"Do you know why I was so good at my job in San Francisco?" His voice was still throaty and laden with lust.

She had no idea where he was going with this. His gentle fingers—caressing her collarbone, her neck, the sensitive spot behind her ear—weren't helping because she ached to her very core for more. "Um, because you're smart and well educated?"

"Because I have a sixth sense. I can predict when companies are honest, solid, and going places. I can also recognize half-truths, inflated numbers to cover flaws, and bullshit when I hear it. That gift has saved my firm from making bad investments with our clients' money." His thumb caressed over the inside of her wrist. "You're not telling me everything."

His directness and how close he was to the truth made her hiss in a sharp breath. Okay, it wasn't just his insight. The taste of him on her lips and the softness of his thumb smoothing over her sensitive skin had something to do with her intake of breath and the fact that she couldn't seem to let it out, making her lungs burn.

When her chest felt as though it would explode, she finally gasped for air. "I don't . . . I can't . . ." She snatched her arm from his grasp and pushed out of her chair. "I'll go through these myself and meet you early in the morning to discuss them."

"Rebel—"

She spun on him. "If you were so good at your big-shot job, then why are you here on this pitiful little island where no one wants to live unless they have to? What are *you* hiding?"

God forgive her. She didn't mean it, but she had to get out of there before she made the mistake of telling him everything.

She fled through the lobby and out the front door to go find Rem for comfort. It was the only source of comfort she'd likely ever allow herself. Because she didn't deserve anything more.

Chapter Eleven

#CrunchTime

Well, hell. Elliott stared at the empty doorway of his office with no idea how to make things right with Rebel. Two half-eaten plates of food on his desk, a burn in his stomach, and a bulge in his pants that could pitch a circus tent wasn't quite how he'd seen the evening unfolding.

He covered both plates with metal lids, leaned back in his chair, and drummed his fingers on the desk.

After he'd overheard Rebel mention extending the camp, he'd honestly thought a working dinner might help improve their working relationship, might help their progress with potential matches, might help keep the camp moving in a positive direction.

He certainly hadn't intended for the evening to end in a kiss and with her storming out the door.

Kissing her was probably stupid. But he hadn't been able to stop himself when she'd opened up about her mother and alcoholism and the destruction it caused, while picking at the food on her plate like it might bite her back if she tasted it. His protective instincts had thundered to life, and he did the only thing that had popped into his stupid male brain.

He'd pulled her into a kiss.

Then all but accused her of lying by omission.

He scrubbed a hand down his face.

Prince Charming he obviously was not.

Extending the camp simply wasn't an option. Not with the partners at his firm about to vote him out and take his life savings as they gave him the boot. Mick had made it clear he could hold them off for a month but no longer.

Spending that month on the island only to have the camp end in shambles because of lack of help and a condensed schedule was even worse.

Canceling might've been best, but it was too late now. There was a garage full of barking dogs on the premises and an angry, stubborn redhead who was likely planning to sleep with them again on an empty stomach.

Elliott might be a hard-ass when it came to business, but he couldn't let her suffer, no matter how hardheaded or upset she might be.

If she was hell-bent on keeping her past a mystery, he should let her. He should.

He blew out his cheeks, disgusted with himself that he couldn't let it go, then got out his phone. He downloaded Instagram and started to set up an account. He paused to decide what to call himself. A smile formed on his lips, and he typed in @NumbersWhisperer. The only account he followed was @WestCoastDogWhisperer.

Then he slowly scrolled through her posts. The most recent was her ferry ride to the island. Obviously, she'd been stressed. He thumbed through a few more, stopping on a trip to a dog park in Portland where she was teaching her dog the proper manners when socializing with other four-legged friends.

Who knew there was dog etiquette.

In the video, her golden retriever was particularly jumpy around a female German shepherd whom he obviously wanted to date.

Apparently, manners didn't just make the man. They made the dog too.

But the video showed Rebel's patience, because as she filmed her interaction with her dog, she finally managed to get him to sit and settle.

Elliott thumbed the screen again. Most of her posts featured clients from up and down the West Coast, and she had thousands of followers. She'd obviously built a name for herself in the world of dog whispering.

Elliott belly-laughed when he tapped a video post that featured a tiny Yorkie with a gigantic attitude. A mammoth-size husband and his perturbed wife were about to give up on the dog. Enter Rebel Tate with her patient but firm demeanor. Within minutes, she had the dog under control and the owners thanking her like she was a superhero.

But what had Elliott's eyes widening and his heart softening was a teenage boy with a traumatic brain injury from a car accident who suffered extreme panic attacks. His family had rescued a dog so he'd have a pet. Unfortunately, the Great Dane puppy had not only grown to the size of a large human, but he'd also grown aggressive toward anyone who wasn't part of their family. Desperate, they'd called in the West Coast Dog Whisperer.

As Elliott continued to watch the video, his breaths grew shallow, and his pulse started to pound in his ears.

When Rebel showed the family that the dog's behavior wasn't because he was mean, it was because he was undisciplined and they were reinforcing his bad behavior instead of deterring it, the dog's demeanor transformed instantaneously.

Elliott closed the social media app and rubbed the corners of his eyes with a thumb and forefinger.

Then he pushed out of his chair to go take care of business the way a real man should.

Fifteen minutes later, he walked into the garage with a picnic basket of reheated food and a heavy blanket rolled up under one arm.

Rebel and Jax were returning several dogs to their crates. He said something to Rebel that Elliott didn't catch, and she and Jax laughed, continuing to crate each dog.

Elliott tried to ignore the burn of jealousy in his stomach.

The easy way they worked together shouldn't bother him, but it did.

As soon as Buddy noticed Elliott, he scampered to his side and panted up at him. Bogart hopped over too.

Rebel unleashed a black Lab, gave it a signal, and the dog trotted into the crate while she latched the door. She looked up and narrowed her eyes at Elliott.

Most men would be put off by her fierce stare. It was bold enough to cause an enormous amount of shrinkage.

Elliott wasn't most men, though. He liked a challenge, no matter what he was doing. Loved the thrill of the chase, whatever he might be chasing. Thrived on assessing risk and rolling the dice when he had a gut feeling that he'd come out on top, even when the odds were against him. It was the reason he was so damn good at his job.

It was the reason he shouldn't just walk but run from Rebel, from this camp, and from the resort. Go back to his life in San Francisco now instead of waiting a month.

But he could still taste her sweetness. Feel her softness. Blood pounded through his veins to settle in parts he'd rather not admit to.

Nope, no shrinkage here.

And he'd given up on the old wrinkly guys. They didn't stand a chance against the sassy dog whisperer who'd invaded his thoughts, his dreams, and his fantasies.

Even though he shouldn't, even though he couldn't, he still wanted more of her.

"Yo," Jax greeted Elliott as he put away a white Lab. "That smells awesome." He sniffed the air just like the dogs.

"It's not for you," Elliott snapped, immediately feeling like an ass. He walked over and set the picnic basket and blanket down on the bedroll that was already spread out in the middle of the garage. He got out his phone and sent a text to Charley. "Jax, why don't you head over to the dining hall. My cousin's making the biggest steak in the house for you. How do you like it cooked?"

"Medium rare," Jax blurted. "Thanks, dude."

Elliott typed in the order and hit "Send." "Go on over. We're treating you like a king tonight."

"You sure you can hang without me?" Jax asked Rebel.

Elliott assumed *hang* meant *manage*, but he wasn't going to ask. Nor was he going to wait for Rebel to respond. If he did, he'd likely be out on his ear. "I'll stay here to help."

Buddy and Bogart returned to flank her.

She hesitated, her blatant stare staying on Elliott. It was full of that same fire that had wowed him when they were young. Reeled him in and stolen his heart.

He needed this camp to fly for the good of the resort. It was going to be a miracle if he could pull that off without giving in to the desire that kiss had stoked to a raging inferno. He couldn't deny the fact that he wanted her. Badly.

Finally, she nodded. "We'll be fine, Jax. Go enjoy your dinner, and take the rest of the night off. I've got this covered."

When they were alone, Elliott started to unload the picnic basket onto the blanket.

"What are you doing?" Irritation threaded through her words.

Buddy leaned hard against her leg.

"I couldn't let this great meal go to waste, and we still have work to do." He finished setting out the thermal foam takeout containers. Then he got out two packages of disposable utensils wrapped in napkins and two bottles of water. "Can we try this again? Unless you've got something against the food here at the Rem?"

Her dog spun in a circle and yelped.

"Settle!" she hissed. She closed her eyes and said it again in a much calmer voice. When Buddy pressed into her again, she said, "Of course I don't have anything against the food here at the . . . resort." She tucked a strand of hair behind her ear, her hand trembling ever so slightly. "It's just that I've spent most of my time either in the garage or in my room and ordered room service instead of eating in the dining hall."

"Why is that?" He arranged their meals on the blanket just so.

"I wanted to stay out of your family's way. They've been fairly welcoming under the circumstances." She chuckled. "In an Angelina-and-Jennifer-reunion kind of way, but there's an edge in the air. This is your space, and I'm the interloper."

The hint of vulnerability in her voice caused Elliott's chest to warm, even in the cold garage.

He wasn't sure about his family, but *he'd* treated her like an interloper. At least at first. Now he was getting used to her being around. A little too much. "I'm not leaving until you eat, I'm not leaving you to do all the work, and I'm certainly not letting you sleep in this cold, dank garage again," Elliott said.

"You might own the resort, but I can sleep wherever I want," she shot back.

When he stilled and looked up at her, his expression must've communicated his thoughts. Thoughts of her sleeping curled into his side wearing nothing but a smile that said she'd been well satisfied.

Her bottom lip disappeared between her teeth.

"That's not helping me concentrate on work," he said, and Buddy and Bogart joined him on the blanket.

Her forehead scrunched. "What's not helping?"

He drew in a heavy breath. "That thing you do with biting your lip."

"Oh," she whispered in a soft voice. "I don't usually realize I'm doing it."

He waved her to the blanket, where he'd opened her takeout container. "I know. That's why it's so . . ." *Sexy. Sensual. Erotic.* "Cute." Good God Almighty, had he just said *cute?* Time to take up arm wrestling or run a marathon to earn back his man card. He handed the water to her as she sat across from him. "Want to finish what we started?"

When her eyes flew wide, he hurried to clarify. "Matching the vets with the dogs." He nodded to the spread of food. "And our meal."

She visibly relaxed. "Okay." She sprang to her feet, found her notes and iPad, and sat down again.

"No picking at your food the way you did in my office," he warned. "Or I'll stay here all night and watch you until the food is gone."

She sighed, digging in. "Fine."

He'd never seen anyone devour a plate of food quite so fast. She wasn't savage or ill-mannered. More like rushed without quite breaching the frantic zone. Like she hadn't eaten in days and didn't know when or from where her next meal was coming.

He froze midchew with a wad of lobster mac in his cheek. That sixth sense, that instinct that'd been gnawing at the back of his mind for days was back. But he couldn't ask. Not after the way she'd bolted from his office.

So he kept eating like he was all business. "After we pick a few possible matches for each vet, how do we decide which one makes the final cut?"

She chugged some water to wash down her meal. "We don't. The dog usually picks the vet." She wiped her mouth with a napkin. "We might start with a few veterans in the room and only the dogs we've earmarked for them. Then we wait, let them interact, and see if any of them click."

Elliott cut off more steak. "And if none do?"

Rebel gathered up her container and utensils and set them inside the basket. "We keep introducing them to more dogs until they find the right fit."

Interesting. Elliott polished off the rest of his meal. "Sounds a lot like human relationships."

She stretched out her legs and braced both arms behind her. She glanced around at each crate, making eye contact with the dogs who were restless. One by one, they each settled.

He'd watched her interact with Buddy, Bogart, and now the service dogs for days. He'd begun to realize she didn't just train them or calm them. She communicated with them on some sort of telepathic level.

"Except that dogs are more reliable than people."

Says the woman who disappeared with nothing more than a vague kiss-off note.

Elliott knew his IQ, but women—

Correction. *This* woman he still found perplexing.

Why would she be so unwilling to talk to him about her past but communicate so well with animals without having to use actual words?

When he'd discarded all their trash, he pulled over a box of supplies and sat next to her on the blanket, using the box as a prop so they could lean against it. "Okay, it's crunch time. Let's get 'er done."

They worked through each veteran's profile, picking a few dogs for each. By the time they were done, it was late.

She yawned and stretched. "I think I'll turn in for the night. You should be going." She got up like she was seeing him to the door of her home after a bad date.

Oh hell no. "If the dogs get noisy, it won't be much of a problem. There aren't that many guests left, since we've booked out the entire resort starting tomorrow when the vets get here. They'll be fine without you."

She tapped her foot and stared him down. Arms crossed, expression bland, body fucking gorgeous. "Keeping even one guest up is too many. If I remember correctly, your dad likes every guest to stay happy. I'm sure that hasn't changed. I don't want to let your dad down."

Elliott knew the feeling. He climbed to his feet. "Give them a rawhide to chew on to keep them occupied, but you are not sleeping out here again."

She threw her hands up, and Buddy and Bogart crowded her. "Follow me." She started toward the garage door, then stopped. "Not just the dogs." She pointed at Elliott. "You too."

She marched just outside the door. When he joined her, she tapped her birthdate into the keypad, and the door slid shut. As soon as it closed, a chorus of howling struck up like a really bad country-and-western band.

She gave him an *I told you so* look.

With an exasperated expression, he looked up at the sky. "Fine. Open it."

She punched in the numbers, and the garage door motor sprang to life, pulling the door up. Rebel pushed past him and through the door. "I'll be fine. I've slept in worse conditions."

And another clue just reinforced his suspicions.

He followed her inside.

Abruptly, she stopped and turned on a heel. He had to grab her upper arms to keep from barreling over her.

"I'll see you in the morning. Good night," she said.

The dogs had quieted but were still restless.

He laughed, went and closed the garage door, and flicked off the lights, only leaving one on in the corner. Then he pushed past *her*. "If you're staying, then so am I." He unfurled the extra blanket, stretched out, and laced his fingers behind his head for a pillow. "Do your thing, Dog Whisperer, and quiet them down so we can get some sleep, because you're stuck with me."

Chapter Twelve

#NoAudienceNecessary

Rebel's jaw fell open when Elliott patted the empty space on the blanket at his side and said she was stuck with him. All night.

There were worse things than being stuck with a guy as good-looking as Elliott Remington. She was sure of it. For the life of her, though, she couldn't think of any at that moment.

She had to get him out of the garage because she was *not* spending the night with him. His presence was too unnerving. His scent was too mouthwatering.

His body was too tempting.

Nope, he had to go.

"You don't seriously expect me to sleep next to you?" she clipped out.

Rem and Bogart practically stampeded her.

"We're in a garage surrounded by a pack of dogs." His gaze coasted over her. "As attractive as you are, I don't particularly like an audience." His mouth curved into that smart-ass smile that was starting to get under her skin.

And into her heart.

"And I especially don't make moves on women who are sneering at me." He crossed his legs at the ankles and got comfy. "Consider yourself safe."

Oh. Well, in that case. She took small, slow steps toward the blanket. "I wasn't sneering." She lay down, keeping at least six inches between them.

"Your teeth were bared." His voice was already relaxed and lazy with sleep.

"What do you expect?" she asked, defending herself. "I'm used to sleeping alone."

He rolled onto his side to face her. "So you don't have a boyfriend? No fiancé? No ex-husband who pops in once in a while?"

"No, no, and no." She gave his shoulder a push to roll him onto his back again.

Didn't work. Probably because his large frame was solid steel.

"That's surprising. I'd think men would be lined up at your door." The timbre of his voice—so rich, so velvety—skated over her.

There was never anyone for me but you almost slipped out.

His words. His tone. His thirsty look that said he wanted to drink her in and let her essence roll over his tongue like fine wine turned her insides to liquid fire. And he wasn't even touching her.

A shiver lanced through her.

"You're cold." He reached for her, running a strong hand the length of her arm. His touch left a scorching trail of heat in its wake. She should pull away, go sleep in one of the Jeeps outside, but that wouldn't keep the dogs quiet. So she stayed put and stared at the muscles that flowed and flexed under his thermal, which was pulled taut across his broad chest.

"The cold won't kill me," she whispered. "I've got a roof over my head."

Elliott's gaze roamed her face. "You've said similar things since you've been here. Several times. That can't be a coincidence. I'd hate to think you were ever"—the wheels in that magnificent mind of his were obviously churning because he seemed to be picking his words carefully—"without a bed to sleep in."

If she'd been standing, her knees would've given way.

She'd kept it inside for so long, she hadn't even realized how much she wanted someone to know what had really happened. Wanted someone to know what she'd been through and how sorry she was for the damage her mother had inflicted.

Wanted Elliott to know how hard it'd been to leave him and why he'd been better off that she did.

She wanted to tell him all of it.

His hungry look said he wanted all of *her*.

"Don't worry about me. I learned to survive on my own a long time ago." At that moment, the loneliness she'd felt since she'd left the island crashed in on her. He'd been her only source of comfort, the only person who'd cared. The only person she'd ever let love her, because her trust in people had been crushed long ago.

"Everybody needs someone." His voice had gone thick with concern.

She didn't know what possessed her to do it, but she reached out and molded a palm to his strong jaw. "Thank you for caring even when you have every reason not to." His stubble was thicker now than it had been when they were teens, and it prickled her fingers, sending a thrilling current of electricity up her arm to settle in her nipples.

She didn't plan to let it go any further, but she wanted to feel him against her hand for just one moment. One gentle touch that she could hold on to for a lifetime.

He covered her hand with his and turned his mouth in to her palm to feather kisses over it.

Her deep intake of breath must've said it all, because he didn't stop. He took the base of her palm between his teeth and sucked, then trailed soft kisses over the inside of her wrist.

"Elliott," she rasped out.

He shifted, closing the space between them, and covered her mouth with his. He kissed her gently, much softer than he had in his office. His scorching lips brushed across hers. Once, twice, then he nipped at the corner of her mouth. "This is the spot that drives me crazy when you nibble at it." He nipped again. "Like this."

Heat rushed through her veins, making her hardened nipples ache and the moist spot between her thighs throb with need. She buried both hands in his hair.

She rubbed her cheek against his so his light stubble grazed her skin and sent another shiver quaking through her. "This is what drives me crazy. The feel of it against my skin. Remembering how it used to feel between my—"

He growled, devouring her with a hungry, mouthwatering, thigh-clenching kiss. She opened for him, inviting him in. His lovely demanding tongue searched and probed, teasing and taunting until she whimpered out his name.

He rolled her onto her back with another impatient growl. Instinctively, her legs wrapped around his waist. He lowered his hips to grind against hers, and she cried out, clawing at his back.

Pure bliss engulfed her, and before she knew it, her shirt was unbuttoned, and he was pulling down her bra with his teeth. The cool air against her exposed skin hardened her nipples even more.

He rose above her, bracing his weight on both arms. "God, woman, but you are fucking gorgeous."

She wasn't sure she could form words. "So . . . are . . . you," she panted out, hardly able to breathe. Definitely not able to think clearly.

When he dipped his head and pulled a nipple into his warm mouth, she couldn't stop another cry of pleasure from slipping out.

He chuckled against her skin, his warm breaths whispering over her flesh and turning her insides to surface-of-the-sun hot. His talented tongue stroked her rigid peak. And being such a gentleman, he moved to her other breast, took it between his teeth, and applied just enough pressure for a sweet sting to make her gasp.

She fisted his hair in her hands and arched into him, filling his mouth with her tender flesh. *"Oh God."* She couldn't take much more. He was about to bring her home without even taking her pants off.

Just when she thought it couldn't get much better, when she couldn't get much closer to the edge without falling into oblivion, he did a wonderful, delicious lick-and-circle trick around her nipple with the tip of his tongue and ground his hips into hers again.

She shrieked. Literally shrieked. *Dear Lord.*

He laughed, his rigid length pressing into her center. "Shhh," he teased. "That high-pitched sound might make the dogs start howling."

She pinched his shoulder. "So much for you caring about an audience."

He pulled the extra blanket he'd brought over their heads to cover them completely. "There. It's just us now." He went back to nibbling on her earlobe and the soft flesh behind it.

She shivered. "Maybe we should stop. Before it's too late." Before they made a mistake they'd both likely regret. Except that her hands found their way between them, and she fumbled with the opening of his jeans.

"I can feel your hot wetness through both our clothes." He suckled the soft skin where her neck met her shoulder. "But say the word and we're done."

She swallowed. She couldn't stop. Why couldn't she stop? His button popped open, and she searched for the tab of his zipper. "This is bad," she whispered against his lips.

"So bad." His tongue delved into her mouth again, and one hand edged in between the blanket and her butt to flex into her cheek.

Finally, her fingers found the tab and eased down the zipper. *Oh God, oh God, oh God.* Was this really happening? Was she really doing this?

Rem poked his snout under the blanket and licked Rebel's cheek, likely sensing her anxiety.

"Rem! Bad dog!" she scolded before she could think straight.

Elliott went completely still, every muscle in his body tensing.

Oh no.

She covered her face with her hands. Not only had she scolded her service dog for doing his job, but she'd just given away top-secret information about his name.

Not one muscle in Elliott's rock-hard body moved. Only his labored breaths washed over her.

She spread her fingers to look at him, too humiliated to move her hands.

He rolled off her and sat up, straightening his clothes. He propped an elbow on his bent knee and pinched the bridge of his nose. "It's time for you to explain a few things." He let his hand dangle over his knee. "Look at me."

The crispness of his tone made her want to shrink away. She scrambled to pull up her bra and button her shirt. Then she sat up, Rem nudging his head under her hand.

"Look at me, Rebel." Elliott's voice was bitter. Brittle. Broken.

It took every bit of courage she possessed, but she met his gaze, and what she saw there nearly destroyed her. It wasn't anger. It wasn't disappointment. It was pain. Pain that she'd inflicted so many years ago, and it was still raw and real.

"I'm so sorry." And she was. For so many things.

"I need answers," he said. "Starting with why you walked away while I was at college. If you didn't care about me anymore, then why would you name your dog Rem?"

"You deserve answers, Elliott." He also deserved better than her, better than the shame she'd bring to him and his family. "But I can't give them to you." Not without dragging him into the same private hell she'd lived in for years.

"Anything, Rebel." His voice was almost a plea. "Throw me a bone here."

If she started, even with just a few ambiguous morsels of information, she wouldn't be able to stop, and those dark secrets could never come to light. She shook her head, fisting the front of her shirt at the collarbone. "I'm sorry."

"Why not?" His voice turned frustrated, and Rem went to his side.

She couldn't blame either Elliott or the dog for not sticking by her side. She drew her knees up to her chest. "I think you should go."

He sat there for a long time.

She couldn't look at him. She just couldn't.

Finally, he blew out an exasperated breath. "I'm staying. You go."

"Elliott, I'm the trainer. It's my job."

"Go!" He lay down on the blanket with his back to her, pulled the pillow under his head, and punched it.

He didn't have to tell her twice. She hurried to the door. "Come on, Rem." She hit the button to open the garage door. As it raised, she turned to look for Rem.

Tears stung the backs of her eyes.

Both Rem and Bogart huddled at Elliott's back and wouldn't budge.

For the first time since that first stray had found her alone on a park bench and she'd named him Rem, she was without the companionship of a dog. Without comfort. Without unconditional love.

And she'd brought it on herself.

Chapter Thirteen

#CHIVALRYISDEAD

Early the next morning, Elliott stood under the shower, letting the hot water sluice over his aching muscles. If he had to spend another night sleeping on the garage floor, he'd damn sure bring in a rollaway bed from the main lodge.

Hopefully, it wouldn't come to that.

The veterans were scheduled to arrive later that morning, and once they were matched, the service dogs would sleep in the guest rooms with their new companions. Or so their expert dog whisperer had told him.

Somehow, she'd also become an expert at driving his mind, his imagination, and his body wild. Which was another reason his muscles were balled into knots.

He dropped his head forward, letting the water drench his hair and roll down the back of his spasming neck. The heat and steam soothed the bunched muscles in his aching back.

He braced both arms against the tile wall, steam swirling around him. Letting his head fall back, he closed his eyes as the water splattered his face. Did no good. Rebel's taste still clung to his lips. Her scent was still fused to his skin. Her touch still invaded his mind.

After the hot shower, he needed one helluva cup of strong coffee to clear his head.

The sponsor had also promised Elliott a conversation today, and he needed to bring his A game. Convince Down Home Dog Food to ship in the handlers so the camp would stand a chance at success. Then he could rejoin the real world.

It was either that or lose his job and his life savings.

His shoulders tensed again.

Rem whined, and his head appeared around the shower curtain. Bogart nudged the curtain, and his head appeared too.

When Elliott had left the garage to get cleaned up, he hadn't had the heart to leave his new furry friends behind. Not after they'd shunned their owner to stay with him last night. How had he gone from animals hating him to babysitting a jumpy service dog and a handicapped stray?

"I'll be done in a sec, guys."

Rem.

What. The. Hell?

It made no sense. Why would she walk away with no explanation, only to name one of her dogs after him all these years later? He'd suspected she had secrets. Since she'd been back on the island, she'd certainly dropped enough veiled clues. Last night had confirmed his suspicions.

Not that he had any room to talk. The guilt he carried over his mom was something he'd take to his grave. He supposed everyone had secrets. Everyone carried private pain.

Something told him the strange way he'd found Rebel sitting in the rain earlier that week across from Morgan's Market fit into the equation. He just wasn't sure how.

A fist pounded on the bathroom door. "Hey, asshat," Spence hollered. "Don't use up all the hot water."

Elliott dragged a hand down his face, wiping away the thick drops of water. He reached for the knobs and shut off the shower. "Keep your panties on, Sleeping Beauty." Growing up in the hotel business, all the Remingtons had been conditioned to rise early, but Spence was never a morning person. He'd still been snoozing in his room when Elliott got home with the dogs. He wrapped a towel around his waist and flung the door wide.

Spence's brows drew together when he saw Rem and Bogart. "Wow."

"You don't know the half of it." Elliott shook out his wet hair, spraying Spence.

Spence held up both hands as a shield. "When are you gonna move into your own place?"

Tightness cinched around Elliott's lungs. He certainly couldn't delve into that subject while he was still trying to process what had happened with Rebel in the garage. He pushed past Spence and walked into the hall, turning left toward the kitchen. "Got coffee made yet?"

"Hold up, bro," Spence said. "You've got—"

Elliott rounded the corner into the den and stopped short.

Rebel was standing by the sofa. Black athletic pants and a fitted top clung to every inch of her. She was covered from her ankles to her neck, yet there was nothing left to the imagination. That was saying something, because he'd imagined plenty.

Her hands were stuffed into a fleece jacket that was unzipped, and she shifted from one black-and-gray camo running shoe to the other, the bright-pink laces snagging his gaze. He let his eyes slide up and over every sensual curve, every lush contour.

When he reached her flushed face, he realized she was doing the same to him.

She chewed the corner of her mouth as her eyes coasted over him. He should be cold and uncomfortable in nothing but a towel, his bare, wet chest exposed to the cool air. But *naw.* His chest expanded at the approval in her eyes, and he let her take in her fill.

"You've got company," Spence said from behind him.

No shit. "Thanks for the heads-up," Elliott smarted off as Rem and Bogart trotted into the den.

Her expression brightened when she saw the dogs but dimmed again when they stayed at Elliott's side instead of darting to her as they usually did.

He gave them the *okay* command, and Bogart hopped to Rebel. Rem didn't move. "You too, boy. Go ahead, *Rem*." Elliott gave Rebel a satisfied smile.

The color drained from her face, and strained silence filled the room.

Rem and Bogart crowded around her legs.

Spence gave Elliott a questioning look.

He responded by scratching his left shoulder, code for *Tell you later*.

Spence cleared his throat. "So Elliott was just asking for coffee. Want some, Rebel?"

"No, thanks," she said. "I just came to get my dogs." She bent to pet them. "When you weren't in the garage this morning, I found Charley in the kitchen. She said I'd probably find you here."

A knock sounded on the front door, and it swung open before anyone could respond. Trace walked in.

"Sure, come on in," Spence said. "All we need is music and a tub of beer, and it'll be a party." He glanced at his watch. "At seven in the morning." He eyed both his brothers. "At *my* house."

"I thought you were making coffee?" Elliott asked.

"Make your own." Spence headed for the front door. "I've got stripes to paint on the new parking lot I just laid."

"Warehouse," Trace corrected as Spence pushed past him. "I need you to finish expanding the boathouse into a warehouse."

"And I need you to make coffee," Elliott called after his youngest brother.

Spence didn't bother with their secret code. Instead, he flipped them the universal hand signal for *Up yours* over a shoulder. "It's Saturday morning." He paused in the doorway. "I get that we can't take many weekends off in the hotel business, but I sure as hell could use a day off from you two." He closed the door in his wake with a *thud*.

"I better get to work too." Rebel took a few steps toward the front door.

"Wait, Rebel," Trace said. "I'm on my way to Cape Celeste to pick up the first plane full of campers." He hooked a thumb over his shoulder. "It's going to take two trips, and a storm's rolling in. I swung by to let you know a flight delay is possible."

Rebel eased closer to the door. "If the vets are late, I've got things to keep me busy in the garage. If you're really delayed, I can go into town to run an errand." Her running shoes squeaked against the hardwood floor as she took another step as though she was looking for an escape route.

Oh hell no. She wasn't getting away from Elliott that easily. Not until he at least tried to get her to open up.

He wasn't above playing dirty, so a) he'd get rid of his brother . . .

"Text me with updates," he said to Trace. "If you hurry, maybe you can stay ahead of the weather."

As if on cue, Trace walked out and closed the door behind him, leaving Rebel alone with Elliott.

And b) he'd be BFFs with her dogs.

He gave Rem and Bogart a signal to return to his side. To his amazement, they obeyed.

Her eyes widened, obviously as surprised as Elliott. Then those eyes turned smoky, caressing over his bare chest, then dropping to the towel that was slung low on his hips.

His skin heated.

So did her cheeks, if the pink seeping into them was any indication.

Which led him to c) he'd stay in the towel instead of getting dressed as long as it worked to his advantage.

He padded into the kitchen, calling the dogs to follow. Since the cottages were designed with an open floor plan, he knew she'd be able to see his backside as he made coffee. "Have a seat."

"I . . . I should get over to the garage. I, I . . . Jax and Ben are feeding and walking the dogs." Her shoes squeaked against the floor as she followed him. "Your dad is even pitching in. More to help Ben with his Scout badge, but it's extra help, nonetheless." Her voice was a little croaky.

Elliott glanced over a shoulder to find her standing on the threshold that separated the kitchen from the den. Her eyes brightened as she squatted and called Rem to her for a hug.

It was obvious how much she'd missed Rem after just one night. Which made Elliott stiffen his resolve to get to the truth. Why *that* name?

"I slept on a concrete floor last night." Elliott looked over his shoulder again. "I need coffee."

She stood, the red in her cheeks spreading down her neck. "I can relate."

"Then have a seat at the kitchen table, and let's talk while the caffeine convinces me that I'm in a good mood." He braced both hands against the countertop while the coffeepot gurgled to life.

The chair legs scraped against the floor as she pulled it out and sat at the table.

When he had two piping-hot mugs ready, he turned to find his plan working beautifully.

Her eyes roamed over him.

He fought off a smile and set a cup in front of her. "Mine isn't as good as Charley's, but it'll do."

He took the chair diagonal to her. As he scooted forward, his knee pressed into hers under the table.

A visible shiver raced over her. Just like it had last night when he'd had her tender breast in his mouth, and she'd quaked beneath him.

She molded both her hands around the mug. "Maybe you should get dressed."

He didn't miss a beat. "And risk you running off like you did last night? Not a chance." He took a sip, eyeing her over the rim of his cup. "Not unless you want to join me in my room while I change so I can keep an eye on you."

Her lips thinned. "You insisted on staying in the garage. *And* you've brainwashed my dogs, so don't expect me to feel guilty about leaving last night."

He lifted a shoulder. "Can't help it if they respond to my charismatic personality and irresistible charm."

She rolled her eyes so hard the unusual color of her hazel irises disappeared. "I've met dope dealers and pimps on the streets of Portland with more charm."

He knew she was joking, but he was also certain it was another clue. "You have experience with dope dealers and pimps." It wasn't a question, but he waited for her to respond.

She circled the rim of her mug with a finger. A finger that had romped through his hair, traced down his abs, and fumbled with his zipper.

"I have experience avoiding them," she finally said.

"You've been on the streets of Portland, and not sleeping in a bed isn't new to you." He paused so she could let his words sink in.

He could swear she stopped breathing.

His chest squeezed, and his heart thudded at the thought of her being alone on the streets with no one except a drug-addicted mother. He drew in a deep breath and leaned toward her, his knee massaging up her thigh. "Rebel, were you homeless before or after your mom died?"

Rebel's sharp intake of breath whistled as her lungs filled. Her heart expanded too, because of the softness in his eyes and the promise of acceptance in his voice. The need to touch him, kiss him, confide in him rained down on her until her chest was ready to shatter.

She stopped herself from blurting *both*. She'd known it wouldn't take much for Elliott to fit the pieces together. He still didn't know everything, though, and she planned to keep it that way.

"What are you talking about?" she asked. Denial wasn't all it was cracked up to be, because a part of her heart splintered, the pain sharp and biting.

He let out a long, frustrated sigh. "Don't insult my intelligence. I can't keep pretending that I don't care about whatever happened to you."

She spun her cup around. "You want answers."

He nodded. "Yeah. I do."

He leaned forward, the friction of his strong thigh setting off a riot of lust that arrowed through her. Drops of water still dotted his muscled chest and starred his long lashes.

"It's been long enough, don't you think?" he asked. "What could it hurt to tell me now?"

If he only knew. Telling him *everything* would make him complicit in a crime unless he reported it to the authorities. It was doubtful he'd be thanking her for being honest once he realized she'd put him between her and the law. If he kept her secret, he'd have to live with the shame the same way she had. If he told the truth, the fallout for the resort could be massive because of their association with her.

She couldn't do such a rotten thing to Elliott or his family.

"How about a game of truth or dare?" he asked. "I'll go first."

"What happened to old-fashioned chivalry?" she asked.

He shifted in his chair and slid his knee between her thighs. Which meant his package, which was so deliciously wrapped in nothing but a towel, was right under the table and ready for the taking.

She couldn't go there. No matter how much she might want to.

He leaned in and dropped his voice. "I'm not all that chivalrous. But I'm especially ungentlemanly when I'm as close to naked as I could possibly get." His tone was sultry and seductive.

Her mouth turned to cotton. Which only made the water droplets left on his pecs even more enticing. "Fine," she croaked out. "Hurry and ask me something, or I'm leaving."

"Why does that not surprise me?" His tone was challenging as he took another sip.

She tried to stand up just to show him she was serious, but he caught her wrist. "Stay, Rebel." His voice turned to a plea. "Come on. The longer we put off this conversation, the worse it's going to be for the camp."

True. She let out a heavy sigh and sank back into the chair. Tension between her and Elliott might throw the dogs off when she needed them to focus on the veterans. "Go get dressed first." His bare, hard chest gave him an unfair advantage.

"No." He leaned harder on the table, and a lock of damp, uncombed hair fell across his forehead. It curled around his ears and the nape of his neck and made her want to run her fingers through it like she had last night.

God, was his body beautiful or what?

The man did have the goods to make a girl swoon. Or drool. Or straddle him and whisper *take it off* like a hussy, then slip a twenty in his towel.

"When did your mom pass?" He leaned back in his chair.

A flock of birds took flight in her stomach at the memory of her helpless dying mother lying in a hospital bed. "I get to choose whether or not I want to tell the truth or take a dare," Rebel protested.

A sly smile curled onto his lips. "The Remington 'dare rules' are a little different."

She glowered at him. When he didn't give in, she decided to offer a small crumb of truth. "Less than a year after we left the island." That was an honest answer without giving away too much intel.

"My turn," she said. "Why did you move back to the island?"

The look on his face told her she wasn't the only one with something to hide. Now she had a chip in the game.

He ran his fingers through his wet hair before he answered. "Dad needed help with the resort."

Fair enough. The Remingtons were a tight family. Still, there was more to it than he let on.

"Why didn't you come back here after your mom died? It would've been better than nothing." He didn't hesitate to spit out the next question, as though he'd already made a mental list of them. But his voice was tender. So tender that it made every cell in her body ache with sadness and regret.

"The bank foreclosed on the house while my mom was in the hospital." The bird wings beat harder against Rebel's insides, and silence hung in the air as she retreated in her mind to recover. Finally, she leaned back and crossed her legs, ready to volley another question back at him. "Why didn't you ever get married?" Rebel wasn't certain he hadn't, but people usually carried scars from divorce, and Elliott didn't seem to have any of the signs.

He shifted, propped his elbows on the counter, and stared into his mug. Then his gaze lifted to hers and caressed over her face. Regret filled his magnificent eyes when they lingered on her mouth. "Because . . . I was . . ."

For a second she thought he'd say, *I was waiting for you.* Foolish, she knew, but she couldn't help but hold her breath.

"I was married to my job," he finally said.

She exhaled, not sure if she was relieved, disappointed, or both. But the way his voice was somber and filled with something akin to regret made her heart do a flippity-flop.

"My job is demanding." He stared into his mug. "I've seen it tear a lot of marriages apart at my firm. I'd never do that to anyone, but especially not to someone I cared about." He shrugged. "So I stayed single."

It was his turn. Instead of firing off another instantaneous question, he stared at her mouth for an eternity. He reached out and brushed a thumb across her bottom lip. "Why didn't *you* ever get married?" The heartache in his eyes and in his tone was her undoing.

Because no one ever compared to you. She wanted to shout it from the depths of her soul.

Where was duct tape when she needed it? Or a staple gun? Since neither was handy, she bit down on her tongue to keep from outing herself.

"Would you rather take the dare?" His stare stayed anchored to her mouth.

Only if the dare required her to unfasten his towel. "No. I'm done here."

Before she could stick her foot any further into her mouth, she stood and stalked for the door without waiting for Rem or Bogart.

"Rebel," Elliott called after her.

She didn't stop. She flew down the steps of his porch and hurried past the garage, all the way to her room. She needed to think. Maybe she even needed to pack her bag and go back to Portland.

Because if Elliott looked at her again with such raw emotion, touched her again with such undisguised passion, she'd strip off every stitch of his clothing and shrink-wrap herself around him.

Chapter Fourteen

#SoBadItsGood

Of all the responses Elliott could've anticipated from Rebel when he'd asked why she never got hitched, silence was the biggest eye-opener.

It made perfect sense. In a completely nonsensical kind of way. The indicators were there, all pointing in one direction. She'd still cared about him.

The silent self-loathing over caring about her all those years was suddenly snuffed out. He hadn't been an idiot. Hadn't been blind. She really had loved him. And she must care about him now. Otherwise, why name her dog Rem?

But why leave the island and break off all communication?

He grabbed his wallet, phone, and keys; called for Rem and Bogart to follow; and drove to the garage. As he parked his Jeep outside at the end of the line of white resort vehicles, the first raindrops splattered the windshield.

Jax ripped open a gigantic bag of food as Elliott walked in.

While Dad supervised, Ben had several bowls lined up by the stacks of food, filling each with a scoop full. "Uncle Elliott! I'm gonna get my badge in no time!"

Some of the dogs became restless at his full-throttle tone.

"Inside voice, Ben," Dad reminded his grandson. "Remember what Rebel said?"

"Hey, Dad. Did Rebel come this way?" Elliott asked.

"Haven't seen her since she left to find you." His dad helped Ben finish filling the bowls.

Elliott motioned for Jax to join him on the far side of the garage. "Have you seen Rebel in the last few minutes?"

Jax pointed to Rem and Bogart. "Not since she left to get those little dudes."

There weren't many places she'd go on the resort grounds. Elliott rubbed the back of his neck. "Listen, would you mind my leaving Rem and Bogart here for a little while?" Jax didn't have much reason to go the extra mile for Elliott, considering how he'd treated the poor guy, but Elliott asked anyway. "The veterans might arrive late because of the storm, so I need to take care of something."

"Sure thing." Jax called the dogs to his side.

They didn't budge until Elliott gave them the signal. Communicating with them wasn't much different from the secret code he and his brothers had invented.

They trotted to Jax, who gave them a few treats.

Elliott turned to go, but then he stopped. "Hey, Jax." This time that name didn't seem quite so ridiculous. He lowered his voice so only Jax could hear. Truth was, Elliott was embarrassed for his dad to know he'd acted like a jealous teenager who could still be led around by his hormones. "I wasn't very nice when we first hired you."

Jax's brows scrunched. Obviously, he hadn't noticed Elliott's sour attitude.

He still owed the guy an apology, though. Not to mention a debt of gratitude for helping with the camp. "I was being an unprofessional douche."

Jax still looked confused.

Wow. "I apologize for taking out my problems on the people around me. I've been out of sorts lately."

Realization dawned in Jax's expression. "Dude, no worries. Women do that to me too."

Elliott tensed. It was his turn to be confused. "What do you mean?" Had it been that obvious? "What woman?"

Jax let out another surfer-like laugh. "Anyone with half a brain can see you and Rebel have a thing for each other." He picked up the bag of kibble and moved it to the corner to stack it with the other bags. "That's why I haven't asked her out. I knew right away I didn't stand a chance because you're the one she wants."

Apparently, Elliott wasn't as smart as he'd once thought. Apparently, the IQ test had lied. Apparently, his numb skull was half-empty because he hadn't seen it nearly as quickly as Jax. *Jax.* Who'd named a dragonfly and sat outside every afternoon waiting for it to come out and play.

Elliott had to let that sink in.

He stared at the concrete floor. Finally, he said, "Thanks, man. If you ever need a reference, just say the word." Then he marched out of the garage; got in his Jeep, since the rain was falling harder; and drove straight to the main lodge.

Going to her room was crazy. Foolish, even.

But he wanted Rebel so much it hurt every time he looked at her. What he wanted even more was for her to tell him the truth so he could help. So they'd both stop hurting inside. Because as much as he hated to admit it, he'd never gotten over Rebel or the way she'd disappeared from his life. No way was she over it either or she would've answered his question before running out of the cottage.

When he entered the main lodge, he didn't even take the time to flinch at Mrs. Ferguson's neon-orange spandex pants, tank top, and headband as he passed the great room, where she had a hot chair yoga class in full swing for their older guests. He took the stairs two at a time, lengthening his strides to get to Rebel.

Standing in front of her door, he drew in a deep breath and knocked. No answer.

He knocked again. Could be she wasn't inside. A more logical explanation was that she was hiding from him. "Rebel, I've got a master key," he said loud enough so she could hear him through the door if she was inside.

The Remington had a strict rule that every staff member followed, including family members: never go into a guest's room without permission. She didn't have to know he'd never break it.

Relief zinged through him when the sound of the lock turning echoed down the hall.

But the door only cracked. "What do you want?" Rebel peeked through the gap with one eye.

"To finish talking," he said. "And I'm not leaving until we do."

"I have nothing left to say."

His heart pinched when the door shut in his face.

Rebel paced the length of her room, waiting for Elliott to go away. She couldn't let him in. She couldn't let herself be around him at all if she was unable to hide her feelings for him any longer.

She went to the closet and got out her suitcase. Only to toss it back inside and slam the door. Running away was not an option. Not with all she had at stake. She retrieved her phone from the desk and pulled up the commercial real-estate listing. After flipping through the photos of the property, she tapped the real-estate agent's number.

When the call connected, she said, "I'm calling about the abandoned animal shelter you have for sale."

"At the tone, leave your name and number and one of our premier agents will contact you shortly," an automated voice said.

Shee-ot. Rebel growled at the phone, then held it to her ear again to wait for the beep. When it finally made a blipping sound, she rattled off her name and the listing. "I'm working out of town right now, but when I'm back in Portland, I'll contact you. I *will* be making an offer soon."

There. A verbal commitment gave her a reason not to run. That property would be hers in the near future.

As soon as she got the paycheck from Down Home Dog Food in her hot little hand. She'd make the offer over the phone on the ferry ride back to the Cape, with Angel Fire Falls in her rearview. No one would ever have to know that she'd spend the rest of her life helping others who'd been damaged, abused, or abandoned by society as penance for covering up her mother's crime.

She'd never have to see Elliott Remington again. Never have to answer any more of his questions.

She walked to the desk where his jacket was draped over the chair. She picked it up, held it to her nose, and breathed in his scent.

She'd never have the pleasure of seeing him, touching him, kissing him.

She pulled on his jacket and snuggled into it, closing her eyes against the pain of eventually having to leave him all over again without a full explanation. Which was why she couldn't let herself get more personal with him than she already had.

A *thud* sounded on her balcony. Slowly, she walked to the curtains and pulled one to the side.

Her eyes rounded. "Elliott!" She jerked open the curtains, unlocked the sliding glass door, and threw it wide. "What in the world are you doing?" She ran out onto the balcony, where he was clutching the wrought-iron bars for dear life. Rain had soaked his clothes.

"The wind blew the ladder out from under me. I grabbed the bars," he ground out. "But they're slippery."

"Give me your hand!" She wedged her knees between the railing for leverage.

"I'm too heavy. I'll pull you over with me." With an *oomph*, he eased a foot up onto the ledge, then used his strength to hoist himself up and over the railing. He leaned back against the balcony, closed his eyes, and tried to catch his breath. "I thought I was a goner."

"Would've served you right. What possessed you to climb up to my balcony in the rain?" she demanded.

Finally, he opened his eyes. "I need to talk to you." He took her in, his green eyes growing heavy with desire. "You're wearing my jacket."

She looked down at herself. *Oh. Yes. How 'bout that?*

"I was cold, and it was handy." She fidgeted. "I'm not ready to talk." She waved her arms in the air. "I'm not ready for *this*. Why are you here, Elliott?"

He moved like a superhero and was on her before she could protest. "Because you still care enough about me to name your dog Rem." A firm hand found her waist, and he backed her into the room. When they were inside, he reached behind him without looking and slid the door closed. He pulled her close, holding her against his chiseled body with a firm, possessive hand. "Because you still care enough about me to wear my jacket. I like seeing you in it."

With a dip of each shoulder, she shucked his jacket. "I'll take it off."

His look said he wanted her to take off more than just the jacket.

"Why are *you* here, Rebel?" He dipped his head so his nose was a fraction from hers.

All the air rushed from her lungs.

She'd been asking herself the same question for days. It was for her career. For her future. For her dream. But she'd be lying to herself if she couldn't admit that it had been her first—and probably her last—chance to come back to the island and see him while hiding behind a good excuse.

His hand inched around to the small of her back and dropped to her ass. He cupped her cheek and pressed her hips into his. The rock-hard shaft pulsing against her belly made her gasp.

She mumbled something incoherent, hoping she hadn't just offered him a towel in exchange for his clothes. Because seeing him that way— or in nothing at all—was the only thing she wanted at the moment. "I can't stay on the island forever. I'm going to use the money from this event to open my own training facility in Portland. I've got some property in Portland in my crosshairs already." Her voice was a throaty whisper, but she needed him to know that she'd be leaving eventually.

Because she couldn't resist a man who'd risked falling from a second-story balcony just to see her. Just to touch her. Just to grind against her.

His nose brushed hers. "I'm not asking you to stay. I've learned never to expect forever, but I'll take whatever amount of time you can give." He grabbed two handfuls of her ass and lifted her off the ground.

She squeaked and wrapped her arms and legs around him. When his shaft pulsed against her center, she moaned and let her head fall back.

He took full advantage and devoured her neck with his mouth, his lips, his teeth, his tongue. "Do you want me to leave?"

Good God, yes. She couldn't make herself form the words. "No," she breathed out. She stabbed a set of fingers into his hair at the back of his head and pulled his mouth to hers. Her kiss was deep and desperate. She breathed against his mouth, "Don't go." She crushed her lips to his once more.

When she broke the kiss to look into his eyes, what she saw made her heart stutter. The raw need. The hungry desire.

Maybe it was her imagination, but the unrequited feelings shimmering in his eyes seemed to match hers.

It tore her heart into a thousand tiny pieces. With a fingertip, she traced along his jaw and whispered, "I *had* to leave you ten years ago. I'm sorry." And she was. So, so sorry.

He swallowed her words with a smoldering kiss and carried her to the bed. When they came up against the mattress, he broke the kiss and looked down at her, his lips curling in the sweetest way. She knew he was giving her an out.

No way could she take it.

Her body hadn't just come to life. It had shifted into warp speed, the flames of desire engulfing her.

She framed his face with her hands. His masculine beauty caused an ache that curled and coiled at her core. She put her feet on the ground and tugged off her fitted shirt. When she inserted both thumbs into the waistband of her athletic leggings, he covered her hands with his.

"Let me." Sexual electricity crackled through his voice. Gently, he inserted both hands into her pants, the spandex fabric molding his palms to the sides of her butt. His nimble fingers flexed into her aching flesh. He slid her pants down.

She kicked off her shoes and stepped out of the leggings, leaving her in just a black lace bra and matching panties.

He stepped back to look at her, his eyes turning the deepest shade of green she'd ever seen. They traveled the full length of her and back up again.

Those eyes. Always those beautiful eyes. They scorched a trail of heat over her. "You're even more fucking beautiful than I remembered," he rasped out.

Swear to God, her panties practically flew off on their own.

The ache coiled tighter, making her thighs quiver oh so decadently.

She couldn't wait another second to touch him. Spinning an index finger in a tight circle, she said, "Now I want to see you."

He gave her a naughty smile.

When she felt a blush coming on and looked down bashfully, he growled and took a step toward her.

"Uh-uh." She held up a hand. Then waggled her fingers while letting her own gaze slide down all six feet plus of him. Then up again. "Off."

One satiny brown brow arched high. "You're giving commands now?" He reached behind his head and one-handed his shirt off, dropping it to the floor. "More subtle training that I'm not supposed to realize is happening?"

"I don't think I'm being all that subtle." She glanced at the bed. "And would it really bother you if it was?"

"Not a bit." He kicked out of his boots, hooking his eyes into hers as he unbuttoned and unzipped his jeans.

When he dropped them to the floor, she licked her lips. A pair of navy-blue boxer briefs clung to his powerful thighs. Slowly, he circled and came up behind her. She let out a tiny gasp as one arm slipped around her midsection, the other around her chest, and he put his mouth to her ear.

"Do I get a reward if I'm a really good boy?" His sultry whisper sent a current to her nipples, turning them to hard peaks.

"Yes." She could barely speak. "A really good reward." She reached up and let her hand wander through his hair. "Just tell me what you want, and it's yours."

He growled against her ear, sending another shiver rioting through her. Then his fingers dipped between her thighs. "This." He taunted her with slow, mesmerizing circles.

She leaned her full weight back against him.

Gently, slowly, he scraped his fingers along her neck until they caught on her bra strap and tugged it down her arm. His big, warm hand molded around her aching breast, kneading and massaging until she had to bite her lip to keep from screaming. He took her rock-hard nipple between his fingertips and toyed with it.

"And this." He suckled her neck, trailing hot kisses to her ear. Then he sank his teeth into her earlobe with just enough firmness for her to let out several tiny gasps, each one searching for small bits of air to stem the tide of orgasm that was threatening to send her over the edge.

His satisfied chuckle against her ear caused another shock wave of desire to arrow straight to her core.

She fisted his hair and turned her head to the side, hauling his mouth down to hers. His kiss scorched her lips.

"You're wet." His voice, so thick with lust, made her shiver.

"You're hard." She pressed her butt into his groin and did another shimmy and shake.

"*Christ*, woman." He bit off each word as though fighting for control. He released her breast to unhook her bra and slid down her panties. They coasted to the floor, and she stepped out of them.

He spun her around and guided her onto the bed, the comforter soft against her bare skin. When he started to crawl up her body, she opened to wrap her legs around his hips. He stopped and looked up at her with softness and warmth that was meant to ease her frantic nerves.

It worked, her rigid body relaxing as she softly sighed.

He settled between her legs and hooked her thighs over his broad shoulders.

"Do I get an even better reward if I'm a really *bad* boy?" He parted her with his tongue, delving into her heat.

"Absolutely," she moaned, arching into him.

He groaned and went back for more.

"That's . . . really . . . bad," she rasped out.

"So bad, it's good." His hot breaths against her moist folds sent a shiver racing through every molecule in her body.

His nimble tongue circled and stroked her clit until she writhed under him. Her fingers curled into his shoulders as she held on for dear life.

"*Elliott,*" she gasped out. "I'm about to—"

He inserted two of his nimble fingers, searching out the deepest, most intimate part of her, and did a twitch-and-curl number.

She came undone.

Tumbling end over end into oblivion, she cried out. The exquisite pleasure of orgasm swallowed her whole as his tongue and fingers kept milking every drop of her essence. Every cell in her body burned with sweet satisfaction.

While she was still soaring above the clouds, he moved away from her, his heat receding. He fumbled through the pockets of his jeans, and then he was back and covered with protection.

This time he did crawl all the way up her body, his incredible erection poised at her pulsing center. He braced a hand on each side of her head and stared down into her eyes. He entered her slowly and lovingly, pressing in until she was filled and aching for the delicious friction of his movement.

She bit her lip and let her eyes flutter shut, the entire room falling away as she concentrated on his pulsing shaft that filled her so exquisitely. Just as slowly, he pulled out until only his tip was left inside her wickedly wet center. Her eyes clamped tighter, and she turned her head to the side.

"Look at me." The roughness of his voice and the tenseness of his body said he was fighting for control too. "Look at me, baby."

She opened her eyes, fixating on the deep green pools that stared back at her. Only then did he start moving again. Slowly, entering and withdrawing, his measured strokes and deliberate rhythm hurtling her to the brink again.

She let her hands glide over his cut torso, around his waist, and she gripped his muscular ass.

Involuntarily, her eyelids drifted shut again as she tried to hold on to her sanity.

He stilled, deep inside her. His cock pulsed and throbbed, making her want more.

"Look at me."

She blinked him into focus and shook her head. "I don't want to."

"Why?" he asked. "Tell me, sweetheart."

Tears stung the backs of her eyes. Tears of regret. Tears of loss. Tears of fear. "Because I'll fall apart so much quicker that way." And she didn't want it to end too quickly, because it might be their last time.

He took her mouth with his, kissing, biting, nipping. He braced an elbow on the bed next to each of her ears and gently massaged his fingers through her hair. He kissed down her neck, biting at the sensitive skin of her collarbone, then back up to her mouth for another long, sultry kiss.

He brushed the tip of his nose across hers. "I want you to look into my eyes when I make love to you so I can see the real you."

She swallowed. That was exactly what she didn't want him to see. Yet she couldn't look away. She dug her nails into his hip so he'd start moving inside her again.

He obliged, reaching down to grasp one of her thighs just above the back of the knee. He pulled her leg up, spreading her wide.

"*Oh,*" she gasped. "*Yes.*" Another gasp.

She kept looking into his eyes, the building storm inside him clouding them over. He picked up the pace as they both reached for that blissful climax that was drawing ever closer.

His strokes deepened, quickened as he rode her hard and fast, never looking away.

As though he were looking into her soul.

It terrified her and excited her all at once.

A powerful orgasm barreled through her, and her muscles exploded around him, plunging them both over the brink.

He collapsed against her, dropping his head to the mattress. He turned his face in to her ear, so his heavy, erratic breaths feathered across her skin.

They lay there for a long time, their hearts beating in unison. She swirled her fingertips along his dewy back.

"Hey," she whispered, stroking the hair from his forehead.

He lifted his head. "Hmm?"

"I owe you a treat," she teased.

His eyes sparkled with mischief. "Yeah? Give me a sec." He rolled to the side of the bed and discarded his protection. Then he was hovering over her again. With one swift movement, he rolled onto his back, taking her with him.

She straddled him, and he raised up to nuzzle the space between her breasts. "My kind of treat."

She braced both hands against his shoulders and pushed him back on the bed. "Lace your fingers behind your head."

He frowned.

"Do you want your treat or not?" she warned.

When he did as he was told, the muscles in his arms flexed.

"Yum." She lowered her torso to meet his, rubbing her breasts along his skin, which was still moist from round one. With her mouth and her tongue, she trailed hot, openmouthed kisses down his body and gave him the reward of a lifetime.

Chapter Fifteen

#MeAgainstTheUniverse

After a few more rounds, Rebel curled into Elliott's side, twining her bare legs with his. Long-term, getting naked with him might've been a mistake, but at the moment, it seemed magical and perfect.

She hadn't lived in the moment since her last night of sleeping on the streets. Maybe it was time.

Wind whistled outside as rain pelted the windows.

He wrapped his arms around her, caressing her arm and shoulder with his palm. It was the safest she'd felt since she'd left the island. The first time she hadn't felt alone since she'd driven her mother's car onto the ferry.

She wished she could say she hadn't looked back that day. But she had. She'd gotten out of her mom's car and stood at the rear of the ferry, watching Angel Fire Falls fade into the distance.

She'd been scared as hell. Turned out, she'd had every reason to be afraid. Her sad life growing up on the island had seemed like heaven compared to being eighteen and homeless. But now, lying in Elliott's arms again, that fear was gone, even if it was only for a few brief hours.

It was time for her to ask a few questions of her own. Time for a little soul baring, now that they'd bared everything else. "What will you do after the camp is over? Go back to your regular responsibilities?" She traced the outline of his pecs with a finger.

He drew in a weighty breath and held it like he was trying to make a difficult decision. Finally, he blew it out. "I haven't had the heart to tell my family yet, but I've taken a leave of absence from my firm to help with the resort. I'm going back to San Francisco . . . as soon as I can." He ran a hand over his face. "God, it feels good to finally tell someone."

"I always knew you'd be a success," she whispered against his chest, clamping her eyes shut against the reality of what that meant. Ten years ago, she hadn't wanted to be the person who held him back. He'd been going places she knew she'd never belong because of her miserable background. If he was going back to his corporate job, then she was still caught between the same rock and hard place. A woman who'd barely finished high school and came home from work every day smelling like dogs wouldn't stand a chance in his circles.

He scoffed. "So successful that I chose to work all the time to make partner as fast as possible and didn't come around for years. So successful that I let the resort decline instead of helping my aging father take care of it. My hours are only going to get worse now that I'm a partner, so I'll be even more neglectful of my family once I go back to work at the firm." He let out a sarcastic laugh. "I'm a superstar all right."

"That lifestyle doesn't sound like you." She nuzzled his neck. "Your family has always been a priority." The selfish description of himself didn't match his decision to put a successful career on hold now to come home and help the resort. "Is that why you lied to your dad the other day about the camp going so smoothly when it's not?"

Elliott rubbed his eyes. "I just can't stand to let him down again."

Again? Since when had Elliott let anyone down? He was one of the most responsible people she'd ever known.

He placed a finger under her chin, tipped her head up, and kissed her. "Hopefully, I won't have to. With an expert trainer here to save our asses, maybe I won't be such a disappointment." He placed a tender kiss on her forehead. "I shared a secret with you. Now, will you tell me what happened after you left the island?"

She flattened a hand over the dip in the center of his chest. The gentle rhythm of his heart pulsed into her palm. *Okay, here goes.* He wanted to know what had happened *after* she left the island. She could be honest without telling him what had happened before she fled with her sick, frantic mother who didn't want to spend her last days in prison.

"The drinking destroyed her liver. She'd been feeling poorly for a while. By the time she finally went to a doctor, she needed a transplant." Rebel suddenly felt cold. So cold. At the same time, it felt good to talk about it. "Her doctor on the Cape referred her to a specialist in Portland because she wasn't going to make it much longer."

Elliott rolled onto his side to face her. He brushed her hair back and tucked it behind an ear. "She didn't get the transplant?"

Rebel swallowed past the thickness in her throat. "No. She stopped drinking but had to stay clean and sober six months before they'd put her on the list. She died in the hospital right before qualifying." Rebel brushed a lock of hair off his forehead.

Rebel had been nagging her mom to clean up because she hadn't been feeling well. Then she'd come home crazy with fear because she'd woken up from an alcoholic blackout with no memory of how she'd driven her car into a ditch. Word spread that Dan Morgan had been hit by a car while riding his bicycle. The driver hadn't stopped, leaving the scene of the accident without helping the little boy.

The dent she'd found in the fender of her mother's car was the last straw. Rebel threatened to go to the authorities if her mother didn't stop cold turkey. They'd packed up what fit into their old car and checked into a hotel on the Cape. A few days and an urgent-care appointment later, they were on their way to a hospital in Portland. Her mother kept her promise and never touched another drop of liquor, but it was too late.

She swirled a fingertip through the smattering of hair on his chest.

Elliott's hand rested against her jaw, and his thumb caressed the soft skin above her cheek. "No one on the island knew why you'd left. Why didn't you tell anyone?"

She molded her hand on top of his. Knew that he was chipping away at solving the mystery, one question at a time. "It happened so fast. We were desperate to get to the hospital."

Her chest tightened because she figured what was coming next. He'd want to know about the note. About why she'd asked him not to look for her.

Instead, he said, "Now that I know what happened to your mom, tell me what happened to you."

It shouldn't have, but it threw her. She'd thought he'd be more interested in how her sudden secret departure had affected him. It was so like him to focus on how it had affected her. "Um, well . . ."

He placed a soft kiss at the corner of her mouth where she was chewing it. "Stop worrying and just tell me. You know you can trust me."

She did know. That wasn't the problem. The problem was that she couldn't reward his loyalty by putting him in a situation where he had to choose between his conscience or her. It would tear him up inside. She should know. That impossible choice had shredded her to pieces for years.

"You were homeless." Softly, gently, he kept stroking her cheek and the skin under her eye.

White-hot tears stung the backs of her eyes as she nodded. "I slept in Mom's car as long as I could. I still feel overwhelmed when I have to eat in front of people. It's like they'll know I was a street rat by the way I eat."

His body went as rigid as a plank of wood. "Don't ever call yourself a street rat again. None of it was your fault."

But it was true. She couldn't forget it any more than she could forget how much it'd hurt to leave Elliott without an explanation. Even back then, she'd known he was going to move up in the world, just as much as she'd known she wouldn't. That part hadn't changed and never would.

"After Mom died, I had to sell the car for cash just to eat." Rebel hadn't missed the car a bit, since it was the weapon her mother had inadvertently used to hurt Dan Morgan. "After that, I slept on a park bench."

A deep, guttural sound of agony escaped through his lips, and he pulled her into his embrace.

"That's how I became a dog whisperer." She snuggled into him. "A stray dog found me."

Elliott chuckled. "You were homeless, yet you rescued a stray dog. That's so you."

She hadn't rescued the dog. Not really. "He rescued me. Looking after him was the only thing that kept me from giving up." She smoothed a hand over Elliott's tight abs and around to his muscled back. "When I couldn't feed him anymore, I took him to a shelter. The manager asked me if I wanted a job cleaning out the kennels, feeding the dogs, getting them water." She lifted a shoulder. "The same stuff Jax is doing to help us. She let me sleep on a cot in her office. I worked with the dogs constantly, and one thing led to another."

His phone dinged. Instead of answering it, he kept stroking her arm, her shoulder, her hair.

"We should check that." She wrinkled her nose. "We do have a lot of responsibilities we're neglecting at the moment."

He got up and searched through the clothes strewn on the floor. When he found his cell, he blew out a heavy breath. "The storm blew in faster than expected." His face paled, and he stared at the phone like he wasn't really seeing it.

She rose onto an elbow. "What's wrong?"

"Trace is grounded on the mainland until the weather lets up. He's putting the vets up in a hotel so they'll be comfortable until the airport opens again." He tapped on the screen of his phone. *"Fuck me."*

"What is it?" she asked.

"I pulled up the weather report. The storm might last two days."

She fell back on the bed. "We're already on a condensed schedule. Losing two days is critical. We'll have to ask the sponsor to extend the camp—"

"No." His tone was more than firm. It was bordering on harsh. "I'll have to cancel before I do that." He started to pull on his clothes.

She sat up. "You'll cancel? Just like that?" She got out of bed and gathered her clothes too.

"If I have to." He sat on the edge of the bed to put on his shoes.

She hurried to get dressed. "Elliott, we'll get a better result if we have more time."

He stood, his stare unwavering.

It was like someone had flipped a switch.

"What happened to not disappointing your dad?" she asked.

He ignored her question. "I'm going to my office to call the sponsor again. Are you coming?"

Rebel couldn't help but wonder how they'd gone from whispering sweet things to each other to Elliott threatening to shut down the whole camp.

She pulled on his jacket. "Let's go." She wasn't about to let him cancel because of a storm.

When they got to the top of the stairs, she said, "If we can get Down Home Dog Food on the phone, we should discuss the situation and try to figure out possible solutions."

He practically jogged down the stairs. "As long as the solution doesn't require extending the camp, then sure."

She hustled to keep up. "Well, canceling isn't an acceptable solution either."

He stopped on the landing where the stairs switched back in the other direction. "You're the dog expert, but I'm the businessman. I make the final decision, because the resort has the most to lose."

Her mouth fell open.

The resort has the most to lose?

Hardly.

A dull throb started behind her eyes.

He had no idea how much was at stake for her. No way could she afford to build a facility from scratch. Ever. No matter how many camps she led or dogs she trained. The property in Portland was her one and only chance to have her own place outfitted to train and match dogs with people in need.

Her one and only chance to make up for what her mother had done.

She poked his shoulder with a finger. "I need this camp, Elliott. I don't have an expensive education. I don't have another career waiting for me. This is it. My only option. I loved you enough to let you go ten years ago so that I wouldn't hold you back. I need you to return the favor."

Hell. The last part had slipped out.

His head snapped back. "You *loved* me enough to ditch me through an ambiguous note? You *loved* me enough to leave me wondering where you were, if you were okay . . ." He threw his hands up. "Or if you were even alive?"

"I did it for you, and it wasn't easy." She planted both hands on her hips. "And now I need you to think of what this opportunity can do for me. Just because this poorly planned and inefficiently managed disaster of an event fell into my lap shouldn't mean I have to go down with it."

A throat cleared at the bottom of the stairs. "Excuse me."

As if on cue, she and Elliott both clamped their mouths shut and leaned to peek around the banister.

Lawrence stood at the bottom of the stairs, his eyes wide with warning.

A fortysomething man in a dark suit stood next to Lawrence, a wary expression on his face, a green tint to his skin, and a disapproving look in his eye. Dark water stains were splattered over his shoulders, and his hair was wet from the storm.

"This is Mr. Collins." Lawrence paused like the name should mean something.

Elliott didn't speak, like he was trying to refocus on what his dad was trying to say.

Rebel didn't respond either, her hackles still up from their unfinished argument.

"Mr. Collins is the head of Down Home Dog Food's public relations department," Lawrence clarified, his lips thinning.

Oh. Shee-ot.

"Mr. Collins, this is Rebel Tate, our dog whisperer extraordinaire." Lawrence made the introductions with a reassuring tone. "She stepped in at the last minute to save the camp."

Elliott may not have to end her dream by canceling the camp. By the look on Mr. Collins's face, he was ready to cancel it himself.

"I brought Ben over to the kitchen to eat with Charley's little girl and found Mr. Collins getting off the shuttle," Lawrence said.

"Wonderful to meet you." Rebel's voice shook. "But I, um, we weren't expecting you."

"Obviously." Collins rocked back on his heels. "I made it over on the last ferry before they shut it down. It was a choppy ride."

That would explain the Kermit-green tint to his complexion. It might also explain the disapproving Grinch look on his face. Catching the trainer in the middle of a heated squabble while she called the camp a disaster might have something to do with it too.

She hurried the rest of the way down the stairs. "Sponsoring a camp like this is such a great thing you and your company are doing. You have no idea how this will impact the lives of the veterans who served our country. Thank you for allowing me to be part of it."

His dim expression lightened a bit.

She may not have experience in the corporate world, but if she could charm unruly dog owners into doing things her way, then surely she could charm a company suit.

Rebel looked up at Elliott, who was still rooted in place on the switchback. Charming a brooding Remington was another matter entirely.

"This is Elliott Remington," she said. "He's the family contact person for the camp."

"Yes, I've gotten your messages." Collins hitched his chin at Elliott.

That finally spurred him into action, and he came down the stairs. "When you said we'd talk today, I didn't realize you meant you were coming to the Remington in person."

Collins didn't have to repeat *obviously* out loud. He communicated it quite clearly in his expression.

Elliott shook his hand. "Thanks for moving the camp to the Remington." He gave his father an uncertain glance. "We're working hard, despite the obstacles we've encountered." Elliott could obviously do some charming of his own when he wanted.

"I'm counting on it." Collins looked at Elliott, then at Rebel. "The camp is ready? You can resolve your differences?"

"Of course," Elliott assured him. "I do my best work with challenging people around me." He gave Rebel a smart-ass grin.

She narrowed her eyes a fraction.

"Iron sharpens iron, as the saying goes." He extended an open palm to Rebel. "Our expert trainer can give you the details."

"Why don't you pull your Jeep under the portico, and we'll give Mr. Collins a tour of our setup," she said to Elliott. If she could get Collins alone for a few minutes, she could pitch extending the camp. Then she'd talk sense into Elliott.

He dug a set of keys out of his pocket. "Dad, can you pull it around?" Elliott gave her a dazzling smile. "I don't want to leave Rebel's side for a second." His white teeth glinted under the light. "I need to stay apprised of all the details so we can make this event a success."

"Now that's the team spirit I'm looking for." Collins beamed. "It's the reason we selected a family-owned resort and insisted a family member be in charge."

"We aim to please." Elliott's smile couldn't have gotten any wider. Swear to God, he could've starred in a toothpaste commercial.

Damn that pantie-melting smile.

Less than ten minutes later, they walked into the garage. Rem and Bogart ran to her instead of to Elliott, which gave her a little satisfaction. She introduced Collins to Jax, then gave him a tour, explaining every aspect of their setup and how the camp would unfold over the following weeks.

"The real training won't start for a few days." She kept her palm on Rem's head, mentally scrambling for a way to ask for more time without alarming the sponsor. She glanced at Elliott, who wasn't giving her a minute alone with Collins. "The veterans are stranded on the mainland. When they get here, they'll need a chance to settle in at the resort to reduce their anxiety. It'll take a few days to match the dogs, and then a few days after that for the matches to bond. Our schedule isn't—"

"We'll work around the clock to make sure we get the job done," Elliott interjected.

She pasted on a thin smile. "Mr. Collins, when will the handlers arrive? I have to say, I was surprised when they didn't show up with the service dogs." She gave Elliott a look meant to pacify him. "We can speed things up quite a bit with one-on-one training once they arrive."

Several wrinkles appeared between Collins's dark brows. "Handlers? Didn't anyone tell you?"

Obviously not.

"Could you refresh our memory?" Elliott asked.

Collins slid both hands under his suit jacket and shoved them into the pockets of his slacks. "The dogs have been in training with handlers who reside at the women's state correctional facility."

The sharp breath that whistled through Rebel's lips had Rem pressing into her leg and Elliott frowning.

"That's . . . that's brilliant." And it was. "But . . ." And this was going to be a really big *but*. "It does leave us shorthanded."

Elliott beamed at both of them. "Lucky for us, we have Jax here to help out."

"Aiya?" Jax finally looked up from a graphic novel he'd been reading in the corner of the garage.

Rebel's eyes slid shut. She forced them open. "Mr. Collins, it's fairly standard procedure for handlers to help the dogs transition to their new matches. Not having them here presents a prob—"

"Rebel is a veritable magician with dogs, though," Elliott assured Collins. "I have no doubt we'll make the camp work."

How? HOW? She bit her tongue to keep from blurting her frustration.

Collins rubbed his hands together. "Excellent. Now, I'd like to see what the service dogs can do."

"Of course." She tried to put on a confident smile. "But our compressed schedule may need to be adjust—"

"We'll be ready," Elliott said.

Would they? And if he interrupted her one more time, she might have to kick him in the shin. Then she'd be happy to strip off his pants and kiss it to make it better.

She cleared her throat, trying to focus on the problem at hand and not the smoldering hottie standing next to her. Wasn't it just her luck that they were one and the same.

Well, it had been Rebel against the universe when she was alone at eighteen, and she'd handled it. She'd have to do the same now.

Chapter Sixteen

#OpticsAreEverything

Elliott unwound the cord of another space heater he was setting up in the garage to stem the cooling temperatures, while Rebel put the last of the dogs in their crates for the night. The storm had the veterans stranded on the Cape for two days and counting, so he and Jax took turns sleeping in the frigid garage.

Once Rebel told him the truth about living on the streets, Elliott wasn't about to let her sleep anywhere but a warm bed.

A lump formed in his throat at the thought of Rebel spending nights alone in a park. How terrifying it must've been for a young girl. He glanced in her direction as she led a large black Lab to its crate.

She went about her work like the professional she was.

In high school, he'd known she was resilient, but surviving on the streets as a teen? It turned his stomach inside out, and respect for her mushroomed in his chest. And something else bubbled up and knocked at the door of his heart. Something he couldn't quite put a name to. Something he was *afraid* to put a name to.

While they waited for the storm to pass, Rebel devised a schedule to rotate the dogs out of their crates for both mental and physical exercise using the obstacle course she'd created in the center of the garage.

Collins had been thoroughly wowed by both the Remington as a venue and Rebel's skill as a trainer.

Rebel, on the other hand, wasn't in the least bit thrilled with Elliott's refusal to ask for an extension for the event. She'd given him an arctic-level cold shoulder ever since that could've ended global warming.

And he'd been in a foul mood because he missed her more than he cared to admit.

Rem and Bogart had been hypervigilant because of the tension, constantly darting between him and Rebel.

"Okay," Rebel said to Jax when she closed the last crate. "I'm going to my room. Let me know if you need anything."

"Will do." Jax got out a graphic novel and got comfy on the fresh bedroll Elliott had delivered to him.

She completely ignored Elliott, called Rem and Bogart to follow, and went to press the button to raise the garage door.

"Hold up." Elliott switched on the last heater and jogged to catch up with her while pulling up the hood of his rain slicker. "The rain is still heavy, and the wind hasn't completely died down. I'll drive you to the main lodge."

She hesitated. Then stepped out of the garage, lifting the hood of her jacket as she watched him.

Heat crept into his chest as he punched her birthdate into the key panel to close the door.

Rem whined, and as usual, Bogart mimicked him.

When they were all in Elliott's Jeep, he turned up the heat. The headlights streamed over the lane that took them to the covered portico at the main lodge's entrance.

He pressed his finger on the door lock and kept it there so she couldn't jump out. "How can I make things better between us?"

"Extend the camp," she spit out without a second thought.

Damn. That was fast.

"Anything but that," he said.

"Why?"

Rem stuck his head through the seats.

Elliott exhaled, propping his elbow against the window. "Okay." He finally turned to her. "I'll tell you. But you have to give up your secrets too."

She scoffed like she was insulted.

"Don't even try to pretend that you've told me everything, because I know you haven't, Rebel." He tapped his temple. "I've got a really high IQ, remember? Your story might be true, but you've left something out, because your mom's illness still wasn't enough of a reason to cut me off without a word."

She crossed her arms and stared through the front windshield into the dark. "More of your rigged version of truth or dare?"

"No." His voice was a near whisper. "Just truth this time."

Her lips parted, and she turned to look at him. Finally, she nodded. "Why won't you extend the camp?"

He didn't hesitate. "If I'm not back at work soon, they're going to fire me and take my life savings too. All partners are required to buy in to the firm. I gave them everything I had except for my apartment."

"Oh," she whispered. "I suppose that's a good reason."

"I've got a few questions for you, but I'll start with the easiest." He slung a hand over the steering wheel. "Why did you name your dog Rem?"

Her chin quivered. "I . . . I've named all my dogs Rem as a way to stay connected to you."

A thrilling rush of heat pounded through his veins so hot and fast that it scored his insides.

"I used your birthdate as our garage code for the same reason. My apartment security code too." He blew out his cheeks. "Now that we've established we both never got over each other, why did you leave without telling me where to find you? I get it that your mom was sick, but I could've helped. My family would've been there for you too, Rebel."

Her bottom lip trembled along with her chin. "I haven't told you everything for your own good. I shouldn't—"

"I *have* to know." Knowing was the only way to end his torment.

"My . . . my mom hit Dan Morgan," Rebel whispered.

Elliott stilled, shock rolling over him in waves.

She dropped her face into her hands. "God, you're right. It *does* feel good to finally tell someone."

Elliott gave her a moment. Really, he was giving himself a moment to recover too. The revelation of what her mom had done, what she'd put Rebel through, sickened him.

When she laced her fingers in her lap, one thumb rubbing the other, he covered her hands with one of his. "What happened?"

"Mom didn't remember the accident because she passed out. She woke up in a ditch on Sunset Road, and then she stopped in town to get more liquor on her way home. There was a dent in her car where she'd hit something, so when the news broke about Danny, she just knew it was her fault."

His pulse kicked when a tear trekked down her silky cheek.

"Shh." He shooed Rem to the back seat, then leaned over the console, pulling her into an embrace. "Why didn't you call me? I would've come home."

She nodded. "I know you would've. That's why I didn't tell you or your family." She leaned back and gave him a pitiful look. "I loved you too much to let you give up your scholarship. I would've hated myself for it."

"So you disappeared." He framed her face with his hands and pulled her into a sweet, gentle kiss. "You survived on your own without anyone looking out for you."

Another tear slipped down her cheek. "I loved you enough to let you go."

His heart shattered into a million tiny pieces.

"It's okay, baby." He cradled her against his chest. "I've got you now." He wasn't sure how to process what she was telling him or what to do about it. He only knew that if she was brave enough to survive all she'd been through and trusted him enough to confide in him, then he had to protect her. To help her somehow, someway.

It didn't make sense that Dan would've been all the way over on Sunset Road on a bike. Elliott knew where the Morgans lived, and it was nowhere near Sunset Road. If nothing else, maybe he could find out some of the details about Dan's accident. "Do you remember what time your mom got home that day?"

"Well, it was late on a Saturday morning. She'd been out all night. That's all I remember." She sniffed. "I wouldn't blame you if you turned me in."

He placed his finger under her chin and lifted her gaze to meet his. "We'll figure something out. Keeping this secret so long has obviously torn up your life like it did Dan's." Elliott stroked a palm across her silky hair. "You shouldn't have to keep paying for your mom's mistakes, sweetheart."

He kissed her. Soft and sensual and so, so sweet until his comforting kisses made her rigid posture relax.

"Hey." He tilted his head to look into her eyes. "You go on up to your room and get some sleep. I'm going to stop in and see how Dad is faring with Mr. Collins. Since he's been trapped on the island during the storm, I'm sure he's getting antsy."

Elliott walked her to the stairs. "Good night." Jeez, he felt like a teenager again on a first date. But instead of asking if he could kiss her on the cheek, he wanted to ask if he could meet her upstairs, strip her naked, and kiss her *everywhere*.

His expression must've registered his thoughts, because she blushed. "'Night." With an index finger wandering over the banister, she took each stair slowly, glancing over her shoulder like she was unsure about leaving him at the bottom. Rem and Bogart followed her up.

When she finally disappeared without inviting him up, he sighed in disappointment. Then he went to find his dad and Mr. Collins.

Only two days had passed since Elliott and Rebel were caught arguing in the middle of the main lodge, wearing the fresh scent of sex like they'd been attacked by a cologne salesperson at a department store. Those optics hadn't made an ideal first impression, but besides Rebel's impressive skills, Elliott had managed to dazzle Collins with his knowledge of business.

The thought of business, his firm, and the world of high finance usually got his adrenaline pumping.

Not tonight.

A dull throb started at his temple.

Tonight, all he wanted was to fix things for Rebel so she could let the guilt over Dan Morgan's accident go. So she could have a life. With him. Somewhere. Somehow . . .

Fuck.

Had to be the great sex they'd had causing his brain to cramp because his life and his savings were waiting several hundred miles down the coast. Unfortunately, the long hours that went with his job wasn't the life she deserved.

He breezed past the kitchen and turned right toward the family den, drawing in a weighty breath.

He had to admit he'd gotten used to showing up to work every day in jeans and work boots. The power suits he wore at the firm were stiff. Uncomfortable. Not to mention damn expensive, because looking the part was half the battle when it came to reeling in big clients.

He'd take his relaxed jeans any day over those stuffy suits.

Hell, he'd take the resort and a cottage any day over his corner office and penthouse apartment in San Francisco.

That thought squeezed the air from his lungs.

Definitely the incredible night they'd spent together doing the thinking for him. He needed to keep his head in the game and keep the camp on track so that he could keep his life savings and his lucrative career. He and Rebel could figure out some sort of arrangement once they both went back to their real lives. For the life of him, though, he didn't see any arrangement that would be fair to her. Because asking her to move to San Francisco to his empty apartment where he was never home would suck for her.

When he got to the den, his father and Collins occupied two wing-back chairs with a half-empty bottle of expensive brandy sitting on the table between them.

"*There* he is." Collins slurred his words slightly and wore a cheery expression.

Thank God for Dad. Elliott had planned to do the schmoozing with the hope of landing Down Home Dog Food and their camp as an annual event. Since they were shorthanded, his father had stepped in and was obviously doing a fantastic job.

Collins lifted his glass of brandy in salute. "Your dad was just telling me how valuable you've been to the resort since you've been back."

Not really. Anyone could do Elliott's job. His dad was giving him far too much credit because he was glad to have his three boys home for good—or so his dad thought.

He'd been quick to sign over ownership of the resort to Elliott and his brothers. And Elliott hadn't had the guts to stop his father from doing it, because the gesture had brought him so much joy. It was the happiest Elliott had seen his father since Mom died.

Scratch that.

Since Elliott had caused her death.

He raked a hand across his jaw. His mother's death hadn't crossed his mind the past two days. A record.

And he wasn't sure if he should be thankful for the reprieve from the guilt or more ashamed than ever.

On top of that, it was going to kill Elliott as much as his father when he finally broke the news that his prolonged stay wasn't permanent. "Enjoying the evening?"

"Absolutely." Dad had the same twinkle in his eye he got when entertaining guests. "Get yourself a glass and have a seat."

Elliott went to the wet bar and got a glass, filling it with the dark-amber liquid. He sank into the seashell-print sofa across from his dad and Collins. Lifting the snifter to his nose, he let the rich scent drift up so he could breathe it in. Something he often did with both potential and existing clients.

It was nice, but he preferred Charley's coffee or an occasional long-neck bottle of beer.

Collins rolled the brandy around in his glass. "Just shooting the breeze and trading stories from our military days. Different wars, but the details are always the same."

And that's why Elliott loved his dad so much. He found that special something, that soft spot in a person's soul.

Elliott gave his dad a subtle smile that communicated *thank you*.

His dad's glittering eyes said he was happy to pitch in.

"Quite the place you've got here," Collins said. "Definitely the kind of place our company likes to utilize."

Ah. Elliott's business prowess sprang into action. "Would your company consider attending employee team-building events here?" His firm required similar company-sponsored activities. "If you're interested, we can put together a proposal." He shrugged. "If your company signed a contract for, say"—he stroked his chin—"five years, we'd make our prices extremely competitive, especially if you schedule during our off-season."

Landing two annual events from a big client would help stabilize the resort's year-round income. A coup d'état in Elliott's not-so-humble opinion.

Collins nodded as though he was giving it serious thought. "I'll finally be able to leave first thing tomorrow, but I'll be back soon for our first round of interviews. It'll be time to start the publicity side of this project. We can discuss additional events then."

"We'll be ready." Elliott hoped like hell they could get the campers ready. Because his time was about to run out, and this was his last chance to do something good for the resort. Then he and his family would be even.

At least as even as he was ever gonna get.

His phone dinged, and he retrieved it from his pocket.

He stared at the screen. And almost swallowed his tongue.

A picture of Rebel wrapped in his jacket—he tilted his head to the side—and, it would seem, nothing else made his mouth go dry and everything else go hard. The text that came with it was even better.

I'll be in the shower. Dare you to use your master key.

"It's been a long day." He knocked back the brandy in one gulp. "I think I'll hit the sack." They didn't have to know he wouldn't be alone. He said his goodbyes and cantered up the stairs with a spring in his step. On the way up, Elliott sent Lily a text about the potential new event.

When he got to Rebel's door, he pulled out his wallet and opened it.

Master key. *Check.*

A long strip of condoms. *Check.*

He touched his key to the pad below the knob, and Rem and Bogart greeted him at the door.

"Hey, guys." He gave them a scratch as he locked the door behind him. He shed his jacket. "Stay here."

The bathroom was directly to his right, and the sound of running water filtered through the four-inch crack. With his fingertips, he pushed it open. A wall of steam engulfed him, moistening his skin. The naked silhouette behind the foggy glass shower door set him on fire.

But what stole his breath and had his heart skipping a beat or two was the message etched into the condensation on the glass. It was a creatively drawn heart. A simple thing.

Except that it wasn't all that simple.

Rebel used to sign her love notes to him the same way. No name. No scrawling signature. Just a heart. It had been her way of telling him she loved him.

He swallowed. That heart should make him happy. He wanted to deepen their relationship instead of ending it once the camp was over and they left the island. But he had absolutely zero to offer her because his career would consume him the moment he stepped through the front doors of his firm.

The shower door cracked a few inches, and she peeked out. Then she slid the door completely open.

He forgot what fucking century it was.

Her wet red hair was slicked back. Wetness starred her eyelashes. And water sluiced down her perfect, naked body.

"Whoever said optics are everything was pretty damn smart in my opinion," he said, deep and throaty.

A wicked smile curved her lips.

His stare licked over every inch of beautiful skin as he slowly unbuttoned his shirt and tossed it to the floor. Next, he kicked off his all-weather boots. When he got to his pants, her expression turned hungry, and she chewed one corner of her mouth.

Her nipples hardened into glorious peaks. Tempting. Teasing. Tasty.

"The optics from where I'm standing don't get much better." Her voice was sultry and seductive as she watched him undress.

He left one foil square on the counter and was in the shower with another condom, pulling her into a white-hot kiss so fast she squeaked. But then she melted into him, their need fogging the room just as much as the hot water. He eased her against the back wall of the shower and placed the condom on the soap dish. With a firm, possessive touch, he smoothed a hand down her toned back, over her contoured waist and hip, then down her thigh to grip the back of her knee. He lifted her leg so her foot would rest on the edge of the tub.

He slipped a hand between them, letting his fingers glide through her moist curls as he searched out the hot space between her thighs.

She broke the kiss, letting her head rest against the shower wall as he circled and massaged.

Her lashes fluttered down, and a soft breath whispered through her plump lips.

"Is that what you wanted?" he murmured against her mouth.

With her eyes still closed, she was too in the zone to answer.

"Or did I get my signals crossed?" He bent and pulled a tight nipple into his mouth, swirling his tongue over it.

She opened glazed eyes, spearing her fingers through his hair. "That's what I want."

Another swipe of his tongue and another circle of his fingers had her moaning.

One of her hands left his hair and wandered down his chest and over his abs.

He hissed in a sharp breath as her warm palm closed around his shaft and stroked its length.

"Baby, if you do that again, we'll have to skip the rest of the shower," he said, biting her neck.

She angled her head to give him better access. "You can't last through a shower?"

"I can." He suckled the soft spot where his teeth had just been. "You won't."

"That sounds like a promise." She chuckled, using her other hand to trace the outline of his six-pack.

"Or a dare." He massaged one lush breast, letting his other hand find her ass. He dipped his knees, placing his pulsing flesh at her hot entrance. "Either way, you'll see stars, and I'll have you screaming for more in a few seconds."

"You're pretty sure of yourself." Her index finger wandered lower and lower still.

He put the foil square to use, and then his fingers circled her wrist. He guided her hand to the bar on the shower wall next to them. "You should hang on." He filled each palm with her fine ass and lifted her so her legs circled his waist. He slid into her with one scorching stroke, filling her to exquisite perfection.

She cried out, and he swallowed it with a hungry kiss. He stilled, giving her a second to adjust. His forehead rested against hers, and their labored breaths created more fog that mixed and mingled with the steam from the water.

She laced her arms around his neck, letting one finger play with the back of his hair. "I . . ." she said in a soft, shaky voice. "I missed you, Elliott," she murmured against his neck, and he knew she wasn't talking about the two days since they'd slept together.

"I missed you too, baby," he whispered back. And he had. So damn much it still made him ache. He just hadn't wanted to own up to it.

He started to move his hips. Slowly at first, then faster, stroking deeper with each thrust.

She nipped his bottom lip. "God, that's so good," she panted out.

Her nipples tightened, grazing his chest with each rock of his hips. The glimmer of orgasm sprang up from his depths. His fingers flexed into her soft flesh as he picked up speed. Gritting his teeth, he held back the tension coiling tighter inside him.

The way she moaned and dug her nails into his back told him she was close. So he reversed his hips and drove into her to the hilt.

She let out a short, sharp scream as her muscles contracted and quivered around him, pulling him over the edge too. Their heartbeats drummed in unison as they floated on the clouds, then slowly descended.

Rem whined from the door.

He smiled against her neck. "I'm surprised he actually runs toward that kind of scream. I bet it rattled windows on the mainland."

She bit his earlobe.

"Ouch," he said with a playful laugh. He set her down and turned off the water. "Come on."

She followed him out of the shower, and they toweled each other off, getting hot and bothered again in the process. She reached for the condom he'd left on the counter.

"Uh-uh." He grasped her hand and brought it to his lips to feather soft kisses across the inside of her wrist. "I'm hungry. Let's order room service." He trailed more kisses over her soft skin. "I'll even turn away if you don't feel comfortable eating in front of me." He placed a soft kiss at the corner of her mouth where she nibbled it when she was nervous. "But I'd rather you let me feed you."

More pink seeped into her cheeks.

While they waited for their food to arrive, Elliott pulled on his pants and got a fresh terry-cloth robe from the closet with THE REMINGTON stitched onto the front. He lounged against the headboard and patted his lap. "Room service said they're pretty backed up in the kitchen. It's going to be a little while before our food gets here."

Rebel finished brushing out her wet hair, gave Rem and Bogart the command to stay on their mat in the entryway, then climbed onto his lap. She turned onto her side and cuddled against his chest as he circled her in his arms. He placed a gentle kiss in her hair.

"How do you feel about inviting Dan Morgan over soon so we can introduce him to Bogart?" Elliott asked gently, trying to ease into the subject. Following through with her plan to help Dan might help relieve some of the guilt she still carried over her mother's role in his accident.

Elliott was an expert on the subject of pent-up guilt and self-recrimination.

She tensed from head to toe. "I'm . . . I'm not ready."

Rem whined from his mat in the entryway.

"Come on." Elliott called him over.

Rem rocketed onto the bed and nestled next to them. Bogart, unable to jump very high, settled on the floor next to the bed.

Elliott stroked the length of her damp hair. "Don't we have to pair them soon?"

"I . . ." Her voice went croaky, and she cleared her throat. "Sure. I mean, this is kind of a test case, but it's ideal if they meet early in the training to see if they bond. And of course we need to speak to Dan's parents—that is, if he still lives with his parents, since he's . . . well, you know, but we've got so much to do, and the vets will be here tomorrow, *finally*, and we're already behind schedule, and I really need this camp to work out, and—"

He framed her face with his hands and tipped her head up. He kissed her long and lovingly until a soft, sexy sound escaped from the back of her throat. When she relaxed against him again, he broke the kiss.

"It might make you feel better," he said. "Especially since we won't be on the island forever. Before you know it, we'll both be going back to our lives." He wanted to get lost in the fantasy that they both had a lifetime. But that was more than a fantasy. It was an outright lie.

The lamplight glinted off the wetness that filled her beautiful eyes.

"You're . . ." A tear slid over her creamy cheek, and he kissed it away. She sniffed. "You're so sweet. You always were."

He chuckled. "Of all the adjectives used to describe me, *sweet* has never been one of them."

"That's my point." She curled into him. "To everyone else, you're a badass. But to me, you're sweet."

"I want to help. I want *you*." He tightened his embrace so she'd feel safe. He hadn't been there for her when she lived on the streets, lonely and vulnerable, but he could be there for her now. He wanted her to lean on him. "But I won't lie to you. I don't know where we go from here. My life in San Francisco wouldn't make you happy." He wished like hell it would, but he knew better. "Most of the partners at my firm have been through more than one divorce because they're never around for their families."

But that didn't mean he and Rebel couldn't discuss potential solutions to their dilemma.

"I don't expect forever, Elliott," she whispered. "I let you go once. I can do it again."

His heart skipped a few beats.

Not what he expected her to say after the secrets and the intimacy they'd shared. Rebel had always been strong. Tough. Independent. Things he'd admired. Now he wasn't so sure he liked those traits at all because they were working against him. Apparently, their time together hadn't meant nearly as much to her as it had meant to him. And probably never had if she was willing to let go so easily. For the second time.

Chapter Seventeen

#MatchMadeInHeaven

The next morning, Rebel hustled around the garage after matching the first four veterans with their new companions.

Besides an unfortunate leg-hiking incident that soiled an ex–Army Ranger's backpack, it had gone smoothly. That veteran—all six feet four of high-octane testosterone and bad attitude due to a strategically placed roadside bomb—was now on his knees, hugging a black female Lab named Fiona with tears streaking his cheeks.

Rebel flipped through her notes and read the names of four more veterans to Elliott. "Can you escort these out and bring the next group in?" she asked, trying to keep things moving along at a fast clip. It was her only option, since he'd confided his reason for not pursuing an extension for the camp. She'd try her best to make it work, because just as she couldn't have allowed Elliott to give up his scholarship because of her problems, she wouldn't ask him to let go of his dream so she could pursue her own. She cared too much for him to be that selfish.

"Sure." Elliott gave her the same vacant smile he'd had on since he'd told her his life in San Francisco wasn't suited for long-term relationships.

Probably for the best. As a partner in a prestigious financial firm, he'd need a woman on his arm who fit the part. Immaculately dressed, well educated.

Not someone who wore rubber boots to clean out dog runs and barely finished high school because of her mother's drinking binges.

It sucked, but no one knew how bad life could suck more than her. She was a big girl, and she'd deal.

"Which dogs should I take out?" Jax asked from behind her.

She jumped, her notepad clattering to the floor.

She scrambled to pick it up, then flipped through them. "Let's take out Nestlé, Simba, Harley, and Valentine."

"When's the little dude coming back to help?" Jax asked.

"Ben will be here after school," she said.

A few minutes later, Elliott walked in with four vets following. His natural-born leadership was so obvious just by the way he carried himself. He took charge the same way in bed.

She couldn't stop her tongue from darting out to trace her top lip, his taste still there from the previous night's romp. But a switch had flipped in the few hours that had passed, and he was distant.

Jax got the next set of dogs ready and leashed.

When the vets were lined up in front of her, she said, "Are you ready to meet your matches?"

The four veterans mumbled or said nothing at all, which was often how PTSD and TBI matching started. Once they were paired, they came out of their shells.

"We're going to start with these dogs. When you're matched, you can explore the grounds, maybe pop into your room so your new companion can get familiar with it before bedtime."

Normally, she'd give new pairings several days to bond at home before starting their training. Because of their condensed schedule, they had to start immediately.

She reached into her pocket and pressed the clicker. All four dogs went still and focused on her. She retrieved a treat for each Labrador from her fanny pack and nodded for Jax to unleash them.

Then she watched and waited.

Elliott eased up beside her. "When do we start matching this group?"

Rem came to his side.

"We've already started." She nodded to the dogs. "Watch."

Three of the dogs stayed close to her, waiting for another treat. But the chocolate Lab named Nestlé went to a veteran who could pass for an eighties rock star. He knelt and draped his arms around Nestlé's neck.

She lowered her voice so only Elliott could hear. "The dog often picks the person. When a pair clicks so quickly, it's almost always a lock."

Sergeant Rock Star leaned his forehead against Nestlé's and scratched behind both ears. The dog didn't pull away but sat still, already reading his companion's cues.

"This initial bonding sets up the next step in their training process." She turned a satisfied smile on Elliott. "The way they're already trusting each other tells me it's going to be a match made in heaven."

Her favorite hashtag. And one she used with an uploaded pic to Instagram every time a dog found its perfect companion.

"Trust between companions. I'm guessing that nonverbal bond is how they learn they'll always be there for each other." He met her gaze, his lovely eyes raking over her face. "I can see why it's an integral part of the relationship."

She got the feeling he wasn't just talking about the campers. "Trust . . ." She glanced at the new match. "Trust is more difficult for humans because it makes us vulnerable."

"True." Elliott's gaze still licked over her. "But isn't vulnerability what makes us human to begin with?"

"Is everything okay?" she asked.

"Yup." He folded his arms. "Just getting familiar with how things work in your world."

"Um . . . well, let's move on, then."

She didn't offer the dogs any more treats. Instead, she led them to the veterans. "Interact with them, get on their level, and play with them or pet them." She went and got several toys and balls out of a box and passed them around. It took a full hour, but two more of the veterans had been paired with only one left.

A young woman by the name of Maggie, who had one maimed arm and was using a cane for her severe limp, hadn't found her match.

Rebel flipped through her notes, then pointed to two more crated dogs. "Jax, can you bring out those two?"

Maggie's posture was stiff, and she wasn't overly friendly with any of the dogs.

Rebel sat on the floor with her legs crossed, and the dogs surrounded her. "Maggie, can you sit like this?"

Maggie gave her a timid nod. It took a minute, but she finally lowered herself to the floor, using her cane for support.

None of the dogs went to her.

"Now call them to you." Rebel sat still, not petting or encouraging the dogs in any way.

Maggie smooched to get the dogs' attention and patted her leg. Squeaks stayed by Rebel, but a cream Lab named Rooney and a strapping red Lab named Bear went to Maggie.

She glanced at Elliott, who was watching with such intense interest that it filled her with pride. "Can you hold Rem back?" The next step in the matching process might get high stress, and she didn't want Rem intruding if he decided to respond to the vet's anxiety.

Elliott knelt and gripped the handle on Rem's vest.

She motioned for Jax to take away the dog who hadn't shown any interest in Maggie.

"Maggie, give them both a treat." Rebel lowered her voice so the dogs would keep their attention on the veteran. After Maggie retrieved the treats from her fanny pack, Rebel said, "Now, try to stand up as fast as you can." Rebel knew it would be a struggle with her physical handicaps.

Maggie gave Rebel a distrusting look that said *hell no.*

"Trust me, okay?" Rebel said in a soothing tone. She glanced at Elliott, because the fact that they'd just been talking about trust wasn't lost on her. She shook it off and concentrated on Maggie. "I don't want you to be cautious when you stand. I want you to try to get up fast."

It took Maggie several minutes to work up the nerve. Her eyes darted around as her anxiety obviously escalated, and a sheen of perspiration beaded on her forehead.

Oddly, Rem didn't respond to her stress but stayed focused on Elliott and Rebel.

Rebel didn't break eye contact with Maggie, but she kept a confident, encouraging expression on her face and patiently waited.

Finally, Maggie awkwardly tried to use her cane to climb to her feet. When she lost her balance, Bear stepped into the path of her fall, and Maggie grabbed on to him.

And there was the perfect match Rebel had been hoping for.

Maggie knew it too, because she sat back down, threw her arms around Bear's neck, and broke down into a sob that racked her entire body.

It never failed to fill Rebel's eyes with tears and her heart with pure joy.

Elliott still hadn't spoken. Hadn't moved a muscle. She got up and went to him, watching the new pair as they bonded.

He let go of Rem and stood, never taking his eyes off the new match.

She kept her voice low to give Maggie time to empty out her emotions and recover. "After what wounded veterans have been through, they tend to shut down emotionally and throw up walls, quietly living in their own personal hell. Until they reach a breaking point and finally let themselves rely on another being."

For a second, Rebel's world tilted off-balance.

She had done the same thing. For ten long years, she'd existed in a private purgatory no one could understand. Until she'd finally confided in Elliott.

Then he'd proceeded to emotionally, if not physically, withdraw.

"It's a very moving experience," he whispered.

"Yes." Her voice was thick with emotion. "But it's so much more." Pulling her ponytail over one shoulder, she twisted it around her finger absently.

Rem whined at her side. It wasn't a comforting whine like when her anxiety level spiked. It was more urgent.

"What is it, boy?" She knelt to his level.

He barked and took off to the corner where Bogart lay on a foam mat. She'd been so busy with the veterans that she hadn't noticed his listlessness. She went and sat next to Bogart, feeling his nose. It was bone-dry and warm. Strange, since he'd been fine when they arrived at the garage early that morning.

Elliott's forehead scrunched as he joined them. "What's up?"

She shook her head. "Bogart isn't feeling well." She stroked the dog's head. He didn't bother to lift it he was so lethargic. "There's a veterinarian on the island?"

Elliott nodded. "Lily has Dr. Shaw on alert for the camp, and she even asked him to make house calls if necessary."

Rebel stroked the length of Bogart's frame again. "I think it's necessary."

Before she could ask Elliott to make the call, he had his phone out. When he finished dialing, he held the phone to his ear. "Hi, this is Elliott Remington. We have a sick dog here. Can Dr. Shaw come take a look?" He looked at Rebel as he listened.

She forced a confident smile.

He did the same. "Uh-huh. Thank you." He stuffed his phone back into his pocket. "Dr. Shaw has a full schedule today. He'll try to get here as quickly as possible, but it might take a while."

She put on a brave face. "Maybe it's nothing."

There were two likely chances of that—fat and slim. Rebel had a decade of experience with canines, and her instincts said Bogart wasn't just having a bad day. If he was contagious, she might not be able to get a job as a professional poop scooper after all was said and done because bringing a sick stray into the camp wouldn't scream *success* when the sponsor showed up to conduct interviews for the media. What it *would* scream was that, as a trainer, she sucked. Hard.

Her dream of using the boot camp as a springboard into opening her own facility and attracting donors just got a little further out of reach. And if Bogart's condition was serious, she'd never forgive herself for not taking him to the vet as soon as she'd taken him in.

Elliott had graduated at the top of his class from the most prestigious business school in the country. He'd outperformed the best financial analysts on both coasts. He'd doubled his firm's megaclient list in record time.

Damned if he knew what to do with a sick animal and a trainer who looked nervous enough to set off every service dog between Angel Fire Falls and the Canadian border.

After they'd matched the last of the veterans, Dr. Shaw still hadn't shown up. So they loaded Bogart into the back of Elliott's Jeep, left Rem with Jax, and headed to the veterinarian.

Fifteen minutes later, they parked in front of Dr. Shaw's office.

"I've got Bogart." Elliott got out and jogged around to the back passenger door. Bogart hadn't budged from where Elliott had laid him in the back seat, bundled in a blanket he'd dug out of one of the supply boxes. He scooped him up in his arms and carried him the same way he'd seen Trace carry Ben as a baby.

The assistant led them to an exam room right away, and Elliott laid Bogart on the metal table. Rebel stroked the wiry coat across the dog's rib cage. Elliott stepped close so the front of his shoulder and chest brushed against Rebel's back. She leaned back into him just enough for the contact to warm him. Soothe him. Relax him.

The same way Rem seemed to do for both Elliott and Rebel.

How had she so quickly become the Elliott Whisperer? Because she was balm to his driven type-A soul.

He stared down at her as she worried her bottom lip.

He wanted to have the same calming effect on her, but she hadn't hesitated to say she'd be able to let him go. Apparently, his presence didn't provide the same comfort that he got from hers.

The sting of rejection settled in his gut just like it had years ago.

Dr. Shaw walked in. "Sorry for the delay. I'm swamped today." He put Bogart's patient file in a holder on the wall. "Mabel called several days ago to let me know Bogart had been adopted." He pumped sanitizing gel onto his age-spotted hands and rubbed them together thoroughly. "So, Mom and Dad. What's wrong with your new baby?"

A thrill hummed through him.

Back in the day, they'd made plans for a future and a family. Of course, they'd been naive teens. Those plans had been shredded, right along with his heart, once the harsh realities of life barreled over him like a freight train. But even after the way she'd ended things, even after confessing she'd be able to walk away from him again, she was still the only woman who'd ever turned his head and caused him to think there might be more to life than work and building a career.

He couldn't deny it. It was working beside her every day, knowing she was on the resort grounds and back in the Remington fold that blanketed his heart every moment, making him feel full and content for the first time since he was a kid.

Like they belonged together. And like the resort was their home.

"Oh, we're not . . ." She leaned away from him so they were no longer touching. "Bogart isn't ours." She shifted from one foot to another. "We're working together on the service dog boot camp at the Remington."

Dr. Shaw glanced from Rebel to Elliott.

He schooled his expression to hide his annoyance at how she'd just dismissed their relationship. Regardless of the hurdles they'd have to clear to have a future, what the hell had they been doing the last few days if not acting like two people who belonged together?

The doc gave Bogart a thorough exam, which included an unfortunately placed thermometer that no doubt left Bogart just as embarrassed as Elliott.

"He's got a fever." Dr. Shaw undraped the stethoscope from around his neck and listened to Bogart's breathing. When he was done, he removed the ear tips and let the scope hang from his neck. "His breathing isn't normal. It could be a number of things." He pulled the patient chart from the hanging file on the wall and flipped through it.

"Has Bogart had all his shots?" Rebel asked. "And are you aware of any health issues?"

Dr. Shaw shook his head. "Other than the missing leg and whatever he's got going on right now, no. Besides being undernourished from living on the streets . . ."

As soon as Dr. Shaw mentioned living on the streets, Rebel seemed to stop breathing.

Elliott wanted to touch her. Mold a hand against her back and administer comforting strokes to help heal the scars she obviously suffered from that awful period in her life. Tell her he'd never let anything like that happen to her again. But she'd been quick to tell Dr. Shaw that she and Elliott weren't together, so he kept his hands clamped to his sides.

"He was in fine health when Mabel brought him in." Dr. Shaw flipped to the next page. "I administered the proper vaccinations when he became a patient, so they're up to date. I'd like to keep him for a few days for blood work and tests."

Rebel's head bobbed up and down. "Do whatever it takes. I can't stand the thought of him being uncomfortable."

Neither could Elliott.

He also couldn't stand the thought of her walking away from him again and taking Rem and Bogart with her. Elliott was smart. He was successful. Surely he could find a solution so they could spend time together. So they could see if it might morph into something long-term. Something permanent.

She just didn't seem to want the same.

Chapter Eighteen

#HowIsThisMyLife

Elliott got up extra early Saturday morning to catch up on work in his office before heading to the camp. He fired up his computer and sat down at his desk with a strong cup of joe.

The campers had been matched for several days. So far, so good. Rebel had their training cranked into overdrive, giving the campers breaks throughout the day to rest, both physically and mentally. Jax was a huge help and never seemed to run out of energy. Ben had proven to be quite the helper too, doing whatever they needed every day after school. He was going to earn that community outreach Scout badge fair and square.

Elliott logged in to their bank's online bill-pay system and started typing in payments.

His dad had even found a way to contribute in an incredibly helpful way. He mingled with the vets after every training session as they wandered the grounds to practice what they'd learned. He'd organized a few field trips into town via the shuttle when Rebel insisted they needed to start integrating into real-life situations with their dogs.

While Rebel did one-on-one boot camp exercises with the dogs, his dad chatted with veterans. Their powwows had transformed into informal therapy sessions where the vets got to vent and let out pent-up anxiety. She'd even started to reach out to other dog trainers on the mainland who were close to the veterans' homes so they could continue to reinforce their training once the camp was over.

It was a golden arrangement.

Except that Rebel had refused to talk about a long-term plan with *him*. Even though he'd approached the subject several times.

Every night, she morphed into the old Rebel once they were alone in her room. When their clothes came off, it was as though they were one. Each an incomplete half without the other.

It was amazing.

Until they put their clothes back on.

And each day that passed, bringing him closer to returning to San Francisco, caused the knot in his stomach to grow bigger. Moving back to Cali wasn't as appealing as it used to be. And if it didn't make him happy, would it be fair to expect her to join him in the misery?

He logged the bills he'd just paid into his budget spreadsheet and frowned. He loved numbers because they didn't lie. He loved spreadsheets because he could easily identify inconsistencies and trends.

One of their major vendors had gradually hiked their prices each month.

An uncomfortable tingle slithered through him. There had been inconsistencies in Rebel's behavior.

He forced it out of his mind, got a calculator from his desk drawer, and crunched the numbers. Exactly an eight percent increase every month for the past three months.

He picked up the phone and got the account rep on the line. He didn't mince words, letting Business Elliott come out to play.

Or come out to fight.

"Explain your monthly price hike, or we'll go to another vendor." Before Angel Fire Falls had a reliable person delivering their supplies, the mainland vendors had every business on the island by the cajones.

Trace's new cargo delivery business had given local business owners more leverage and negotiating power.

It was an amazing contribution his brother had made to the resort and to the entire island. Elliott, on the other hand, was a wizard with spreadsheets and calculators, which no one seemed to care about. Because, hello. They were spreadsheets and calculators. His skills were utilized to the max at his big-city firm. At the resort, he wasn't much more than a bookkeeper.

By the time Elliott was done with the vendor, their costs had been returned to the original amount.

The seed of an idea sprang to life in his mind. What if the island businesses formed a coalition? There was definitely power in numbers. They might be able to negotiate better prices if they ordered in bulk from the same vendors.

Problem was, he wouldn't be around long enough to see it through.

He rubbed his eyes.

Wow. This failure was a record, crashing and burning before he even got it started. Unless he could find someone else to turn his idea into a reality for the good of the island.

His phone rang, and he snatched it up, welcoming the distraction. *"Yellooooow,"* he said.

"Elliott," Mick barked into the phone.

"Jesus," Elliott said. "Did you chase off another assistant? Or did the stock market crash, because I don't think I've ever heard you so sour this early in the morning."

"If you haven't already checked the stock market yourself, this call isn't as undeserving as I thought." Mick's tone was harsh.

Elliott sat up. "I'm joking." Actually, it was the cold, hard truth. He hadn't looked at the stock market in . . . He clicked on the calendar icon at the bottom of his computer screen and counted the days. *Shit.* He hadn't bothered keeping up with the outside world at all for several days.

And he hadn't missed it. Not one bit.

"I'm not in a joking mood," Mick snapped.

Obviously. Elliott picked up a pen and tapped it against the papers on his desk. Something told him he wasn't going to like what Mick had to say. "You've got my attention, boss."

"That's my point," Mick said. "I won't be your boss much longer unless you come back to work soon."

Elliott's head snapped back. "You gave me a month. I've still got a few weeks."

"I said I'd try to hold off a vote for a month. But some of the partners are getting nervous. We've lost a few big clients who don't feel we're well staffed enough to handle an investment portfolio their size."

The exhaustion in Mick's tone made Elliott recoil. The long hours, the lack of a personal life, the stress. Once, he'd thrived on it. Now it left a bitter taste on his tongue.

And Rebel had been a sweet remedy to the awful aftertaste of his life back in San Francisco.

"Which clients?" Elliott suspected they were his.

Mick rattled off the names, and bingo. Elliott had landed those clients, and they'd been happy with their returns when he was still managing their accounts.

"Who's been working on those accounts while I'm on leave?" Elliott could guess.

Mick hesitated, the grinding of his teeth confirming Elliott's fears.

"Lucas Foster," Elliott said, more to himself than to Mick.

"Yes," Mick growled.

"So the firm promoted an asshat with substandard financial management skills because of nepotism and turned over my hard-won clients to him." Elliott swiveled back and forth in his executive chair. "And the firm is ready to fire *me*."

That was the most corporate America, every-man-for-himself bullshit he'd ever heard.

"We didn't have much choice, since we were shorthanded," Mick groused.

And because Lucas Foster was related to one of the senior partners.

"Really?" Elliott bit off.

If Rebel could manage a service dog camp with no dog handlers and no on-site counselors for the vets, utilizing the inexperienced help she did have to maximize the results and keep a national chain happy, and do it in record time, then his firm could've handed off his bigger clients to someone competent during his absence.

"Let me ask you something, Mick." Elliott's words were measured and deliberate. "When you went through *each* of your divorces . . ." Elliott paused to let that sink in. "Who covered your client load and gave you all the credit?" He didn't give Mick a chance to respond. "And who had your back when you needed to spend a few weeks with your dying father because you hadn't taken time off from work to visit him in years?"

There must've been an infestation of crickets at the firm. It was the first time he remembered Mick being speechless.

"I deserve better from the firm, and you know it," Elliott said. "But if you can hold the partners off just a little longer, I might be able to deliver a major dog food chain to you on a fucking platter. They'll be here in a few days." Just as soon as Elliott got on the horn and invited them. "I'll seal the deal then."

Mick let out a gasp, because that was the kind of client that made the firm truckloads of money. "Okay. I'll do what I can, but you better deliver."

He left off the *or else*, but Elliott knew it was implied.

He'd better reel in Down Home Dog Food as a client for the firm, or else he'd be out of a job.

Amazing that the veiled threat of unemployment didn't bother him all that much. The only thing that did bother him was giving up his life savings to a greedy, ungrateful firm that didn't deserve it. So he'd have to dial up his kick-ass-and-take-no-prisoners business approach another notch and reel in another big client to show them he was still partner material.

He ended the call and dialed up Collins. The camp was going so well; it was a good time to encourage the sponsor to come back with his camera crews and interviewers. Collins and Down Home Dog Food would look like rock stars in the press, and that might create the opportunity Elliott needed to hook a really big fish for his firm and salvage his investment.

Rebel let the campers mingle for a few minutes after leading them through the morning training objectives. Then she stepped outside to call Dr. Shaw's office to check on Bogart like she had the past four days. Several times a day.

After living in Portland, she'd forgotten island life moved at a slower pace. Dr. Shaw had run blood work and several other tests but still hadn't gotten results from the lab on the mainland. In the meantime, Bogart's condition hadn't improved, and he was still under observation at Dr. Shaw's office.

The receptionist didn't answer until the fourth ring.

"Hi, this is Rebel—"

"Tate," the receptionist finished. "I've been expecting your call. Again. Hold for Dr. Shaw, please."

Rebel was worried about her dog, so sue her. Plus, she was equally worried about Rem because he'd been despondent ever since Bogart had been away.

Dr. Shaw's kind voice came on the line. "Ms. Tate."

"Is there any news on Bogart?"

"As a matter of fact, there is." His voice didn't waver. "Has he been around the other dogs at the camp?"

Worry prickled up her spine. "Um, yes. Why?"

"Are any of the other dogs feeling poorly?" he asked.

"Not that I'm aware." She spent enough time with the campers that she would've noticed symptoms. "Please, tell me what's wrong."

"Bogart developed a cough last night. He's got a bad case of Bordetella."

Oh. Hells. Bells. Kennel cough was highly treatable but extremely contagious. "But you said his vaccinations were up to date."

"Bordetella isn't a mandatory vaccine. Owners usually only request it if they're going to board their pets."

"The other dogs aren't showing any symptoms at all." She tried not to panic. Hopefully, they'd received a Bordetella vaccination before they'd arrived like Rem had and weren't susceptible to the illness.

"That's good." He drew out the last word like he really wasn't so sure it was a good sign. "But certain strains can incubate for a while before the symptoms surface. We should keep Bogart here until the camp is over and the other dogs are gone."

They finished up the call, and she covered her face with both hands. How was this her life?

After giving herself a few minutes to regroup, she went inside, pressed the clicker, and everyone stilled. She surveyed the circle of veterans to decide where to start.

She waved over a jittery kid named Kyle with PTSD and a missing arm who didn't look old enough to vote, much less fight a war. "Bring Elmo to the center of the garage." Now that they were several days into the boot camp and the veterans were well on their way to being properly trained—because the humans were always harder to train than the dogs—it was time to advance to the next level.

"Elmo is a big, brawny boy," Rebel said playfully to the whole group of campers while she scratched Elmo behind the ears. "He's a perfect match for Kyle because he's strong enough to push and pull heavy objects to help out around the house." She turned to Jax, who must've conned Charley out of a few doughnuts, because he was shoving half of one into his mouth. "Jax, can you find a toy long enough so I can tie it around a handle?"

"Aiya." He went to search through the boxes, while Rebel dragged a crate to the center of the garage.

When Jax brought her an elongated pink pig that crinkled in the middle, she handed it to Kyle. "Play tug-of-war with Elmo."

Kyle did, and Elmo clamped his teeth around it and flailed his head back and forth, trying to take it from him.

After a few minutes, Rebel tied the toy around a crate. "Kyle, your profile says you need help with laundry and other chores because you live alone, right?"

Kyle nodded.

"We're going to teach Elmo to do that for you." She nodded to the toy anchored to the crate. "Crinkle it and say, 'Pull.'"

Kyle seemed uncertain, but Rebel encouraged him with a nod. "We don't have to get it right the first time. It takes practice, dedication, and reinforcement."

Kyle crinkled the toy and said, "Pull."

Elmo grabbed the toy, waggled his head, then pulled backward until the crate scooted across the garage.

A flutter of murmurs and aahs came from the watching veterans.

Rebel tapped her fanny pack, reminding Kyle to reward his pup. "The second you get the desired result, reward him. Keep practicing, and eventually the command will transform from a game to a regular part of his life with you."

She went through more advanced commands and training techniques for each pair, demonstrating them to the whole group. Then she stepped back to watch.

This was what she lived for. Why she did what she did. Watching the dog and human start to depend on each other, trust each other, and the incredible gratitude a matched pair developed for each other when they realized how their bond would impact their future together.

Hopefully, she hadn't single-handedly ruined it for everyone, including herself, by taking in a three-legged stray that may or may not be a good match for Dan Morgan. At any rate, she'd spent enough time trying to work up the nerve to face the Morgans, and now it was time.

The thought of seeing them made bile rise up and burn her throat.

Maybe Dan wouldn't have the dedication it took to go through the training. Maybe Dan's parents wouldn't want a service dog. Maybe they hated dogs. Maybe he was allergic.

Ack!

She drew in a breath to calm her racing heart and glanced around the garage.

Not one of the Labs looked sick. Not in the least. *Whew.*

Her gaze snagged on Elliott, who must've snuck in through the side door. He was hidden away in the corner, lounging against the wall with his arms folded and his feet crossed at the ankles. The temperature had dropped another few degrees, and he'd added a knit slouchy cap to his casual hired-hand wardrobe.

It only made him look ruggedly handsome and hot as hell.

Her girl parts sighed. So did her heart and her mind and every other part of her anatomy.

She pressed the clicker to get everyone's attention. "Feel free to go exploring for a few hours. Practice what we've learned, then meet me back here for our next session."

As the matches filtered out of the garage, she went to join Elliott.

"How long have you been standing there?" She leaned a shoulder against the wall to mimic his stance.

"Long enough to see how amazing you are." Fire ignited in his eyes.

She must've blushed like a schoolgirl because the corners of his mouth turned up into a cocky grin.

But then she had to be honest and tell him how totally amazing she really *wasn't*. She rubbed the back of her neck, letting her smile fade. "Dr. Shaw called. Bogart has kennel cough."

Elliott's brow scrunched. "What's that?"

She couldn't hide the weariness in her voice. "It's a contagious respiratory infection. Basically, he's got the canine flu."

"Are any of the others sick?" The lines across Elliott's forehead deepened.

"No," she said. "Rem's had the vaccine for it, but I'm not sure about the other dogs. If I ask, it might set off an alarm with the sponsor."

Elliott thought a second. "Since they've already been exposed, I say we wait and see if the other dogs start showing symptoms. No sense causing alarm unless they get sick too."

"Dr. Shaw is going to keep him at the clinic just in case." She waved a hand in the air. "I'm sure it's nothing to worry about. Did you get caught up on your office work?"

Something flashed in his eyes. "Yeah. For now." Then the smoldering look was back. "Listen." He reached out and fiddled with the zipper on her jacket. "I was thinking we could take a break, if you're done."

"You have a dirty mind," she teased.

"Absolutely filthy." He tugged her to him, and her breaths came quicker and shallower from the excitement of just being near him. "But that's not the type of break I had in mind." He squinted and looked up. "Although I could probably be persuaded."

She poked his ribs with a finger.

He grabbed her hand with a laugh and held it against his chest.

A soft sigh feathered through her.

"Would you go on a walk with me?" he asked.

"A walk?" She could hardly wait to see what he really wanted.

"Yep. A walk." He went to one of the supply boxes and took out a new fleece blanket. "This is meant for the campers, but it won't hurt for us to use it first." He motioned to Jax, who was across the garage sweeping up the morning's dog hair with a large broom. "Hey, man. Can we leave Rem with you for a little while?"

"Sure," Jax said, and called Rem over with a handful of treats.

When Elliott and Rebel were outside, he extended his hand, and she laced her fingers with his. He led them along the path toward the dock.

"Thanks for coming." He pulled her to his side to drape an arm around her shoulders. "It's important." When they got to the dock, they passed the pier and veered left around the boathouse, which was under construction and roped off with caution tape.

Elliott still hadn't offered up an explanation, but she kept letting him lead her through the thick overhanging vines and overgrown trees that formed a canopy. "You're being very mysterious."

He stopped cold, pulled her to him, and laid the most electrifying, thigh-clenching kiss on her that had her body humming like a teakettle. His tongue—lots of tongue—commanded her. His hands conquered her. When her toes curled at the tips of her hiking boots, she sighed like she was surrendering.

In a way, she was, because she could no longer deny how much he meant to her.

When he broke the kiss, he let his lips linger over hers. "Mysterious would involve a blindfold."

Her sharp intake of breath communicated her surprise.

He chuckled against her mouth. "And whipped cream."

A shiver raked through her, communicating her curiosity.

Which egged on his sensual teasing even more.

"And maybe a black lace thong and stiletto heels." He nipped at her bottom lip. His teeth closed around her bottom lip with just enough pressure to make her gasp.

"That . . . sounds . . ." Her voice was small and wispy as his tongue moved to her neck, suckling and nipping. "Interesting," she finally finished between pants. "But not that mysterious."

"The mystery is in the whipped cream and where on your body I'd put it, since you'd be blindfolded." He swatted her on the rump. "Come on. We're almost there."

With his erotic needling session over, he grabbed her hand again, and they followed the dirt trail until it ended at a KEEP OUT sign hanging across the path by a single chain. He held up the chain so she could pass under. "Watch your step. It's muddy from the last storm." He crossed under the chain and dropped it back into place.

They followed the trail until a copse of maple trees came into view.

Mystery solved. She knew where he was taking her, and she pulled him to a stop. "Elliott, are you sure you want to do this?" In high school, he'd avoided the cove where his mom had drowned like it was a toxic waste dump.

"I'm sure." He tugged on her hand, and they cleared the trees. The landscape opened up into a sandy beachhead that gently sloped to the water.

Not one muscle in his tall frame so much as twitched. His expression blanked, then filled with sadness as he stared at the smooth water.

She came up behind him, her chest pressing into his back. Her chin rested on his shoulder. "It must've taken a lot of courage to come here."

When she slid her hand around to the front of his chest, he covered it with his. Drew her fingers to his lips to drop sweet kisses over the tips.

"I got that courage from you," he said so softly that she barely heard him. "Watching you. Seeing the amazing woman you've become. Your grit convinced me to stop hiding from my past too."

He turned and pulled her against his chest. "Until a few months ago, I hadn't been here since I was a kid. There was an incident with Ben and his duck. I realized then that I'd have to deal with my mom's accident eventually. It's time." His warm breaths washed over her face, heating her against the cool early-autumn air. "I wanted you with me."

She went up on her toes and kissed him with the gentleness and love she felt in her heart. "Thank you for letting me be with you. It would've broken my heart for you to do this alone."

"Really? Because I've been alone for a long time, Rebel." He leaned his forehead against hers. "Ever since you left." He caressed an open palm over her hair. "Until lately. When you and Rem and Bogart aren't with me, I miss you. It's like part of me is gone when you're not around."

"Oh, Elliott," she whispered, snaking her arms around his head to pull him into the notch of her neck. "You've always owned a piece of my heart." And he always would, even though his career stood between them. She leaned back and gave him a lusty look. "You've officially passed the hot test, by the way."

He gave her a teasing frown. "That's all it took? I've wasted a lot of valuable time trying to wow you with my brainiac routine and all the window-shattering orgasms."

She tilted her head. "I see your ego has surpassed your massive IQ."

He placed the edge of his index finger under her chin and tipped her face up to his. Seriousness replaced his playful expression. He filled his lungs with fresh air like he was gathering courage. "It's my fault my mom died. And I was too chickenshit to tell anyone the truth."

Rebel's lips parted, because of all the things Elliott could've said, that was the last thing she'd expected. It would seem she wasn't the only one who'd been harboring a deep, dark secret.

She cradled his head with both hands, and he buried his face in the nook of her neck.

"Tell me, babe," she whispered against his ear.

He took her hand again and led her to an old dried-out log that had fallen on its side. He shook out the blanket and laid it on the sand so they could sit, using the log as a backrest. They snuggled together with her nestled into his side. With one arm circling her shoulders, he brushed a thumb back and forth across the back of her hand as it rested in his lap.

"I was jealous that Trace and Dad went on a campout without me. A friend of mine called and said his dad had taken him out fishing on the south side of the island around Devil's Point. That's not too far from here, and the steelheads were biting." He hesitated as though to keep his emotions in check.

Rebel rested her cheek against his shoulder, the rhythmic rise and fall of his labored breaths telling her how difficult this was for him.

"I wanted to have a trophy to rub in Trace's face when he and Dad got home from the campout." Elliott let out a hollow laugh. "Childish, right?"

She molded her palm against his cheek and turned his face to hers. "You *were* a child, Elliott. You shouldn't beat yourself up over acting your age."

Rebel wished she could've acted like a child when she really was a kid. Instead, she'd had to be the adult as soon as she started walking and talking because of her mother's irresponsibility.

"Most children aren't selfish enough to cause a parent's death." His voice cracked, and he took a moment to regroup. "I told Mom I wanted to go fishing. She said no because a storm was rolling in." He kept stroking the back of her hand, staring out over the cove. "I snuck down to the boathouse and got a life vest." He pointed to an old oak to the left. "I dragged one of the small rowboats here so she wouldn't see me launch from the dock, but Spence ratted me out." He shook his head and sighed with sorrow. "*He* was mad because I wouldn't let him go with me. How fucked up are we?"

"Oh, Elliott." Rebel snuggled closer.

"Mom caught me just as I was pushing off, but I refused to pull the boat out of the water. She said the storm might sweep over the island quicker than expected, and we couldn't risk it." He scrubbed a hand down his face. "I threw a pity party and wouldn't get out of the boat." He bent a knee and draped an arm over it. "Mom made Spence stay ashore, but she waded out to the boat in waist-deep water and climbed in because she didn't want me going out alone. When we were alone, I accused her of not loving me as much as she did my brothers. Trace was the oldest and most responsible. Spence was the youngest and needed more of her attention. I was the middle child, constantly squeezed out of the limelight." With a thumbnail, he traced an imaginary line along the center of his pant leg. "I guilted her into going out on the water with me when I knew it was dangerous. Essentially, I killed her." His voice cracked.

Rebel closed her eyes against the heartache in his words because she knew what was coming. She molded both of her hands around his.

"Mom was right. The storm rolled in quicker than expected, and our little boat didn't stand a chance. We started taking on water." His words were strangled. "I paddled as fast as I could, but the wind blew us against the far bank." He nodded in the direction of the cove. "The boat broke up, and Mom didn't have a life jacket. She yelled at me to swim for shore. She kept yelling for me to keep going and not look back."

Rebel placed a hand over his chest, and his heartbeat hammered into her palm.

"So I did what she said." His voice was gravelly and strained. "I made it to shore, and she didn't. And I never told anyone she drowned because I was throwing a childish tantrum."

Rebel moved onto his lap, showering his face and neck with gentle kisses. "I'm so sorry you've had to keep it bottled up for so long." A feeling Rebel knew far too well. "No child should have to live with that." She wanted to tell him it wasn't his fault, that it was an accident, but she knew he wouldn't accept it.

She also wanted to tell him she'd move to San Francisco just to be with him, if that was what he wanted. She'd take the long hours alone and the empty apartment if he promised to always come home to her bed and no one else's. But she had nothing to offer him in return. At least nothing that would help his career.

A woman who was usually covered in dog hair and ate like the homeless person she'd once been didn't exude the image of a partner's wife.

Wrapping her arms around him, she held him for a long time. When he smoothed both hands up her back, she smothered his mouth with a hot and heavy kiss. Before she knew what was happening, he'd tugged her pants down, so she toed off her shoes. She got up just long enough for him to shuck his shoes and jeans too. He pulled her back down onto his lap so she straddled him.

"Can you handle the cold?" She lifted a brow, glancing down to where their bodies connected.

"Baby, things are about to get so hot you won't notice that you're bare-ass naked in this weather." He took off his knit cap and pulled it onto her head to cover her ears. "But since I'm a gentleman and all, I'll give you my hat."

He grabbed his pants to search the pockets for a condom. As soon as he was covered, he eased two fingers between them.

"Jesus," he hissed. "You're already so wet."

Slowly, she unzipped her jacket, then went to work on the buttons of her shirt. "I get excited just looking at you."

He let his head fall back to rest against the log and enjoyed the show.

When her shirt fell open, exposing a pale-yellow satin bra, he moaned and sat up to kiss her tingling flesh.

"Elliott," she whispered. "I do need your help with something."

"Anything, baby," he said. "Just as soon as I make you orgasm."

She gasped when his hot mouth closed around a nipple, and he suckled.

She lifted, then eased down onto him, his hard shaft filling her so completely. So perfectly. She shimmied and shuddered, which made him groan.

He grasped her hips and moved her up and down, grinding into her.

She rode him fast and hard, with him guiding her hips until they both climaxed, and she collapsed against his chest.

Their heartbeats intertwined and intermingled, finally slowing.

She wrapped both arms around his head. "I love being with you like this."

"Then let's find a way to stay together," he murmured against her neck.

A strange sound roared to life inside her head, ringing in her ears. It was the snipity snap of her self-control. The crisp crackle of her composure. The pop, pop, pop of her perseverance. It was like the secret she'd harbored had kept her closed off and feeling as alone as she'd felt on the streets. Not anymore. Not after Elliott had just trusted her with his heart.

"Will you come into town with me after we finish the next session with the campers?" she asked.

He nodded. "Of course. What's going on in town?"

"I need to go see the Morgans." She sighed. "That's what I need help with." She'd put it off long enough. Unfortunately, it was time.

Chapter Nineteen

#Adorbs

After the afternoon training session, the service dogs needed a break as much as Rebel did. So she gave the campers the rest of the evening to bond, doing whatever they wanted.

"Thanks for going with me," she said to Elliott as he veered around a big puddle still there from the last storm. Unfortunately, her evening break wouldn't be as relaxing as the campers' time off would be, since her destination was Morgan's Market. "It was a good time to take a break, because when service dogs train as hard as we've been training, they get mentally exhausted and they need downtime just like humans. I mean, we all need downtime, right? Because—"

Elliott reached across the console and gave her thigh a reassuring squeeze. "I'm going to be with you the whole time, baby."

Right. She was rambling again.

His thumb stroked her thigh.

Ladyland sighed at the safety she felt from his touch.

"I couldn't have faced Dan's parents by myself." She covered Elliott's hand with hers. "Especially since I left Rem with Jax because he's depressed without Bogart around."

"Do you think Rem's getting sick?" The concern in Elliott's voice was unmistakable. And adorable.

If she had to caption a photo of him and the dogs with a hashtag for her Instagram account, it would be #adorbs.

It made her fall a little more in love with him.

Because she did love him.

She always had.

When he glanced at her expectantly, she realized she hadn't answered his question and was staring. Memorizing. Because even though he wanted to find a way to stay together, she didn't see how it could work. He was a highly educated, successful businessman with a prestigious position.

She was a dog trainer who couldn't walk in a pair of party heels if her life depended on it.

And he'd mentioned how image and entertaining clients was a big part of making his career successful.

"Rebel?" Elliott squeezed her thigh. "Do you think Rem is coming down with kennel cough?"

"Um . . ." She shook her head. "No, he's been vaccinated. I think he's grieving because he misses Bogart."

"I miss him too. He's like my family now. Rem too. And you." Elliott let his gaze smooth over her face for a second before returning it to the road. It made her squirm with guilt all over again.

She swallowed. "Remember why we're going to see the Morgans." She needed to prepare him for the eventual separation. Handlers went through the same thing every time they had to relinquish a dog they'd been training for months or even years. It was hard, but it was part of the job. "We're going to offer Bogart to Dan."

Elliott stared straight ahead without replying.

Oh boy.

This from a man who couldn't stand dogs just a few weeks ago. She was used to the relinquishing part. Elliott was brand new to it.

When they pulled up along the curb in front of Morgan's Market, the sunlight had all but disappeared. He killed the engine and reached into the back seat to retrieve the umbrella Dan had loaned them the morning she'd jogged into town. "I'll return this while we're here. Ready?"

She shook her head. "No. I don't think I can do this." She still wasn't sure what she was going to say. After she offered Dan a potential service dog, she wasn't sure she could tell them the reason she wanted to help.

"You're the strongest person I've ever met. I know you can do it." He smoothed the backs of his fingers over her jaw. "Just start with Bogart, then go with your heart."

She nibbled the inside corner of her mouth. "It's now or never. Let's go."

They got out and waited for a car to pass, its high beams stabbing into her eyes. Then they trotted across the road to the market's storefront where the lights lit the window. Elliott turned the old brass doorknob and opened the door, the bell overhead jingling.

When Rebel stepped inside, a teenage girl was checking out a customer at the register. The old-fashioned register beeped with each keystroke.

Elliott stepped over to her. "Are any of the Morgans here?"

The teenager smacked a wad of gum and blushed, obviously shy because Elliott was such a hottie.

Rebel couldn't disagree.

The gum-smacking teenybopper pointed to the rear of the store. "Mr. Morgan is in the back."

Elliott laced his fingers with Rebel's. "Come on. You're not alone, okay?"

She nodded, a burn starting in her stomach and spiraling outward to every limb.

Elliott led her down the center aisle. At the back of the store, he used a knuckle to rap against the door that was marked PRIVATE.

A whistling Mr. Morgan opened the door. Instead of aging ten years since she'd last seen him, he'd aged twenty-five.

Rebel couldn't help but wonder how much of that was due to his son's accident.

"Hi, Mr. Morgan," Elliott said. "I don't know if you remember us, but I'm Elliott Remington and this is Rebel Tate."

"Yes, yes." Recognition dawned in Mr. Morgan's eyes. "You kids are all grown up now."

"Yes, sir." Elliott squeezed her hand. Then he held out the umbrella. "I need to return this. Do you have time to talk?"

Taking the umbrella, Mr. Morgan nodded and waved them into his small office. He sat at a tiny writing desk that was shoved up against the wall and cluttered with stacks of bills. He took the chair in front of the desk and swiveled it toward a small sofa. "Have a seat."

She let go of Elliott's hand and perched on the edge of the love seat. Elliott sat next to her, one elbow braced against his knee, the other arm resting behind her.

He gently stroked her lower back.

How did he know that was what she needed? Her racing pulse calmed at his touch.

"What can I do for you?" Mr. Morgan asked.

Rebel couldn't untie her tongue.

"Sir," Elliott started.

"It's about Danny," she finally blurted. "I, um, mean Dan."

Mr. Morgan frowned. "I thought you might be here about your mom's outstanding bill." He scratched his balding head. "What could you possibly want with my son?"

She shot an uncertain look at Elliott. "Um, my mom has an outstanding bill?"

Mr. Morgan got up and shuffled through a metal ledger box that had to be from the sixties. He pulled out a tab and handed it to Rebel. "One of the biggest tabs I've ever let accumulate at the store." He gave her a sympathetic look. "I allowed it because she had a daughter to feed."

"Oh . . ." Rebel's lungs locked.

Elliott extracted it from her fingertips. "We'll make sure it's paid as soon as we can."

What she wouldn't give for this visit to be as simple as an unpaid bill. "Um, Mr. Morgan, I understand Dan has a brain injury." She laced her fingers in her lap, and one thumb furiously rubbed the other as she returned to the point of her unfortunate visit that had been a decade in the making.

Mr. Morgan's curious expression turned grim, and he took off his reading glasses. "Yes, he does."

"U-um . . ." she stammered, searching for the right words. "Well, I'm a dog whisperer who specializes in training and pairing service dogs with people who suffer from PTSD and traumatic brain injury."

His expression turned back to curiosity again.

It wasn't much, but she'd take it. She squared her shoulders. "I was wondering if Dan might be interested in a service dog. It's a big commitment, but I'd be happy to get him started with a dog we got from—"

"Actually, the dog we have for him may not be a good match after all," Elliott said like he was the expert. He gave her a knowing look. "I think Bogart might be better off paired with Rem."

Of course he would. Why hadn't she seen it? Rem hadn't been jumpy or hard to manage since he'd bonded with Bogart. They were the perfect match.

And Mr. Dogs Hate Me who had zero experience until a few weeks ago had been the one to see it.

She gave him a smile that said she understood.

Then she returned her attention to Mr. Morgan. "We're up to our elbows in a service dog camp at the resort. If you think Dan might be interested, bring him by the Remington this week to observe. When our camp is over, I'd be happy to help him find a dog"—she would love to train the pair herself, but she wouldn't be around—"and a trainer close by who can work with them."

Mr. Morgan breathed in, tapping his glasses against his knee. "We don't have any pets. Mostly because we've got our hands full taking care of Dan and running the store."

"There would be some responsibility involved, of course, but a service dog would relieve some of your load when it comes to looking after your son. And he could easily learn to feed and bathe the dog himself," she said.

Mr. Morgan scrunched his lips like he was considering the proposal. "Sounds interesting. Let me talk to my wife." He tilted his head. "But why? What made you think of Dan?"

Her heart hammered against her chest so hard and fast that she was sure Elliott and Mr. Morgan could hear it.

She went to tuck a strand of hair behind an ear, only to realize her hand was trembling.

She clamped it to her thigh, and Elliott covered it with his. His touch steadied her nerves just like Rem did.

She took a deep, calming breath.

"Because I . . . I . . ." *I know who did this to your son. I've known all along and was too chicken to say anything. And I still am.* "I saw him not long ago when he was cleaning the front window. That's when he loaned us the umbrella. I just thought a service dog might help with his . . . condition . . ."

Elliott's hand tightened around hers.

"Think about it, and let us know what you and Mrs. Morgan decide," Rebel said, losing her nerve to go any further. "It couldn't hurt to bring Dan by the camp to check it out."

She stood, which cued Elliott to do the same.

"Thanks for your time, Mr. Morgan." Elliott rubbed his chin. "I know it's probably hard to talk about, but do you mind if I ask a question about Dan's accident?"

What? Rebel stiffened.

Mr. Morgan's face fell, his expression going grim again. "Go ahead."

"Where did Dan's accident happen?" Elliott asked.

Mr. Morgan's brows bunched. "On Sunrise Road."

Rebel froze.

"It was Sunrise Road and not Sunset Road?" Elliott pressed.

"Yes, why?" Mr. Morgan asked.

"Oh, just curious." Elliott waved a hand in the air. "I heard someone talking about it the other day, and I thought they might have the details mixed up. And if it's not too painful for you to talk about, can I ask what time Dan's accident occurred?"

Mr. Morgan scratched his temple. "We found him in the evening. Because the bruising hadn't fully formed, the doctors estimated he was hit sometime that afternoon."

Rebel's mind raced. Not only had her mom woken up in a ditch on *Sunset* Road, but she'd come home before noon that day. There was no way her mom could've hit Dan.

"I'm sorry." She put one hand on her stomach and covered her mouth with the other. "I'm not feeling well. I need some air."

She didn't wait for Elliott. Didn't say goodbye before rushing from the room. As soon as she stepped onto the sidewalk, she sagged against the brick storefront and bent over, putting her hands against her knees to gasp for air.

The doorbell tinkled again, and Elliott's shoes appeared on the sidewalk directly in front of her.

"You okay?" he asked.

"No," she wheezed. "All this time—" She choked.

"Hey." Elliott pulled her upright and into his arms. "Now you know. It's over."

She let out a sob, pouring out the years of pent-up misery. "How did you know to ask?"

"It was just a hunch." He stroked her hair. "When you told me your mom's story, it didn't make sense. Dan was little and on a bike. I wanted to find out why he would've been on Sunset Road because it's so far from where he lives."

"But my mom's car was dented," she said, still unable to process that she'd believed the worst for so long. And her mother had gone to her grave thinking she was responsible for Dan Morgan's accident.

"Maybe she hit an animal." He shrugged. "At least we know she didn't hit Dan. Today didn't give the Morgans any closure, but it helped you. I'm thankful for that."

She framed his face with her hands. "I'll still help Dan, because that's what I do. It might be over for me, but it will never be over for him."

He smiled down at her with the warmest smile. "That's why I . . . I . . ."

Her breath hitched as she waited for him to finish. To say the three little words that she wouldn't likely be able to walk away from again.

He glanced down the street. "That's why I think what you do is so special."

Her chest deflated when she let out the breath she was holding. She should be relieved.

Instead, she was disappointed.

"I don't want to go back to the resort yet," she said. "I've been avoiding this town because of my mother, but I don't have to do that anymore. We've got the night off. Let's enjoy it."

"The stacks of unpaid bills on Mr. Morgan's desk gave me an idea." He brushed her hair back, changing the subject. "Want to tag along while I try to plant a seed that will help the island?" He glanced around the boulevard like maybe he was taking it in for the last time. "It'll be my way of contributing to Angel Fire Falls before I leave."

"Sure," she said, her voice just above a whisper. Her relief from finding out her mother hadn't caused Dan's brain injury evaporated like mist. Her time with Elliott was drawing ever closer to the end, and she still didn't have any more to offer him than she had the day she'd sailed away on the ferry.

When they left the island, they'd still be on the same coast. Unfortunately, the lives they were each going back to might as well be on separate continents, and Rebel didn't see any way to bridge that gap.

For the first time in her adult life, she was finally free to fully open herself up and build relationships, friendships. Free to open herself up to love.

Yet she felt more isolated and alone than ever.

Standing on the sidewalk outside of Morgan's Market, Elliott typed in an SOS text to both of his brothers and Charley. He couldn't tell them why, but Rebel needed family to rally around her, and the ragtag bunch of Remington yahoos was all she had.

She'd just been released from ten years of hellish agony and needed people around her to share the moment.

He'd been so caught up in the moment that he'd almost told Rebel how he felt about her. But her eyes had widened in fear, so he'd backed off.

His phone dinged three times in quick succession, and he smiled at the screen. His family always came through.

"The fam is meeting us at the Fallen Angel." He stuffed his phone into his pocket and laced his fingers with Rebel's. "They'll be here shortly. Let's celebrate your victory, and I can do a little community outreach of my own for the island at the same time."

"Why is your family joining us?" Rebel asked as they crossed the street.

"Because that's what families do." Too bad he wasn't going to be as reliable as they were once he moved away.

Heartburn gurgled in his chest.

"Oh." Her chin quivered.

They ducked into the Fallen Angel, entering through the glass door on Marina Boulevard. The door led to a set of dark wood stairs that descended into a basement, and retro rock-and-roll music played in the background as they occupied two barstools at the corner of the long bar.

Elliott draped his arm around the back of her stool.

It was still early evening, so the place was virtually empty.

"Hey." Mason, a friend from high school and the most recent owner of the Fallen Angel, came out of the storage room and took up his usual position behind the bar. "Rebel Tate?" He looked surprised when his eyes landed on her.

"That would be me." She fiddled with a napkin, folding and unfolding it. "Good to see you again. You don't look a day older than you did in high school."

Elliott hadn't thought about it, but she was right. Mason's black hair and gray eyes still gave him a boyish look.

"What brings you back to the island after all these years?" Mason asked.

"Work," she blurted.

Mason's stare volleyed from her to Elliott, then back again. "Welcome to my establishment. Beer?"

"Water for me." She kept folding the napkin.

"I'll take a beer," Elliott said.

When Mason stepped away to fill their order, Elliott leaned over to Rebel and said, "What's wrong?"

She lifted a shoulder. "I . . . This was my mom's regular hangout. She came home drunk every single night from here."

Elliott swallowed hard. He hadn't considered what this place represented to Rebel and had delivered her from one hell right into another. "I'm sorry. Let's go." He started to get up.

"No." Rebel grabbed his arm and pulled him back down onto the stool. "I'm done running because of my mother's mistakes. Let's stay. It's a different place now with new owners."

He slid his arm around the back of her seat again and caressed her shoulder. "You're amazing." He'd spent most of his life avoiding the cove because of the horrible memories. But Rebel didn't just face her fears. She barreled through them like a charging bull.

They shot the breeze with Mason until the rest of the Remington clan arrived. Trace slapped Elliott on the back as he and Lily took a seat to his left. Spence took the barstool on the corner next to Rebel.

Charley finally sat next to Spence. "I dragged Briley along. Since we're business partners, she might as well be family too." Briley stayed quiet and took the seat on the end.

"What are we celebrating?" Spence held up a finger, code for Mason to pour him a beer.

Mason hadn't looked away from Charley since she stepped inside.

To get Mason's attention in the most smart-ass way possible, Spence snapped his fingers. "Keep 'em coming, because asshat over there is paying." He hitched a thumb at Elliott.

"Gladly, because we're celebrating Rebel." He lifted his glass.

Her eyes grew wide.

"And all the great things that have happened since she's been home," Elliott finished.

Charley raised her glass. "Congratulations, Rebel. It's good to have you back home again."

If that wasn't proof that the Remingtons had welcomed Rebel back into their lives, Elliott didn't know what was.

Briley and Mason toasted her too. So did Trace and Spence, but they did with the biggest smart-ass grins on their faces as they both stared at Elliott and gave the code for *You're whipped.*

He ignored them and focused on Rebel. Her incessant napkin-folding had stopped, but she was still stiff as a two-by-four. He smoothed a comforting thumb against her back.

She seemed to relax a little more but stayed quiet while the rest of them chatted and drank, Mason joining in the conversation mostly when Charley was doing the talking.

When the conversation lulled, Elliott decided to bring up his idea. "We're all in business here on the island." He may not be staying much longer, but he could make as many strides toward prosperity as possible for the island before he left.

He angled his chair toward Rebel so his knee pressed into her thigh. He needed a comforting touch as much as she did.

"*And*, Thing One?" Trace prompted him to continue.

"I . . . I . . ." *Fuck.* He pushed aside his guilty conscience and kept going. "Well, I have a couple of ideas."

Spence drummed his fingers against the bar. "Hit us with them. As much as it pains me to admit it, your business ideas are usually good."

"Well." Elliott rubbed his chin. "What if the resort, every restaurant, and every establishment that serves food on the island collected up their leftovers and Trace delivered them to the homeless shelter on the Cape during his first morning run each day?"

Slowly, Rebel turned an awed look on him. The wetness shimmering in her eyes made him want to hold her. Kiss her.

"That's a fantastic idea," Charley said. "We spend so much more having our food supplies shipped to the island than restaurants on the mainland, and it bothers me when our leftovers go to waste."

"Hear, hear!" Mason fist-bumped Charley, who blushed. "It would be great PR for the island, and we'd be helping people in the process."

"One problem solved." Elliott unhooked his stare from Rebel's before he got choked up too. "How 'bout forming a coalition so island business owners have more leverage and bargaining power?"

Everyone went quiet, listening.

"If they organized and ordered from the same vendors and suppliers, they could negotiate better prices." He stressed the word *they*, since he wouldn't be included in the venture.

Mason seemed impressed. "Sounds like a great idea."

"I'm in." Charley held up her glass. "Briley, give them the short version of our new business plan."

Briley looked uncomfortable. When she finally looked up, her eyes darted to Spence, then cut away just as quickly. *Ah.* Little brother either wasn't aware of Briley's interest, or he wasn't telling Elliott everything.

"Charley and I are working on a long-term plan to expand our menu, so we need to cut costs without cutting quality." Briley spoke to everyone, making eye contact with everyone except Spence.

"Then we need someone to take charge, and I was thinking . . ." Elliott zeroed in on Mason. "Mason, you'd be a good choice."

Before Mason could respond, Trace spoke up. "No offense to Mason, but this gig is perfect for you, Thing One." He leaned around Elliott and looked at Rebel. "What do you think, Rebel?"

All heads turned to her, putting her square in the spotlight.

"I . . ." She stared down at her folded hands, picking her words carefully, obviously not wanting to give up his secret. "Elliott makes solid business decisions, so I trust his judgment if he thinks Mason should take charge. As long as he's doing what makes him happy, I'm all for it."

What makes him happy? Good question. One he'd been asking himself a lot lately.

And for the life of him, he wasn't so sure of the answer anymore.

Chapter Twenty

#DejaVuIsABitch

After two more days of hard work with the campers and two late nights in bed, Rebel pushed Elliott out of the shower when he tried to get in with her.

"We're late. The campers are waiting for us." She shut the shower door and squirted soap into her palm.

"I had Charley send coffee and doughnuts over to the garage. They'll be fine," Elliott said. "We'll get there quicker if we shower together."

Rebel lathered up her body, then cracked the shower door. She didn't say a word. Just let his smoky, lust-filled gaze drift over her soapy skin.

She lifted a brow. "That's my point." She closed the door again.

Elliott grabbed it before it shut. He rolled it open, pulled her into a kiss that turned the insides of her eyelids white while he massaged one sudsy breast into an aching mound, then smacked her bottom with an open palm and stepped away.

"I'll go to Spence's and shower." Elliott—in all of his six-feet-plus alpha glory—actually sounded pouty.

Which caused a wonderful flutter to take flight in her stomach.

She was in love.

Head over heels, one hundred percent, crazy in love. Okay, she'd never stopped loving Elliott, but that love had grown deeper until she couldn't imagine a life without him.

How was she going to pick up the pieces of her heart and move on once she went back to Portland and he went back to San Francisco? They might be living on the same coast, but their worlds were in separate universes, and there was no way she could assimilate into his.

And after the way his family had warmed up to her, it was going to destroy her all over again to leave both Elliott and the rest of the Remingtons. So she'd started trying to put up emotional walls.

Like the veterans she worked with.

Impossible with Elliott's effort to feed the homeless as a veritable tribute to her.

She finished drying her hair and got dressed, just as a text dinged her phone. It was from Elliott.

Take your time. I texted Jax and he said the campers are busy helping him pick out a name for his dragonfly while they all scarf down doughnuts and coffee.

Rebel laughed out loud. A few weeks ago, Elliott would've smarted off by comparing the dragonfly's intelligence to Jax's. Now Elliott acted like a big brother.

She took Rem outside, leading him around to the back lawn so he had plenty of options to mark as his own. Then she headed for the back entrance that led into the kitchen.

She stopped. A whole new kind of pain vibrated through her.

The back entrance was for family.

Once upon a time, she'd been expected to use that entrance. Walking through that door was symbolic in so many ways that it made her heart fill with sadness.

She took a deep, satisfying breath and tugged it open. The delectable aroma of freshly baked sweets spilled out along with the clatter of pots and pans.

"Sit." She gave Rem the command to stay put just inside the back door.

"Hey!" Charley waved Rebel in.

She pulled out a stool at the counter where Charley was glazing a pan of doughnuts.

"Coffee? Doughnut?" Charley wiped her hands on a towel.

"Both. Your doughnuts could win a Nobel Peace Prize."

Charley dished up a doughnut and set a cup in front of Rebel, pouring liquid heaven into it.

"Oh. God." Rebel let the bold brew roll over her tongue.

"I'm the only restaurateur on the island who serves it. No one else can land a contract with the coffee company." Charley winked. "Helps to have connections. Plus, my family back in Seattle knows I'd organize picket lines in front of their building for the rest of eternity if they dared sell beans to anyone else in Angel Fire Falls." She went back to glazing.

"Do you miss Seattle?" Rebel let the cup hover at her lips.

"Sometimes, but I came here to get away from . . ." She paused. "Toxic people. I didn't think I'd stay on the island forever, but this opportunity opened up, and I took it. I'm definitely happier here than I was in Seattle."

Rebel swirled the caramel-colored liquid around in her cup, taking stock of what was waiting for her back in Portland. Besides a lot of acquaintances she couldn't really call friends because she'd kept them at arm's length for fear she'd accidentally say too much about her mother's accident, there wasn't much left in Portland. No toxic people making it easy for her to leave for good. No one at all, in fact.

The commercial property on sale for a rock-bottom price was the only pull Portland had on her. It was her one and only chance to open her own training facility. But the one and only chance she had at love wasn't in Portland.

"So how is it being back on the island?" Charley asked.

"It's been good." *Great, actually.* "I didn't realize how much I'd missed it." Or how much she'd missed Elliott.

"But you're still ready to go home as soon as the camp is over." It wasn't a question. Charley was sizing up the situation, obviously looking out for her cousin. She just didn't know that Elliott was just as ready to leave as Rebel.

Rebel's heart beat at an odd rhythm.

Truth was, she wasn't all that ready to leave Angel Fire Falls or the resort or the Remington family. And especially not Elliott. But she had to. There was no commercial training facility for sale on the island. No training facility at all, and she'd never be able to afford to build one herself. Even if she could come up with the money, Elliott wouldn't be on the island, so what would be the point?

"Be back in a sec. I need cinnamon and sugar." Charley tossed the hand towel over a shoulder and disappeared into the pantry.

Rebel picked up the doughnut and took a big, mouthwatering bite. And realized she'd literally bitten off more than she could chew. Her mouth was so stuffed that the warm chocolate smeared around her lips and dribbled down her chin.

She swiped at her mouth, which only smeared the warm glaze more. She stood and looked around for a napkin. A towel. Anything.

With the doughnut still in her hand, she hurried toward the shelves near the back door in search of something to wipe her mouth.

The door swung open, and Elliott stepped inside. With Mr. Collins right behind him.

She froze, doughnut in hand. Mouth full. Face chocolatey.

Dear Lord.

Elliott's expression blanked as he took her in.

She covered her mouth with the back of her free hand to offer a *morning* greeting. "Wourn-ing."

Awesome. She wasn't just a dog whisperer anymore. She could add Scooby-Doo imitations to her résumé.

Elliott's blank expression turned to worry, and Rem moved from his spot by the back door to lean heavily against Elliott's side.

He grabbed a roll of paper towels off the shelf, tore it open, and held up a few sheets. "Mr. Collins came in on the first ferry this morning."

She chewed, swallowed ten thousand calories of heaven, and snatched the paper towel from Elliott's fingers to wipe her mouth. "I, um, didn't realize you'd be here today, Mr. Collins."

"Obviously," Collins said flatly.

Déjà vu was an even bigger bitch than karma.

Charley reemerged from the pantry. "Hey."

"Charlotte, can you get Mr. Collins a cup of coffee and a pastry?" When any of the Remingtons called their cousin by her given name, it was serious.

Charley's hesitation was invisible to anyone who didn't know the Remingtons. She waved Collins to the stool Rebel had just vacated. "Have a seat, Mr. Collins."

"We'll be right back." Elliott took Rebel's elbow and all but hauled her outside.

Rem followed, getting more agitated.

As soon as the back door swung shut, Elliott said, "I fucked up."

"What happened? You're scaring me." The shrill tone in her voice made Rem whine. Honestly, she was surprised the dog wasn't the only one who could hear the high pitch.

Elliott pinched the bridge of his nose. "I invited Collins. The camp was going so well, I thought it would be a good time to start doing interviews." He jammed his hands in his pockets and wouldn't look at her. "I wanted him to see us . . ." He closed his eyes. "I wanted him to see you working with the campers in person."

"Good idea." She bent to look up at Elliott, making him meet her gaze. "And?"

"After I got dressed at Spence's, I stopped in at the garage. Collins was there with a couple of journalists who have cameras." He rubbed his jaw as though what he was about to say was painful. "Several of the dogs aren't feeling well."

Oh no. No, no, no, no, NO!

Collins showing up was one thing. But pictures and videos didn't lie, and this wasn't going to end well.

She took off at a dead run for the garage.

Elliott's dad was from the generation who didn't keep a cell attached at the hip. So Elliott sent an SOS text to his brothers and Lily asking them to find Dad to help with damage control ASAP. Then he stuck his head in the door and told Collins to meet him at the garage when he'd finished breakfast. Elliott didn't wait for him. He wanted to get to Rebel so she wouldn't have to face the cameras alone.

When he got to the garage, a few of the veterans loitered out front with their dogs, which seemed fine.

Elliott found everyone else inside. Rebel knelt in front of Simba, feeling his nose. "When did this start?"

"He wasn't his usual chipper self this morning, but he didn't seem that bad until a half hour ago," the veteran said.

She lay flat on her stomach, eye level with Simba. He wouldn't lift his head.

Just as Collins walked in, she moved on to Harley. Same thing. As she moved to the next sick service dog, one of the reporters motioned to her cameraman to roll tape by twirling her finger in a circle.

Collins crossed his arms and stewed.

Quietly, Elliott stepped in front of the camera, blocking its view of Rebel. "This is private property, so I'm afraid you're going to have to wait outside until we're ready."

When they didn't budge but glanced at Collins, Elliott said, "Or you can leave the premises entirely. Your choice." His voice was low and lethal. He didn't particularly care about impressing Collins or Down Home Dog Food at the moment. Call him a caveman, but his biggest concern was protecting his woman.

Reluctantly, the journalists and their crews obliged.

Elliott stayed right on their heels to escort them to the door. Only to run headlong into Mick and a woman Elliott didn't recognize. She was dressed like a runway model and had the figure of a pinup centerfold. Mick's usual since he'd sworn off marriage and was still making three different alimony payments.

Here they all were. How nice.

"What are you doing here?" Elliott said to Mick through gritted teeth.

"Nice to see you too after all these months," Mick said. "This is Candy."

She gave Elliott an airy smile that said her body might be a twelve and a half but her brain was much less impressive. Then she offered her hand to Elliott for a shake. When he tried to let go, her grasp linger a fraction longer than appropriate.

Of course her name was Candy. What else would it be?

Mick leaned in. "You said a potential big client would be here, so I came to make sure you don't lose your spot at the firm by helping you close this deal."

Blood pounded in Elliott's ears. "The firm is shorthanded, and you're here? You know damn good and well I can handle closing a client on my own."

"You're welcome, by the way." He lifted both eyebrows. "Your family's resort was all booked up. Must not be doing as poorly as you led me to believe. So a better question is, what are *you* still doing here?"

Before Elliott could explain that the resort was booked up *because* of the potential new client, his dad walked in. "What's up, son?"

Christ.

Mick introduced himself. "You must be Elliott's dad. I'm his boss."

His dad frowned and gave Elliott a questioning look.

Panic flashed through him. "Dad, I owe you an apology, but I'll have to explain later. Right now we've got a garage full of sick dogs. Can you call Dr. Shaw and ask if he'll make an emergency house call?" He turned to Mick. "Sit tight, and you'll get an explanation too." Elliott went to Rebel, who was prostrate on the floor in front of another dog. "Dad's calling Dr. Shaw."

Defeat dimmed her eyes, and he helped her to her feet. "I separated the dogs that seem fine and sent them outside. Maybe these didn't get vaccinated for Bordetella." She motioned to the lethargic canines lying around the garage.

Collins, obviously tired of waiting for answers, stalked over. "What's wrong with them?"

"Mr. Collins, do you have the dogs' shot records?" Rebel asked. "They were never forwarded to us."

"I have no idea where the shot records are," Collins huffed. "They were housed at a penitentiary, remember?"

Oh, Elliott remembered all right.

"What's wrong with them?" Collins snapped.

The tone in his voice as he spoke to Rebel made the hair on Elliott's arms stand up, and he eased closer to her.

"I think they're coming down with kennel cough," she said.

Collins looked down his nose at her like she was stupid. "None of them are coughing."

"Not yet," Rebel said. "But they will."

"How will this affect the camp?" Collins demanded. "We've got a lot of money invested in this event."

"I understand, sir." Rebel's voice was controlled, but a thread of desperation caused the slightest shake. "But the dogs will need to rest for several days while they're taking antibiotics. The boot camp was already on an intensive schedule that I would've never agreed to had I been the original trainer in charge." She gave Elliott an apologetic stare. "Now we'll need to push the campers' graduation date out at least a week. Or cancel it before we're finished, because the dogs won't be able to train until they're well."

Collins scoffed in a way that had the back of Elliott's neck prickling. "You told me the camp was going well." He glared at Elliott. "I came here with *reporters*."

"It *was* going well," Elliott said. "This is a new development."

"Then I'll need your word that you and the Remington will keep the camp going for as long as it takes, or it will be a disaster for all of us," Collins barked, his voice rising.

"Hold up." Mick joined them, obviously eavesdropping. "I need you back in San Francisco."

Mick's date glided over in her platform heels and wrapped a hand around his arm. "I'm Candy." She inserted herself into the conversation, obviously not having enough sense to know it wasn't the right time.

She smiled at Elliott. Then she offered her hand to Collins. When she did the same to Rebel, Candy's eyes roamed over Rebel's work clothes.

With an uncertain expression, Rebel reached out to take Candy's hand, who recoiled slightly. Candy shook with the tips of her manicured fingers like she was afraid to touch Rebel.

Then Candy brushed off her hand.

At Rebel's sharp intake of breath, Elliott fell silent. She looked over Candy's impeccable appearance, smoothing a palm over her hair. The tremor in Rebel's hand told him how self-conscious she was. When she looked down at her fleece jacket and jeans and her eyes widened in horror at the dog hair coating her front from lying prostrate while checking on the sick dogs, Elliott ground his teeth into dust.

"The Remington assured my company that your resort would deliver the results we were looking for," Collins huffed at Elliott. "I'm holding you personally responsible to see this through until those results are achieved."

Shit.

"I'm sure, as one of the best financial managers in the country, you have your reasons for spending valuable time on a dog show instead of watching the Dow like a hawk so you can actually do your job and make brilliant trades for our clients," Mick interrupted. "Meanwhile, we're bleeding accounts at a firm that you now own a share of, so you need to wrap this up and get back to work, or your partnership is history."

"We have a contract," Collins insisted.

"So do we." Mick's tone said he was ready to duel with his rival over Elliott like he wasn't standing right there.

"That's enough!" Elliott erupted. "First of all, this isn't a dog show—"

"Wait." Rebel's shaky plea got everyone's attention. "This is my fault. I took in a stray without asking about its health history. I didn't know he was sick until the symptoms started to surface several days ago."

Candy laughed for no apparent reason.

Fuck. "Jax," Elliott ground out, getting the attention of Jax, who was making his way to each dog. "Can you give Candy a personal tour of the grounds?"

Jax's eyes coasted over Candy. "Absolutely."

"And stop in to the dining hall. Anything you want is on the house, but our coffee and pastries are to die for," Elliott said.

"I don't eat carbs." Candy looked down her nose at Elliott this time.

Of course she didn't. "Then the water is on the house." Elliott couldn't help but smart off. "We'll even throw in a lemon wedge."

"Cool," Jax said and led her away.

Wow. Elliott returned his attention to the problem at hand.

"You mean to tell me you brought a stray around these highly skilled dogs that my company has invested tens of thousands of dollars in and spent two years training?" Collins said to Rebel.

Rebel chewed the corner of her mouth. "I'm solely responsible. Don't take it out on the Remington, Mr. Collins."

Collins shook his head. "I'm sorry, Ms. Tate, but you're fired."

What? Wait. "No, she's not," Elliott blurted.

The color draining from Rebel's face made Elliott's blood boil because of all she was about to lose. Her reputation, the camp, her training facility. Her life's work.

Collins didn't back down. "I have no choice. Headquarters will want someone's head."

So Collins was going to give them Rebel's, when he should be handing them his own.

"We'll compensate you for your time," Collins said to Rebel. "The amount we agreed upon will be wired to your account by the end of the day." He turned to Elliott. "Your hospitality director found Ms. Tate. She'll have to find a new trainer immediately, or I'm pulling the plug on the whole event."

"We're a team," Elliott said. "If Rebel goes, then so does the Rem—"

Rebel's hand closed around his bicep, quieting him. "The vets and the dogs need to finish the camp. So do you, so you can . . ." She leaned to the side as Candy followed Jax through the garage door, her eyes wandering over Candy's perfectly put-together appearance. "So we can both move on." Rebel smoothed a hand over her jacket, then crossed her arms as if to try to hide her work clothes. "Mr. Collins, I know a lot of quality trainers on the West Coast. I'll be happy to provide a list of names. I'm sure someone can step in right away."

"Rebel," Elliott whispered.

She fiddled with the zipper of her hair-coated jacket and shot another wary look at Candy's back as she disappeared with Jax. "Thank you for the opportunity, Mr. Collins. I'm sorry I let you down." Without another word, she walked out of the garage.

Chapter Twenty-One

#BestBadIdeaEver

Rebel managed to hold back the tears until she got to her room. But the second the door closed in her wake, they started to pour.

Rem stayed at her side, whining.

She'd ruined everything. For the veterans, for the service dogs, for the sponsor, for the resort. For herself. But mostly, she'd ruined things for Elliott.

Coming back to the island had to go down in the record book as the best bad idea ever. But reality had hit swift and hard when his boss showed up with a woman who looked like she belonged in Elliott's world, while Rebel looked like . . . a homeless person.

She dropped her head into her hands and bawled.

What made her the saddest was the fact that she and Elliott had become such a great team, working together so efficiently. In another life, they could've made a life together. But the routine they'd settled into on the island wasn't real. It was temporary.

And it was over, now that she'd been fired and his boss was threatening him with the same fate.

Well, she'd done him a favor ten years ago by disappearing. She'd do him another solid by walking away again so he could go back to the world where he belonged. A world that had nothing to do with clinging dog hair or handicapped strays or sleeping on garage floors.

Rebel sniffed, closing the security latch so Elliott couldn't get in, even if he used his master key. Pulling herself together, she got her bag out of the closet and started throwing things in haphazardly. When the closet was empty, she went to the dresser and scooped the clothes out in one armful to toss them into the suitcase.

The mechanical lock on the door activated, and she froze. The door clicked open but snagged on the security latch.

"Rebel," Elliott said through the crack.

She wasn't going to answer. She just couldn't.

She dropped the wad of clothes into the suitcase.

"Baby, open up."

Her head fell forward.

Slowly, she went to the door, pressing her forehead against the cool surface and flattening her hand against it as well. "Go away, Elliott." Her voice cracked when she spoke his lovely name. "I need to be alone."

"I'll sit here in the hallway until you come out. Swear to God, I will."

Oh, she believed him. If he'd crawl up the side of the building onto her balcony and risk breaking his neck in the process, he'd definitely sit outside her door all day and all night.

She couldn't face him. Not when she had to sneak away from him all over again.

She backed away from the door all the way to the balcony, threw open the door, and looked over the railing. She could toss her suitcase over and climb down herself, but how would she get Rem safely to the ground?

Think. THINK!

She stepped inside again, leaving the sliding door open, and clamped both splayed hands to her head. *Oh my God.* She was losing her mind.

She went to the entryway again and tried to steady her voice. "Elliott, go back to the camp and salvage what you can. I'll talk you through it until a replacement gets here." She was such a liar. "But right now, I need time to myself."

The door clicked shut.

Thank God.

She'd give him time to get back over to the garage, then sneak onto the shuttle. She was just thankful it was still early so she wouldn't miss the last ferry to Cape Celeste, where her car was stored in long-term parking. Then again, even if she did, she could sleep on a bench at the terminal. It was cold out, but at least she'd have a roof over her head, if not walls surrounding her. She'd certainly slept in worse conditions.

She took a seat at the desk and stared at the notepad that had THE REMINGTON inscribed along the top. It took her several minutes and a lot more tears, but she finally popped the top off the pen that matched the resort stationery.

Rem laid his head in her lap.

By the time she folded the paper in half and scribbled Elliott's name across the front, she'd cried an ocean. She pushed out of the chair and put the note in the center of the bed. The zipper of her suitcase whizzed as she closed it.

Glancing at the clock on the bedside table, she felt sure Elliott was back in the garage trying to sort out the mess she'd created.

Rem barked and ran onto the balcony.

Just as Elliott hoisted himself over the railing.

Both hands flew to her mouth, and she stilled, caught in the act of deserting him. Again.

His jaw shifted when he walked into the room, breathing heavily from the climb.

He took everything in. The suitcase, the empty open drawers.

The note on the bed with his name on it.

"Are you fucking kidding me?" Disbelief threaded through his voice. Betrayal etched across his face.

"Elliott." She couldn't hide the resignation in her voice. "I love you enough to let you go."

"Oh, right," he said on a hollow laugh. "You're thinking of *me* again." He slapped a palm to his forehead. "How stupid of me to miss that. What about Bogart? Did you think about him, or were you going to abandon him too?"

Shame blazed hot in her stomach. In her mind. In every cell of her body.

"You know what? Don't worry about him. I'll pick him up from Dr. Shaw's and take care of him."

"I've fought hard to survive things that no one should have to go through." She squared her shoulders. "I love you, but I deserve better than being looked down on by someone named Candy. I've earned the right not to feel bad about myself anymore, and the professional circles you move in aren't a good fit for me." She stiffened her resolve. "I'm also strong enough and smart enough to know when something isn't going to work. It's best for both of us if I go, Elliott." She moved toward him but stopped when he took a step back.

"You *are* strong and smart. Which is why I can't wrap my head around your decisions. You have no idea what's best for me." He headed to the door, stopping when he was even with her. "You never did."

She reached out and touched his arm. "Elliott—"

The scorn that flashed hot in his eyes, those beautiful eyes, nearly incinerated her on the spot. He pulled his arm from her touch, glancing at his watch. "Next shuttle leaves in fifteen." The scorching disdain in his tone finished her off, leaving her heart in a pile of ashes.

Then he was gone.

Chapter Twenty-Two

#YouKnowARelationshipIsOverWhen

The pain in Elliott's chest was his own damn fault for trusting the same person who'd ripped his heart out when he was a gullible teenager.

This time he'd handed Rebel the rusty knife.

Scratch that.

He'd handed her the rusty chainsaw. And then he'd turned it on for her so she could run him through.

He found his dad in the family den, finishing up a call to Dr. Shaw.

"He's on his way." His dad put down the receiver.

Elliott nodded. "Thanks." He pulled out a chair at the round table in the corner and angled another so he could face his dad head-on and explain that he wasn't on the island to stay. Something he should've done months ago. "Have a seat, Dad."

When they were both seated, Elliott leaned forward with his elbows braced against his knees. "Dad, I'm sorry, but I haven't been honest with you. I didn't come back home . . ." Elliott stumbled over the word. Because Angel Fire Falls *was* his home. Even after years of living elsewhere, the island was the only place where he'd felt relaxed and satisfied with life. It had taken Rebel and the comfortable, cozy routine they'd settled into for him to see it, but he loved being back at the resort with his family. "I never intended to stay on the island for good."

His dad nodded. "I figured as much."

Elliott's mind blanked.

Not what he expected his father to say.

Elliott cocked his head to the side. "You did? How? Why?"

His dad scratched his temple thoughtfully. "The packed suitcase at Spence's and you not moving into a cottage of your own were the first clues you weren't certain about your future here."

"Why didn't you say anything?" Elliott asked.

"I knew you'd bring it up when you were ready." His dad gave him a sly smile. "When you never did, I figured I'd take advantage of that brilliant noggin of yours for however long you were around. I might be getting old, but I'm not stupid. I know an opportunity when I see one." He tapped his temple with a forefinger. "Where do you think you got your brains?"

Elliott chuckled, then sobered. "Dad, I'm sorry. I should've spoken up when you decided to transfer ownership to us several months back. It's just that it meant so much to you to have us all home and running the resort. I never knew how to tell you I was leaving again. I kept waiting for the right time, but I guess I was just chickenshit."

His dad let a sad smile play at his lips. Then he drew in a deep breath. "I've loved every minute you've been here, but if you ever do come back to the island permanently, I'd want it to be for the right reasons. Because it's where you want to be, never because of me. Which brings me to my point. You're still not being honest. Don't you think it's time?"

Elliott fell back against the chair. "What do you mean?"

His dad drummed his fingers against the oak table and studied him. "Why *have* you stayed so long?"

Elliott stared at the floor. There was no easy way to say it. "The resort was in trouble. I felt I owed it to you and my brothers to pitch in and help breathe life into it again."

His dad's unrelenting stare told Elliott he wasn't getting off the hook so easily.

He drew air into his lungs for courage. "I'd already taken too much from you and from Spence and Trace. I couldn't have lived with myself if I'd gone back to San Francisco and this place went under."

His dad waited patiently with an expression that said he knew there was more.

The old guy was pretty damn keen.

Elliott's heart constricted, and he had to fight for each breath as he spoke. "Mom's accident was my fault. I guilted her into going out in the boat that day, and I didn't give her time to go back for a life jacket." He ran a hand across his forehead, swiping off the sweat beading over his skin. He told his dad everything, pouring out the regret and sorrow over what he'd caused that fateful day in the cove.

When Elliott was done, he laced his fingers and leaned forward again, trying to slow his heaving breaths.

His father's strong hand closed over Elliott's shoulder. "Son, in some ways you're so much like your mother. She was a risk-taker just like you. But you're also different, because you take the time to think things through. You assess the risk and weigh it against how much you could lose. That's what makes you so good at your job."

"I pushed Mom by being defiant. I was going out on the water whether she liked it or not, and she died because of it," Elliott said.

"You were a child. She was the parent." His dad squeezed his shoulder. "It was her job to count the cost of the risk that day. It was her responsibility to say no to you, and when you didn't come ashore, she should've called harbor patrol to go after you. Getting in the boat with you without a life jacket was foolish. There's not a day that goes by that I don't miss her, but I've never blamed you for the accident. I've never even blamed her, because it was an *accident*."

"An accident that was my fault." Elliott leaned back in his chair again. Memories of his mom splashing into the water to climb into the boat with him came flooding back, thickening his throat so he could barely swallow down the pain.

"Your mother did what she did because she loved you. Don't let that be for nothing, son."

Elliott stopped breathing for a second. His mother had loved him enough to follow him, regardless of the risk. He hadn't done the same for Rebel, letting her go far too quickly because of his wounded ego.

"Stop torturing yourself." His dad shook his head. "Your mother wouldn't have wanted that."

He *had* been living in torment since the day his mom died. His guilt was the reason he'd escaped to the opposite coast to go to college. It was the reason he'd rarely come home to visit once he started working in San Francisco.

It was the reason he was still running, immersing himself in a job that was slowly draining him of his soul.

"She would've wanted you to be happy." His dad smiled. "She would've wanted you to enjoy life and take a risk on love, the way she and I did. Lately, you've been the happiest I've seen you in years."

Rebel had been running away most of her life too. It was what they'd had in common. It was what had bound them together.

It was the reason she'd ditched him. Twice. But she'd done so because she'd been thinking of him.

His reasons for running away weren't as noble.

He'd been thinking of himself.

And he'd told her to get lost for thinking of him first.

Could he be a bigger idiot?

"I stayed to help the resort." Elliott took a fleeting look around the room, hovering on each of the watercolor island landscape paintings hanging on the walls. "Spence and Trace have so much more to offer this place. I'm kind of a one-trick pony around here. My business sense is the only tool in my tool belt, and I've managed to screw that up royally. The camp isn't working out."

His dad chuckled. "Son, this place is on the rise because of you and your savvy business skills. It was your idea to hire Lily."

True. But still . . .

"You've automated our financial management when I was still doing things old-school."

Yep. But—

"You've renegotiated contracts with our suppliers and budgeted our money so we can afford to upgrade the resort inside and out. And we've done it debt-free."

His dad's chest puffed out. "And I've been getting calls from the island's business owners who are old-timers like me. As the world around us has changed, they've been fighting for survival just like I was. They're damn excited to have a great business mind like yours helping them."

He lifted both brows. "They're saying something about an island business coalition that will save money? Sounds brilliant to me. How can you possibly think you don't have as much to offer the Remington?" His dad frowned. "The resort wouldn't have survived without you. And now you're spreading the love to the rest of Angel Fire Falls. No one else I know on this island has had that much to offer."

Every good business decision Elliott had made for the resort felt like a victory he'd fought and won for his family. He hadn't spent a lot of time slapping himself on the back for those hard-won victories. He'd still felt like a fraud because of the secrets he'd kept from his dad and brothers.

Truth be told, he'd felt more pride over his accomplishments at the resort than he ever had at his firm in California.

"Thanks, Dad." Elliott stood. "I've got a mess to deal with in the garage. And I've got a lot of decisions to make for my life. This time, I promise to keep you in the loop."

He was going to deal with Collins and Mick. But first, Elliott was going after the woman he loved.

◆ ◆ ◆

"A one-way ticket, please." Rebel stepped up to the ticket window with Rem at her side. The ferry terminal wasn't busy, since the tourist season was all but over, so there was no waiting. No scrambling for a spot on the small ferry that would take her back to the mainland so she could be on her way.

Nothing to stop her from leaving Angel Fire Falls. For good this time.

Sadness sliced through her to the bone.

After Elliott caught her trying to sneak away again, she'd made sure to be on the next shuttle departing the Remington. A person knew a relationship was over when one of them told the other to get lost on the next bus out of town.

Or when one left another Dear John letter instead of breaking things off in person.

He'd hate her forever.

She couldn't blame him.

But it had been the right thing to do because they both deserved better than an empty life together because of his job and her insecurities.

Mabel McGill's penciled brow slowly arched. "I thought you were going to be working on the island for a few more weeks?"

Rebel shifted her weight from one foot to the other. "It didn't work out, so I'm going home . . ." Portland didn't seem like home anymore. Honestly, it never really had. Fate had landed her there, and she'd stayed because of her circumstances. "I'm going back to Portland sooner than expected."

Mabel took her money and slid a ticket across the counter. "Need me to deliver any notes this time, hon?"

Ouch.

Mabel hadn't meant it as a slight, but saying it out loud made it so real. And so much more painful.

Rebel shook her head and picked up the ticket. "No need."

Her heart stuttered, and she swallowed back the burn in her throat.

Mabel studied her. "The ferry is delayed for a bit. Make yourself comfortable on one of the benches." She closed the window and picked up what looked like a handset for a two-way radio system. She pressed the button along the side of the device and spoke into it, turning her back to Rebel.

Back to feeling like it was her against the universe.

She settled onto a bench and snapped a picture of Rem. Then she uploaded it to Instagram with a caption that said *You're never truly alone with a service dog.*

She sighed heavily and turned to look out over the waves crashing against the rocky coastline. The cold breeze pitched the flags on the bicycles and giant trikes back and forth.

She'd likely never return to the island because she didn't have a reason to. But she couldn't lie. She'd take Bogart in all over again, even though the decision had cost her the camp, media coverage that might've attracted donors, and a future relationship with Down Home Dog Food. What kind of dog whisperer would she be if she hadn't been willing to take in a stray that desperately needed a family?

Now Bogart had one. The Remingtons looked out for their own, and she had no doubt they'd take great care of him now that he was one of the clan.

She got up and went back to the ticket window.

Mabel had put down the two-way and was on the phone. She held up a finger, finishing a conversation with a few inaudible sentences. When she hung up, she opened the window. "Can I help you, hon?"

"U-um," Rebel stumbled. "Dr. Shaw has Bogart. He's been sick, but he'll be fine." Rem pressed into her leg. "Elliott Remington is taking him in."

Without breaking eye contact, Mabel picked up a deck of cards and began to shuffle. "I see."

The zip of the cards made Rebel jump.

"He doesn't strike me as a dog person," Mabel said thoughtfully.

He hadn't been.

"I guess people can change if they have a reason to." Rebel gave her a timid smile. "Bogart won Elliott's heart."

The cards zipped and purred again. "Oh, I don't know if I'd give Bogart all the credit. He's a special little dog, but my guess is you did most of the winning over, which isn't easy when it comes to the Remington men. They're heartbreakers."

Rebel's heart was definitely splintered into bits, but she couldn't fault Elliott for that. "Well." She took a step back. "I just thought you should know."

She went back to holding down the bench and got out her phone.

She couldn't dwell on what might've been now any more than she could've the last time she'd left the island. The grief would swallow her whole.

Forward. She had to focus on moving her life forward. That strategy had gotten her through tough times in the past, and it would do the same now. Work and serving others through her new training facility would be her lifeline.

She pulled up the listing of the abandoned shelter and hit "Call" under the real-estate agent's number.

Another shuttle pulled up behind her, but she didn't turn around to look, focusing on the ringing phone line that would bring her to the next step in her life.

Her screwed-up, empty life.

She closed her eyes against the sting of hot tears.

When the agent answered, Rebel decided to take the plunge. Go all in because her career was all she had left.

She tried to clear the croakiness from her throat. "Hello, I'd . . . I'd like to make an off . . ." She hiccupped back a sob. "An offer on"—*hiccup*—"one of your listings."

"Don't do it, Rebel," Elliott said from behind her.

She spun around on the bench and dropped the phone. It skidded across the concrete floor.

He stooped to pick up her phone and held it to his ear. "Can you hold, please? It's a matter of life . . ." He didn't finish the sentence and took the phone from his ear. "It's a matter of our life together, so don't make the offer. Please."

"Why not?" She laced her fingers at her waist.

"Just don't. You don't belong in Portland."

"I don't belong anywhere else, Elliott." Her voice was a plea as she swiped away the wetness under her eyes.

"Sure you do." He took a small step toward her. "You belong with me."

She shook her head, quick and fast. "I'd be miserable in your world, and I'd hold you back." She looked down at the dog hair coating her front from lying on the floor to get eye level with the sick service dogs. "Look at me. If I was embarrassed around your boss and Candy, I can only imagine how you would feel. I wouldn't exactly fit in at your company Christmas party."

He took another step, bringing him close enough to touch if she just reached out.

But she didn't. She *wouldn't*, no matter how much her fingers ached to feel him. It would just make their goodbye even harder.

"Good, because I've never fit in at my company Christmas parties either." He smiled and took another step.

"I don't belong in your world, Elliott." She said it like it was a plea to get him to understand, because it was true.

"That's where you're wrong, baby." He took another step closer. "You *are* my world. Always have been." He closed the last few steps between them, laid her phone on the bench, and framed her face with his hands.

The shuttle lumbered over the hill and came to a stop in front of the terminal. The doors whistled as they opened, and out stepped Elliott's boss, his carbless date, and Mr. Collins. The camera crew stepped out next and waited while the scrawny kid who'd delivered Rebel to the steps of the Remington the day she arrived struggled with their equipment.

"Jesus, they're like a fungus that won't go away," Elliott mumbled.

"There you are," Collins said with a sniff, walking over with Mick and Candy on his heels. "I'm leaving and shutting down the camp."

Rebel couldn't take any more. "No, I'm leaving. That's what you wanted, so there's no reason for you to go."

"No one's going anywhere until I have my say." Elliott angled his body half in front of hers, like a protective shield. "Mr. Collins, with all due respect, you set our dog whisperer and our resort up to fail. We took this event on at the last minute. We found an outstanding trainer. She's done an amazing job with no experienced help at her back." Elliott let it all tumble out at once. "There's been little to no communication from your company. Ms. Tate didn't even know there wouldn't be handlers on-site, and she's still accomplished more than I thought possible."

"Elliott," Rebel whispered, touching his arm. "Don't."

Apparently, he'd lost his hearing without her knowing it, because her plea didn't faze him in the least.

"She did what any humane person with a heart would do, and she rescued a dog who has obviously been through hell, just like the veterans we're supposed to be helping." Elliott stepped back and put his arm around her. "Yes, it caused a problem for the camp, but frankly, it's just one more problem in a long string of problems that started with the way your company has handled this event. Down Home Dog Food didn't even make sure the dogs were vaccinated properly."

Collins's mouth opened, but then he shut it again.

"The camera crew came here for an interview. *We* can either tell them you're shutting the camp down because of poor management on your part . . ." The way Elliott stressed *we* was obviously to let Collins know the sponsor wouldn't be the only one calling the shots when it came to press coverage. Down Home Dog Food would have to take their share of the responsibility. "Or we can explain to them how we've overcome one trial after another without giving up, just like our veterans have had to do."

Collins listened with pursed lips.

"Letting Rebel go would be a bigger loss for you than it would be for her." Elliott motioned to the journalists, who were still by the shuttle sorting through luggage and equipment. "It's your call, Mr. Collins. But if you keep the camp open and let Rebel stay on as the trainer, I personally guarantee that not one of the campers will leave this island until they're thoroughly ready and your company is completely satisfied."

Elliott glanced at Mick. "No matter how long it takes." He returned his stare to Collins. "I'd like to suggest you speak to each veteran and ask *them* about their experience here before making your decision. Because this camp isn't really about Down Home Dog Food or the Remington. It's about them." When he looked at Rebel, his eyes shimmered with passion . . . and so much love that it made her heart soar. "Rebel is the only one who's kept that in mind."

Collins thought for what seemed like an eternity. Finally, he said, "Fair enough. I'll go back to the resort and speak to them." He strolled over to the camera crew.

Elliott pulled Rebel tighter against his side. "Mick, the partners don't have to vote me out, because I'm done at the firm."

Mick sputtered out a bunch of words without stringing together a full sentence.

Candy took a seat on the bench and looked at her nails like she was bored.

Elliott held up his hand. "I appreciate all you've done for me, but let's face it. I've done my share for you too. I've spent years making you look good, not to mention the money I've made for the firm and our clients. It's time for me to do something for myself. This is my home, and I'm staying put."

Rebel couldn't stop a gasp from slipping through her lips.

"You're going to give up everything you've worked for?" Mick asked, obviously stunned.

Elliott looked into Rebel's eyes again. "Nope." He shook his head decisively. "I'm not. Which is why I'm staying here, because this place and my family are what I've been working for the past several months, and it's where I belong."

Rebel shook her head. "I couldn't let you do that for me ten years ago, and I still can't."

His beautiful green eyes smoothed over her face. "I'm doing it for me too. I realized something. We both need to stop running because of our moms. And we both deserve better than what I've got going in San Francisco. I want to be here. With you."

Her throat grew thick, and she nodded. "I want that too."

Elliott placed a soft kiss on her lips.

Then he gave Mick a calculated smile. "If you go to bat for me with the partners so they'll pay back my buy-in"—he nodded to the camera crew—"you can tell the camera crew it's a contribution so the Remington can build a facility to start a service dog training program on the resort grounds."

Rebel tightened her grip around his waist.

"Imagine how that will have the firm's phone lines burning up with high-dollar clients." Elliott glanced at Collins. "I bet his national chain will sign on the dotted line before you even get back to California after you tell the reporter how much you believe in what we're doing at this camp and give Down Home Dog Food all the credit."

Elliott went silent, and Rebel figured it was to give Mick a moment to process the far-reaching implications. Or to calculate his firm's potential earnings.

"You really know how to play hardball, don't you?" Mick asked.

"I learned to swing for the fences from the best," Elliott said. "I have every confidence you'll make the right decision for both of us."

He didn't wait for Mick to respond. He turned his back to block out everyone else and focused on her. It made her feel like the center of his world.

"I should've kept looking for you. I'm so sorry I didn't, but I'm not letting you go this time. I'm nothing without you."

A tear escaped, rolling down her cheek.

He swiped it away with a thumb and pressed a soft kiss across her lips.

Then he squinted and looked at the terminal ceiling. "According to my calculations"—he flashed her a dazzling smile that melted her heart—"and I've been told I'm pretty good with numbers, my buy-in from the firm, combined with the equity I'll get out of my apartment when it sells, plus your paycheck from Down Home Dog Food should cover the cost of building a training facility at the Remington."

The tears kept coming, but this time they were happy tears.

He chuckled, kissing them away. "We'll have to build it far enough away from the main lodge so the barking doesn't disturb our guests."

"As sweet as that is, I . . . I can't take your money." She rested her forehead against his chest. "I almost ruined the entire event for the Remington."

He placed the side of a forefinger under her chin. His gaze hooked into her when their eyes met.

"My guess is that by the time we get back to the resort, the campers will have told Collins that you were the only thing holding the camp together. There's no doubt in my mind your job is still waiting for you if you want it." Elliott shrugged. "Of course, I wouldn't blame you if you didn't want to continue with an asshat like Collins." He gave her an apologetic smile. "Or an asshat like me."

Her arms tightened around him. "It's still your money, Elliott. The kind of facility I need will cost a fortune to build from scratch. I wouldn't feel comfortable sinking your savings into my career. It's too big a risk."

"It's a risk well worth taking because I believe in you. If your last name becomes Remington, it would be *our* money."

She gasped and went up on her toes to give him a kiss that communicated her approval. "I've always liked the name Remington."

"Obviously." Elliott glanced at Rem. "I vote we spend *our* money on a custom-designed training facility. I have a brother who can help us out with the project."

"You have a brother for everything." Her arms circled his waist. "Or a dad or a cousin or a sister-in-law. There seems to be a Remington who can help with just about any problem."

"True." He winked. "There's strength in numbers. So what do you say?" He glanced down at Rem. "You wouldn't split up Team Rem and Bogart, would you? Because we're a family."

She threw her head back and laughed. "You want me and all the rescue dogs I'll likely pick up along the way?"

"I want you, the rescues, the picket fence, Rem and Bogart. All of it. I'm selfish that way." He laid the softest, sweetest kiss on her lips, and she opened for him, running both palms up his back and around his neck. "We can personally escort Dan Morgan to the mainland to pick out another dog at the shelter, because he can't have mine."

When the sexy sound of surrender escaped from the back of her throat, he broke the kiss and smiled down at her with glittering eyes and a smile of victory. "Is that a yes?"

She nodded. "It is."

He hooked his arm around her shoulders and waved to Mabel.

She put down the cards and opened the window.

"Thanks for the call, Ms. McGill," Elliott said.

"Thank *you* for coming right over. I couldn't hold the ferry forever." She picked up the radio handset and pressed the button, her bright eyes sparkling at Rebel. "All aboard. The ferry will depart momentarily."

Rebel's mouth fell open. Then she let a smile form on her lips, so big and heartfelt that it seeped all the way to her fingers and toes.

"I couldn't let you make the same mistake twice, hon," Mabel said.

"I'm forever in your debt, Ms. McGill," Elliott said, molding Rebel to his side.

She snuggled against him, flattening a palm to his chest. "So am I, Mabel."

She smiled as she closed the scratched acrylic window.

Elliott picked up Rebel's phone off the bench and handed it to her. She held it to her ear. "Um, hello? Is anyone still there?"

Silence.

"I guess they hung up," she said.

Just as well, because the opportunity of a lifetime had just fallen into her lap, and nothing in Portland compared. She stuffed the phone in her pocket and resumed her snuggle position under his arm.

Elliott covered Rebel's hand that was resting on his chest with his and brought it to his lips to feather sweet kisses across her knuckles. "Let's go home, baby."

Those words were like velvet, soft and soothing and so, so right. She nodded. "Let's go home."

Chapter Twenty-Three

#POSITIVEREINFORCEMENT

Elliott used an index finger to part the shade in the foyer of the Remington.

His heart softened as he watched Rebel line up the veterans and their healthy service dogs under the portico for graduation day. The vets were receiving their diplomas for completing the camp, and the dogs were getting IN TRAINING vests.

Mick and Collins emerged from the great room, where Elliott and his dad had just finished closing *the deal*. His dad had already joined the rest of the family under the activities pavilion, but Mick and Collins had stayed behind to finish talking business.

Collins shook Elliott's hand. "Thanks for connecting us with your firm."

"Former firm," Elliott corrected.

Mick's eyes flashed, telling Elliott his old mentor still didn't agree with his career change, but he kept a thin smile pasted on anyway.

"They're the best in the country," Elliott added. "You won't be disappointed."

"We've set up a conference call with your hospitality manager," Collins said. "My company has decided to make the service dog matching camp an annual event here at the Remington. It's great PR."

Elliott crossed his arms. "I'll make sure our resident dog whisperer is on the call too. Our hospitality manager can take care of the bookings, but Rebel will be in charge of this particular event."

Collins looked contrite for not thinking of Rebel himself. He might be good at public relations, but an administrator he was not.

"Yes, well, we'll also be booking annual team-building events for each of our departments," Collins said, taking a step toward the front door.

"Excellent, sir." Elliott beat him to the door and held it open. "We'll take good care of your employees. You have my word on that."

As soon as the door closed, Elliott parted the shades again to watch Rebel.

Mick joined him. "You're either the dumbest SOB on the planet or the smartest."

"I'm not the one with three ex-wives." Elliott didn't plan to ever have an ex-wife. Why Rebel wanted him was a mystery, but he planned to spend his life making her happy. "Whether or not my decision was smart is a no-brainer." He decided Mick needed to lighten up. "Where's Candy, by the way?"

"You're an asshole," Mick groused.

Elliott laughed. Candy had dumped Mick right after her first visit to the island and had been back several times to see Jax. Unbeknownst to Jax, he'd likely saved Mick from a fourth monthly alimony payment. Candy and Jax seemed pretty infatuated with each other, so she'd obviously done herself a favor too.

"I hope you know we're going to do a top-shelf job managing Down Home Dog Food's pension fund, even without you at the firm."

"I have no doubt you will," Elliott said. "You can fill me in on the details when you take over the account, because I plan to stay in touch. You need someone to ride your ass as a reminder to have a little fun once in a while instead of working all the time."

Mick nodded. "If you ever decide to build time-shares or condos on Angel Fire Falls, I'll be first in line to buy one. This little island is a hidden gem for vacationing. The firm will be booking team-building events here too. I think we need them."

Elliott finally tore his gaze from his hot new fiancée and her sexy mane of long red hair, and he held out a hand to his friend and former colleague. "Thanks, man. I appreciate your talking the other partners into paying me back. That took guts."

Mick didn't just shake Elliott's hand. He pulled Elliott into a bear hug. "Not nearly as much courage as it took to give up the kind of financial security our firm offered. I admire what you're doing. But if you ever change your mind, you know where to find me."

Elliott slapped Mick on the back and returned his attention to the window to watch Rebel. "Thanks, but not a chance."

Finished with the lineup, she smoothed both palms over the back of her blush-colored sweater and down the black leggings that covered her incredible ass. Her toned legs disappeared into classy ankle boots. It was the dressiest thing she'd worn since the day she'd arrived.

She looked fabulous. He made a mental note to show her just *how* fabulous later when they were alone in the cottage they'd moved into across from Spence's.

"I have everything I need right here." And he wasn't planning to ever let it go.

Rebel had the graduating matches lined up and ready to walk across the stage so they could get their well-deserved awards. When Mr. Collins walked through the front door and started congratulating each pair, Rebel took the opportunity to peek over an Oregon holly shrub.

Her heart punched against her chest.

Even though the temperature had dropped substantially, every row of folding chairs under the covered pavilion was occupied. Elliott and Spence had built a makeshift stage that faced the resort so the campers could cross and receive their diplomas and vests in front of an audience.

Rem and Bogart loitered at her feet, so obviously happy to be reunited now that Bogart was fully recovered and healthy.

Her chest filled with gratitude. Against the odds and a week and a half late, the camp had still ended in success. At her insistence, Down Home Dog Food had even lined up refresher courses at the resort once a month for the next year so the campers could stay on track with their training.

. The front row was reserved for the graduates, but the top brass from Down Home Dog Food filled the next two rows. Some of the graduates' families were in attendance. The media coverage, courtesy of the reporters who were setting up on each side of the venue, had attracted a lot of attention to the resort and to her future training facility.

But what made her chest squeeze was Dan Morgan, who sat in the back row with his parents and the German shepherd–border collie mix he'd adopted from a shelter on the mainland. A week ago, she and Elliott had taken him to Cape Celeste and helped him pick out a dog. She'd made arrangements with his parents to train the new match at the resort once a week for as long as it took for them to function on their own.

Ben came thundering across the lawn with Charley's little girl, Sophie, on his heels. "Can I help?" Even with his Asperger's, he'd started to learn to dial down the volume around the veterans, because some of them were skittish when it came to loud noises.

"Of course." Rebel chuckled and tugged on the community outreach badge that was pinned to his Frontier Scouts vest. The media had eaten it up that a Frontier Scout with high-functioning autism had earned a badge by helping disabled veterans at a service dog camp. "It wouldn't be right if one of our best helpers wasn't included. That's why we scheduled the ceremony on the weekend instead of on a school day. You're going to hand the diplomas to the veterans when their names are called, okay?" She bent to look Sophie in the eye. "And you, princess, are going to help me put the vests on the doggies."

They both yipped and yayed all the way back across the lawn to rejoin the rest of the Remington family, who were greeting the guests.

Collins walked up behind her and cleared his throat, and she turned to face him.

Instantly, the crack in the shades snapped shut, and Elliott stepped outside. He hung back, but no doubt he was listening to make sure Collins behaved.

Rem darted to Elliott, Bogart hopping in his wake. When Elliott squatted to their level so they could nuzzle his neck, he lost his balance. He laughed and hugged them both.

Rebel's heart doubled in size because of all the love that filled it.

Not the best behavior for trained service dogs, but that was okay. They were exactly what she and Elliott needed.

"Thank you for all you've done, Ms. Tate." Collins looked uncomfortable eating crow.

She couldn't blame him. Crow wasn't exactly a tasty meal.

"You've done such an incredible job that we'd like you to head up next year's camp as well." Collins couldn't meet her gaze. "Right here at the Remington."

"Oh." Her gaze shifted to Elliott, and he gave her an encouraging nod. "Thank you. I'd be honored." But they needed to get a few things straight first. "We should start planning much sooner. It will help the event run smoother for the campers."

"Understood." Collins tried to sidestep her. "I'll go take my seat."

"Mr. Collins." Rebel stopped him. "I'd like you to consider lengthening the camp and pairing the veterans with rescue dogs next time. It will be an even bigger outreach program if we're helping both abandoned dogs and our servicemen and -women find a new purpose."

"Excellent idea," Collins said. "I'm ready to start planning whenever you are."

She nodded, and Collins strolled back to the venue.

Before she could give the graduates the go-ahead to start their procession, Elliott grasped her elbow.

"Give us a second, guys," he said to the matches as he led her inside.

Just as the door swung shut, he pulled her into his arms, consuming her mouth with a wonderful kiss that held a promise of more to come.

"What was that for?" she asked, breathless.

"It's for being so gorgeous. So courageous." He took her mouth with his again, kissing her senseless. "So fucking amazing," he breathed against her lips.

Her body went up in flames. "You're pretty amazing yourself."

"Thank you." His eyes softened with so much tenderness that Rebel went weak in the knees. "This event has opened up great opportunities for the resort. You've done a lot for our family, and that means the world to me."

The way he referred to the Remingtons as their family and not just his made Rebel's throat thicken.

She had a family. People who cared about her, even when she screwed up. People who would look out for her, even if she didn't need it. People who would always be there for her no matter what.

And she had a man who loved her exactly the way she was.

She glanced toward the closed door. "Soooo." She fiddled with a button of his dress shirt. He wasn't wearing a suit jacket, but he'd pulled a pair of dress pants and dress shoes from his packed suitcase that was full of tailored suits, then shoved it back under their bed. "Can we pick up this conversation right after the ceremony? In our cottage?"

"Damn straight we will," he promised. "I've got a few other locations where we can converse too."

Lawrence had offered to go to Cape Celeste and get her car out of long-term parking, but Elliott had insisted he and Rebel go get it themselves. Best car ride ever, because they'd christened it while crossing the channel on the ferry.

"But I can't keep you up too late because Trace is flying us to Portland tomorrow to pack up your apartment." Elliott squeezed her butt cheek.

She frowned. "You said you'd be busy for weeks catching up on the stacks of work on your desk. And didn't you say you were meeting with a few of the island's business owners to discuss forming a coalition soon? If you're too busy, I can go to Portland on my own."

"Not a chance, baby." He squeezed her ass harder. "I'm not letting you get on that ferry without me ever again," he teased.

She narrowed her eyes at him. "What if I promise to always come back?"

His eyes twinkled with mischief. "Then I'd reconsider." He cupped her butt cheek again and pulled her against that rock-hard package of his. "And this would be waiting for you every time you return."

A shiver lanced through her. "Are you trying to train me with positive reinforcement?" she asked suspiciously.

"Hell yes," he said shamelessly.

She let her eyelashes flit downward. "Well, it's working. I haven't even left the island, and I'm already looking forward to coming back."

He kissed her hard once more. Someone walked through the lobby, but they didn't break apart because there was no place she'd rather be than right there, wrapped in his arms.

"Dudes," Jax said. "Get a room." He snorted. "We're at a hotel, and you own it. Get it?"

Elliott stared at her and chuckled.

"Seriously, dudes," Jax said. "We're ready to roll out there." He hooked a thumb toward the pavilion.

"Hey, Jax," Rebel said, glancing at Elliott to read his reaction. "I was wondering if you'd like a permanent job here on the island?"

Elliott's eyes sparkled with approval.

"Instead of being an assistant, I think you'd make a great trainer. When my new facility opens, two trainers will be even better than one." She shrugged. "Maybe we can eventually hire a staff and an entire arsenal of trainers."

"Whoa," he said. "I love it here. You got a deal." He fist-bumped her and Elliott, and then he joined the veterans outside.

The sound of graduation marching music filtered into the entryway from outside.

"That's our cue," she murmured against his lips. "It's the sound of success."

"You did that." He tucked her hair behind one ear.

She shook her head. "We did it together. I love you, Elliott Remington." Her voice grew croaky.

"I love you too, Future Mrs. Remington."

Her throat closed.

The music coming from the venue might've been the sound of success. But Elliott's words were the sweetest melody of all because, for her, they were the sound of forever.

ACKNOWLEDGMENTS

As always, I owe my critique partner and friend, Shelly Chalmers, a debt of gratitude for helping me polish this book. I also owe my super-agent, Jill Marsal, a shout-out for her input and for helping me work through my Achilles' heel, the all-is-lost moment, once again.

A few key people helped plot this book with me, and they are angels in my eyes: Skye Jordan, Marina Adair, Michael Hague, and my husband, Blair Alexander. Without you, this book would've likely been about gerbils instead of life-changing service dogs.

And of course, I'm eternally grateful to the entire Montlake Romance publishing team: my editors Megan Mulder and Melody Guy, the cover designers, the marketing department, and so many, many more. Thank you for helping make my dreams come true and for putting my stories out there for my wonderful readers to enjoy.

ABOUT THE AUTHOR

Photo © 2014 Frank Frost Photography

Shelly Alexander's first published novel was a 2014 Golden Heart® finalist. She is an Amazon #1 bestselling author in numerous categories, including contemporary romance, contemporary women's fiction, and romantic comedy. Shelly grew up traveling the world, earned a bachelor's degree in marketing, and worked in business for twenty-five years. With four older brothers and three sons of her own, she decided to escape her male-dominated world by reading romance novels . . . and has been hooked ever since. The author of *Dare Me Once*, the first book in her Angel Fire Falls series, Shelly spends her days writing novels that are sometimes sweet, sometimes sizzling, and always sassy. She lives in the beautiful Southwest with her husband and toy poodle named Mozart. Visit her at www.shellyalexander.net.